# St. Nick

# St. Nick

Alan Russell

**THOMAS & MERCER**

Text copyright © 2013 Alan Russell

Originally published as a Kindle Serial, November 2013.

Published by Thomas & Mercer, Seattle

www.apub.com

ISBN-13: 9781477818459
ISBN-10: 1477818456

Cover design by Cyanotype Book Architects

Library of Congress Control Number: 2013919787

Printed in the United States of America

*To the children that Santa couldn't get to*

# CHAPTER ONE

## The First Noel
### November 28

It was Thanksgiving, but there was no aroma of roasting turkey wafting through the apartment. Nick Pappas had waited until noon to get out of bed. He hadn't slept in, though, and couldn't be sure he'd even slept at all. He had remained in bed because he lacked the impetus to get up, and was afraid of what he might do when he did.

Nick carried cereal and milk over to a warped vinyl dining table that he'd picked up at a garage sale for five bucks. The condiments were already on the table: salt, pepper, and sugar. And there was something else on the table, something metal, and dark, and ugly. He didn't look at the gun, not directly at least, but it was there.

The revolver had been next to the sugar for two weeks. It had started as a game, or that's what Nick tried to tell himself. One day he had taken the gun out of the closet; a few days later it was out of its holster. And then it went from the mantel, to the top of the refrigerator, to the counter, to the table. It kept getting closer to him. He could almost feel its heat.

He poured milk on his cereal, but didn't start eating right away. He wasn't really hungry. Maybe it wasn't cereal he wanted to eat.

No, it wasn't a game anymore. But then it never had been.

The gun was a revolver, a wheel gun—as in, spin the wheel. Young cops thought everything but semiautomatics were

1

antiques—they wouldn't be caught dead with a wheel gun. Nick's was old, but it would do the job. The choice was in front of him: eat or be eaten.

Was that it? Was that the question? Nick wished he could care more, one way or the other, but he didn't. He was just tired. One final disappointment, he thought. But he wasn't ready to act, not quite yet. A small part of him was still holding out.

Maybe the department would reinstate him. Unlikely, he knew, but the Fat Lady hadn't sung yet. He could wait until the suits returned their verdict.

Was that it? Was that his best Clarence Darrow? He hadn't even brought up Teddy, or George, or Corinne. But there were reasons he hadn't. Teddy was an ex-wife, and George and Corinne were ex-kids, or close to it. They were probably all getting together today. Maybe some other man was going to be carving Teddy's bird.

Even if he were reinstated, Nick knew he'd always have the reputation as the departmental screwup. There, he felt something: a twinge of residual pride. He had messed up, done the wrong thing but for what he believed was the right reason. Maybe he could live with that. Maybe. But he'd just been skating on the job anyway, putting in the hours like other burnouts.

He looked at the revolver.

When he had started the ritual, he'd told himself there was no way he really wanted to die.

Liar.

Maybe he should take the bullets out of five of the chambers, and give it a spin. He could pull the trigger. He'd just do it once. And that way he wouldn't really be making the decision. Fate would.

Lying again. Nick knew he wouldn't stop at one attempt. And blaming fate was a *cop out*.

He reached out with his hand. He still wasn't sure if he was reaching for the sugar or for the gun. His hand was halfway there when the phone rang.

Teddy, he thought. She had broken down and decided to invite him over for Thanksgiving dinner. But even as he reached for the phone, he knew it wouldn't be Teddy. They had been divorced for almost five years now, and she had moved on with her life. She only talked with him when she had to, and that wasn't very often. Maybe it was Georgie or Corinne. The kids were a little more forgiving than Teddy, but not much.

As he picked up the receiver, Nick wished he had a cell phone with a display, or at least an answering machine. That way he could have screened who was calling. When he'd furnished the apartment a few years back, he had done all his interior designing around a few garage sales. It was a shame no one had been selling an answering machine. By his own choice, he didn't have a cell phone. He had lost his last cell phone just before everything hit the fan, and since then he'd seen no need to replace it. His home phone rang seldom enough.

"Got your bird in the oven yet, Nico?"

Forster. No one else called him Nico, at least not anymore. Forster had heard Nick's mom call him that. He and Forster had been young then, both of them working patrol. Of course, Forster had been smarter than Nick. He'd put in his twenty years and walked away with his pension and his health. Now he was well into his second career.

"Yeah," said Nick. "It's cooking right now."

"Don't lie to me, Nico. I'll bet you haven't used your oven once since you moved in."

"For your information, I've become quite the cook. I didn't buy some store stuffing. I filled my bird with a cornbread and chestnut stuffing."

"Something's full of it, but I don't think it's your bird."

"Being skeptical of others isn't a healthy way to live, Wally."

Forster hated being called Wally. He went by Walt, or even Walter, but never Wally.

He pretended not to notice. "Our bird is about to come out of the oven, Nico, and I'm not talking some fantasy turkey with chestnut and corn stuffing—"

"Cornbread."

"Whatever. This is a twenty-pound bird. It's got a chest bigger than a Las Vegas showgirl's. And for whatever reason, Maggie wants you to join us."

"I wish you'd told me before I made my stuffing."

Forster played along with the lie. "That's what refrigerators are for."

"I appreciate the offer. But I've got other plans."

"Maggie isn't the only one who wants you here. I was hoping we could talk business. I need you, Nico."

"For what?"

"Come over and we'll talk about it."

"I told you, I got plans."

"I need you starting tomorrow, Nick. That's when it all happens, you know. Christmas season."

Forster was the Director of Security for Plaza Center, one of San Diego's largest malls. "Doors open at five a.m. in some of the stores," he said. "My headache starts at five-oh-one."

"I'm no rent-a-cop."

"Don't need a rent-a-cop," Forster said. "I got enough of those. I need someone undercover. Two days ago we had a mugging. The victim is still in the ICU, and she wasn't the first. Two scumbags roughed her up. I need you on lookout while they're trying to scout other marks. We'll put you in a central location."

"I like the central location of my apartment."

"I'm asking for a favor. I got a lot of people breathing down my neck. Muggings don't help business and these guys are bad news."

Forster didn't give Nick a chance to decline the offer. "Besides, you owe me," he said.

"What do you mean I owe you?"

"You saved my life."

It had happened their second year on patrol. Forster had never seen the second gun. Nick had.

"That's right. So why do I owe you?"

"The Chinese say if you save someone's life, then you're responsible for them the rest of your life."

"You think I care what Confucius says? Here's your newsflash: I'm no Chinaman. I'm one hundred percent Greek, and we're talking the real thing, not the frat boy *I Eta Pi* kind of Greek."

"No, what you are is a cop. And when a cop's partner asks for help, you do whatever it takes."

"You haven't been my partner for years."

"What? There's a statute of limitations?"

Nick took a long breath. Forster sounded like he needed him for real. This wasn't like the charity minimum-wage job he'd offered him when he had first been suspended from the force.

"A week," said Nick, "I'll do it for a week."

"Opa! I need you tomorrow morning no later than seven, Nico. And you better wear your Kevlar vest."

"Why? Are the suspects armed?"

"Who said anything about the suspects? I'm talking about the shoppers. There's nothing quite as dangerous as the day-after-Thanksgiving sale."

Nick could hear the change in Forster's voice: He'd landed his fish. Now he was just playing with it.

"I can hardly wait."

"Do it, Nico. I don't even need to see it. Just do it so I can hear over the phone. That'll be good enough."

As empty as he was feeling, Nick still almost grinned. Anthony Quinn's *Zorba the Greek* character had duped the whole world into thinking that Greeks everywhere loved to dance. Ever since seeing *Zorba*, Forster had been asking Nick to dance. That phony Quinn wasn't even Greek. He was Mexican.

"I don't dance, Wally."

"It's in your blood, Nico. You know it. You're denying yourself. That can't be healthy."

"I don't dance."

"Maybe not yet. But you're like an active volcano that's just waiting to erupt. And when it happens, I want to be there."

"Don't hold your breath."

"See you tomorrow, Nico."

Nick hung up the phone and went back to the table. He had this feeling the governor had called and given the condemned man another week to live. Nick wasn't sure whether he felt relieved or not.

He sat down and reached for the sugar.

# CHAPTER TWO

*O Come, All Ye Faithful*
*November 29*

Forster had been right about the early-bird shoppers; every one of Plaza Center's parking spaces seemed to be taken. Nick maneuvered his Chevy up and down the aisles and finally spied a car pulling out, but he wasn't quick enough. A green and red MINI Cooper pulled around him and squeezed into the space.

He rolled down his window, ready to give the other driver an earful. There were roof racks on the MINI that housed surfboards bigger than the car. Two bumper stickers, one that read "Miracles Happen" and another that stated "My Other Child Is an Angel," sandwiched a personalized license plate that read "XMASELF."

The driver's door opened, and a woman hopped out. Her back was to Nick, but she carried an enormous purse blinged out with rhinestones and holiday decorations. Just as he was about to start venting, she reached into her purse and tossed something into the air. Nick stretched out his hand and caught it. The lady had tossed him a green and red candy cane, and now she was blithely skipping away—and making damn good time.

Nick's driving luck suddenly changed. Right in front of him a driver began pulling out, and Nick claimed the spot. He left his car unlocked, the driver's window open. The best security system was driving a junker with nothing of value in it.

He started sucking on his candy cane, but it didn't sweeten his disposition. Plaza Mall was dressed up in loud, gaudy colors that were supposed to entice. Red, green, and silver were everywhere. The mall was only missing stiletto heels and fishnet stockings. There wasn't a sign or street lamp without garland on it, and holiday music was being piped everywhere. He was only minutes into the holiday season, but it already felt old.

"Bah humbug," Nick announced.

He walked across the parking lot, and then stepped into one of the department stores that anchored the mall. The shortcut came with a price. The department store seemed to be doing a Las Vegas version of Christmas, complete with lights, sights, and sounds. Over the store's speakers, "O Come, All Ye Faithful" played to a disco beat. He wished he'd worn dark glasses and earplugs.

The merchants were desperate this year. You could sense it. Thanksgiving had come late, and December was only a few hours away. Their time clock was running.

Nick forged forward. Security offices were always in the recesses of any building. He walked the length of the department store, wondering why it was always easier to enter a store than to leave one. Eventually he found his way into the mall proper. He went down two flights of stairs and followed some "Employee Only" signs. That got him to the other side of Candy Cane Lane and an area with little color and no ornaments. There was a veneer of respectability around the administrative offices, but it didn't go much further than that. Security was at the end of the hall.

Forster looked like a fire chief working three fires with two fire trucks. His phone was ringing, and he was talking on the other line. Two rent-a-cops, by the looks of them moonlighting Marines, were standing around, waiting to be told what to do. Forster hung up the phone, dispatched his officers to a store on level three, and then greeted Nick by tossing him some paperwork.

"Like old times," he said. "I did your paperwork for you. Just sign wherever you find an X."

Forster punched a button to take the other call, and Nick started applying his signature. When they had worked together, Forster had always been the one writing up their reports. He had been good with the paperwork, whereas Nick had been the talker, at least back then. Forster had been a four-year veteran when Nick was a rookie, and had always treated him like a younger brother.

Nick finished with the forms before Forster finished his call. The job suited Forster, Nick thought. His former partner was looking fit and young for a fifty-five-year-old man. His light-brown hair had turned mostly gray, but that didn't age him so much as accent him, like one of those frosted Christmas trees that were everywhere around the mall.

A small knock sounded at the opened door. Two things struck Nick about the woman standing there: her smile was about as big as her body, and she was dressed as an elf. Her vest and skirt were green and red with silver highlights. She was wearing a pointy hat, and pointy slippers, with little silver bells attached to all the points. Forster motioned for her to come in and sit down.

She entered the office to the accompaniment of her bells. On anyone else, Nick decided, the outfit would have looked stupid, but on her it somehow wasn't that ridiculous. She was blonde and pixyish, with freckles and blue eyes and dimples that went with her big smile. If she had been smaller, with larger, pointed ears, and had traded in a few of her freckles for rosy cheeks, she could have qualified for a real-life elf.

Nick stood up and the woman directed her larger-than-life smile at him. Only then did he remember the personalized license plate and the woman who had stolen his parking space. He frowned at her, but that didn't discourage her smile any.

"You must be the police officer," she said.

"Yes," said Nick. It was the easier answer. "You must be the Elf."

"Angie Gordon," she said, bouncing closer to shake his hand, her bells jingling.

"Nick Pappas."

Angie's handshake was vigorous enough to set off a few more bells.

"Is your name really Nick?" she asked, clapping her hands.

"It really is."

"That's so exciting!"

"I'm glad you think so."

Forster got off the phone before Nick could ask her how she knew he was a cop, and why his name was exciting.

"I guess introductions aren't necessary," he said. "You'll be working with Angie for the next few days, Nick. She'll be cuing you. Angie's in charge of the department you're being assigned to. She's the closest thing there is to a professional elf."

Leave it to Forster to make that sound like a compliment. But Nick still didn't understand how this Elf could be his boss.

"You work security?" he asked Angie.

"No, I have a different calling."

Nick didn't trust people who had *callings*. This Elf was beginning to creep him out. He looked over to Forster and raised his eyebrows, demanding an explanation. He listened while sucking on his candy cane.

"We need you center stage, Nick. But the problem with any large mall is that there really is no center stage."

Nick started to get an inkling of what Forster was about to say—a premonition—and he choked on his candy cane. Shaking his head back and forth, he tossed the candy cane into the trash basket.

"No way," Nick said, "no how."

"Think about it," said Forster. "It makes sense. We got an amphitheater set up, and this time of year it's always the most popular attraction at the mall. Everyone stops to watch the kids go up to Santa, and I do mean everyone. We figure it will be a magnet for our muggers. They'll be scouting out the shoppers who will be watching you. From where you're sitting, you'll have a perfect line of vision to see what's going on."

Nick's head hadn't stopped shaking. "You're kidding, right?"

It was Forster's turn to shake his head. "I had to sell management on the idea, Nick. I think the only reason they went for it was that we could get double-duty out of you."

"Santa Claus and surveillance?"

"Santa Claus and surveillance."

"And what do I do when I spot the bad guys? Invite them over to sit on my lap and ask if they've been good?"

"There'll be a two-way radio in your sleigh. Either you or Angie can call security."

"Are you serious?"

"No one can pick up on vibes like you, Nick. You've always been the best. Just one look and you could always tell what was going down. You've got the gift."

"Then make me an eye in the sky."

"I would if I could, but I don't have the budget. This isn't the force."

"No, this is insanity."

"I didn't think you'd mind, Nick. You're a people person."

"I've reformed. I am a hermit who hates the world now, and the last person who could, or should, play Santa. You know that."

Forster lowered his reading glasses and gave Nick his "don't kid a kidder" look. Then he raised his glasses, turned to Angie, and said, "Kids always loved him. We would go to a school, and they'd flock around him. And when we were working cases, they'd always talk to Nick. Kids who wouldn't talk to a cop, kids who came from families where it was tradition not to talk to a cop, kids whose fathers and grandfathers and great-grandfathers never talked to a cop, talked to Nick."

Nick shrugged. "Things happened. Things changed. And I changed."

"I need your eyes, Nick. I need your instincts. I need you."

Nick shook his head. "I'm not the only one who changed. Doing a bait and switch isn't like you, Walt."

Forster nodded in agreement, but continued nodding as he answered, as if trying to win Nick over with his bobble-head imitation. "You're right. I should have told you from the start, but the way you've been hibernating in that apartment I knew you'd just say no. I figured once you got here and I explained things, there wouldn't be a problem."

"You figured wrong."

"Just give it a day or two."

"After what happened, there's no way I can work with kids."

Angie decided that was her signal to speak up: "I think you'd be a good Santa." She nodded vigorously for emphasis, and her head jingled.

Nick figured her bells covered up the sound of rocks. Of course, Forster was sitting there still doing a lot of nodding of his own. Tough.

"You better get one of your rent-a-cops to suit up," Nick said.

"You and I both know that a murder could be happening right in front of them and they wouldn't even notice."

"Hire someone who will notice."

"I thought I did." Forster kept silent until Nick was forced to look at him. "I want to get those muggers. They didn't need to hurt that woman."

"What am I supposed to say to that? Should I feel some responsibility? Once upon a time I did. But I gave at the office. I can say that with all honesty: I gave at the office."

"Two days, Nick. If you want out at the end of your second shift, I won't say a word."

Nick had every intention of saying, "No." But the word stuck in his throat. He tried to cough it out, but it just stayed in his windpipe.

"You can't say *no* to your partner," said Forster.

Nick tried to say it, but his throat tightened on him again. "Two shifts," he finally said. "That's all. Better have my replacement ready."

Forster smiled. The Elf smiled too. That annoyed Nick. "What?" he asked Forster.

"You are a beautiful man when you dance, Nick Pappas."

"I don't dance."

"I'll go get your uniform," said Angie. She did some skipping and ringing on her way to the door. "It was so nice meeting you again."

"But we never met before," Nick said.

"Well, not in this lifetime," Angie answered, and then disappeared.

Nick turned to Forster and shook his head. "Next stop," he said, "the Twilight Zone."

"Christmas is a special time of year for Angie."

"Why? They let her out of the asylum?"

"Angie's unique, you'll see."

"You ask me, I think she's been hitting the elf juice too hard."

# CHAPTER THREE

## Deck the Halls

For years Nick had been fighting to squeeze himself into his police uniform, but now he had the opposite problem. Given his druthers, he would have just stuffed a pillow under the coat of his new uniform, but that wasn't good enough for Angie. She said if it looked fake and felt fake, the kids would know. Needle and thread in hand, she had come prepared. Her solution was to design Nick some formfitting batting extending from his chest to his crotch. Now, for the third time, he emerged from the dressing room to display the results of her efforts.

"This better be good enough," he said.

Angie didn't comment save to start pinching and poking the padding. When it came to this Santa business, she was all seriousness.

"I feel like a stuffed goose," he said.

"What you should feel like is Santa Claus."

"Ho, ho, hokum."

Angie stopped her prodding. In the sudden stillness her disapproval was magnified. "Do you remember when you were a young boy, Mr. Pappas? Can you recall your expectations of Christmas?"

"What's your point?"

"My point is that you're stepping into some very large shoes. When this uniform goes on, you become Santa Claus. You become the legend."

Nick decided he liked the Elf better when she was smiling and playing the happy sprite. He didn't enjoy being lectured by a woman half his age.

"I was hired as Nick," he said, "not Saint Nick."

"You've been promoted," Angie said.

She finished smoothing the batting, and announced, "It'll do." From elf to drill sergeant, he thought. The woman had a lot of faces.

"We have three suits on the premises," she said. "The uniforms aren't to be taken off the site except to be one-hour dry-cleaned. All of the mall Santas need to have at least one suit and one spare available to them."

"Why a spare?"

"Contingency," she said. "As for the padding, I suggest you take it home after every shift and hang it out on a line. You'll find that a little sachet of potpourri tucked into its folds will render aromatic wonders."

Nick didn't need her Martha Stewart advice, especially since he was a short-timer and had a short-timer's attitude. He reminded her of that. "I'm only here two days."

Something about his declaration made her smile. It was kind of like Forster's smile when Nick told him that he didn't dance. Angie continued talking as if she hadn't heard.

"The first thing you should do is to lay out the accessories to your uniform and make sure you have everything. You'll want to smooth your beard and your wig. You do that to make them look better, and to rid them of some of the static electricity."

Nick watched as she smoothed the beard with the fur of the hat.

"Before putting on the beard and wig, do your eyebrows. They'll need to stand up and out, so you apply the eyebrow stick from the edge of the brow toward the nose."

She handed Nick a white-colored stick. He passed it across his eyebrow once. Angie shook her head and held up a compact mirror.

"More," she said. "You'll want your brows to be as white as your beard."

He did it a second time, and when he finished Angie impatiently extended her compact toward his face. Nick looked at his reflection. He opened his mouth, and was about to say, "Good enough for government work," but then he saw the Elf's expression. That was enough to convince him to do it a third time.

When he finished, she was smiling. "Good," she said. "The next thing you put on is your beard. You'll want the children to be able to see your lips, so you have to allow for good separation of the mustache and beard. That's what these white bobby pins are for. Just run your hair through the pin, and clip it to the mustache's backing. That'll keep the mustache from drooping downwards."

She handed Nick his beard. He took hold of it uncertainly, and after a few false starts put it on. It seemed to fit, but it was scratchy and heavy.

"Wig next."

Nick took the wig from her and fitted it atop his head. His once full head of hair had thinned considerably, his hairline receding more every year. It felt strange to have a luxurious mop on his head again. Angie took out two of the white bobby pins and attached the wig to the beard, then held up her mirror again.

"What do you think?" she asked.

Nick didn't know what to think. A stranger was looking back at him, some white-haired, hairy old man. He shrugged.

Angie studied his appearance critically. "Avoid rouge and lipstick. I know that artists like to draw Saint Nick with red lips and rosy cheeks and rubicund nose, but those kinds of colors play havoc on a white beard."

As if, Nick thought, he'd put on any makeup.

She looked at his brown shoes critically. "The boot covers will mostly cover up what you're wearing, but in the future wear black shoes or boots so that they'll match the boot tops that go over them."

"I'll remember that *tomorrow*," Nick emphasized.

Angie looked at her watch, and then shook her head, apparently not liking what she saw. "Let's hurry with your accessories. Belt, boot covers, hat, and gloves. Put the gloves on last."

Nick felt a little self-conscious dressing under the time clock and her watchful eyes. His fingers kept fumbling with the boot covers and the belt, but when he finally finished putting everything on, Angie was pleased.

"Now you look like Santa," she said. "Go and see for yourself."

Nick walked over to the mirror above the sink. At first what he saw embarrassed him. What if one of his friends saw him? But these days he had few enough of those, and besides, it wasn't likely he would be recognized anyway. With the getup, very little of him really showed. His cap came down to his eyebrows, and the beard covered everything beneath his nose. Only his cheeks and eyes and nose were visible.

But even with his disguise he felt uneasy. Part of the reason, he knew, was that he was nervous. What was he going to say to a bunch of kids? But the bigger part of it was that he was ashamed. He didn't feel worthy of the costume. He was supposed to be a happy saint who loved children and humanity. He wasn't any of those things, and he knew that would show. Even with just that little window of his face on display, everyone would know. The costume couldn't hide what he was.

He tried smiling for the mirror. Someone had once told him it took twice as many muscles to frown as to smile. He'd obviously been doing the harder workout. His smile muscles weren't in shape. He hadn't used them in weeks, in months. It hurt to even try.

Maybe it would be easier with words. "Ho, ho, ho," he said, and flinched at the results. He'd make a far better Grinch than a Santa Claus.

Behind him, Angie's reflection showed up in the mirror. Her smile was genuine, her happiness no act.

"That's it," she said. "But a word of warning: no booming laughter around children. It frightens some of them."

Booming laughter. There wasn't a booming laugh inside of him. That was the least of his worries.

"That's the kind of thing they go over in Santa School," she said. "I guess I'll have to give you the abbreviated version while we walk over to the North Pole."

"I need to get my walkie-talkie," Nick said. He wanted to remind her about his *real* job.

He grabbed the two-way radio, but was at a loss for where he would put it. For all its bulk, his Santa suit had no pockets. Angie opened up a large, drawstring bag for him.

"I'll put it in Santa's bag with the candy canes," she said. "We'll be handing those out as we walk."

Nick dropped the walkie-talkie into the bag, and then slung it over his shoulder. He followed Angie through a utility tunnel that led from the administrative offices out to the mall. Nick's footsteps, and the Elf's bells, echoed around the confines of the tunnel. In high school Nick had played football. The walk through the tunnel reminded him of how he and his team used to come running out into the stadium. He had always gotten goose bumps during those runs. Nick pulled up his jacket sleeve and saw the goose bumps.

"We'll bring the children up to you," said Angie, "and tell you their names. Use the child's name as much as you can. That personalizes things. Ask if they've been a good boy or a good girl, and then stress, 'I know you'll be extra good between now and Christmas.' You can even tell them that you'll be watching. The parents love that.

"The biggest no-no is *do not* promise a particular toy. The most you can commit yourself is to say, 'I'll try,' or 'We'll see what Santa can do.' Got that?"

Nick nodded. He was good about not promising anything. That was the story of his life.

"If the parents want a photo, we'll help you position the child. All you have to do is smile and keep your eyes open during the flash."

"Forster didn't say anything about any photos."

"You need to remember we are a revenue center for the mall. And you need to remember even more that people want their pictures taken with Santa."

"How am I supposed to do surveillance with a flash going off in my eyes?"

"I don't know, Mr. Pappas. In my opinion, being Santa Claus is tough enough without adding *any* additional responsibilities, but then nobody asked me."

They exited from the relative darkness of the tunnel to the mall's bright lights. Instantly, Nick was in the spotlight, with shoppers calling out, "Santa! Santa Claus!" People were pointing at him like he was some celebrity.

"Smile and wave," whispered Angie through her smile. "Yell out, 'Merry Christmas.'"

Nick did as she'd told him, and found people of all ages waving back and smiling.

"Don't stop waving and laughing," said Angie. "People like that. They expect it."

"I feel like a politician."

"You'll be kissing your share of babies, that's for sure."

He wished he could find a quiet place to hide. If this was what it was like being a star, he could live without it. He had worn a uniform for most of his life, but it had never drawn this kind of scrutiny. Angie made it worse. She liked being a spectacle, liked laughing and waving and frolicking. Nick couldn't frolic if his life depended on it.

Angie patted his stomach, and then patted his bag. "Candy cane time, Santa," she chirped. Nick stopped so that she could pull out some candy canes. Then the Elf started dancing and handing out the freaking candy canes. Even worse, she did it with a song.

"Deck the halls with boughs of holly," she sang, her notes high and dulcet and clear, "Fa la la la la la, la la la la."

People cheered the Elf's singing. That was good, Nick thought. The more eyes that were on her, the fewer that were on him.

"Quick," said Angie, coming back for more candy canes. "Tell me the names of the reindeer."

Nick flunked the pop quiz. All he could remember was that one of the reindeers had a drinker's nose and was barbershop red.

"There are nine of them," she said. Remember the rhythm and the rhyme if you can: *Now Dasher, Now Dancer, Now Prancer, and Vixen, On Comet, On Cupid, On Donder and Blitzen.* And of course there's one reindeer not mentioned in the poem: Rudolph."

The Elf went skipping off again, and Nick trudged behind her, glad to be mostly lost in the glow of her song and dance routine. She returned for candy cane refills half a dozen times. He finally caught up with her at an oversized planter.

"We're there," she said. "The North Pole and Santa's Workshop is just around the corner."

Nick felt his stomach tighten.

"You're lucky," Angie told him.

"Why?"

"The mall usually makes a big splash about Santa's arrival. He came by helicopter last year, and two years ago he was delivered in a fire truck, sirens and all. But this year management decided they didn't want the hoopla."

Nick was grateful for that, but suspicious. "Why not?"

"I'm told money's tight," she said. "And because it's a shorter Christmas season they didn't want to distract the shoppers. Besides, they knew there would be no shortage of kids waiting to visit Santa today."

She danced around the corner. Nick walked after her, and then came to a complete stop. The open area of the mall had been designed for display purposes, and extended upwards to all three levels. The atrium allowed for an enormous Christmas tree, topped by a winged angel, to stretch skyward. Gaily wrapped boxes sat at the foot of the tree. Among the branches were a number of special Christmas "nests," and emerging from the eggs were toys and treats.

On the ground floor, a North Pole workshop had been brought to San Diego. Mechanical elves were pounding and assembling. Red carpet had been rolled out, and it led to Santa's throne. Lining the way were figures of snowmen and carolers and reindeer. The carolers looked like something from a Dickens novel, with top hats, and long skirts, and longer scarves. Their mouths opened and closed in fish-like rhythm. Christmas carols were piped out of nearby speakers. Santa's sleigh was there, and stretched out in front of it was a line of reindeer. At the head of it was the red-nosed one. Nick blanked on his name again, but the reindeer's nose was glowing. It was probably, Nick thought, the same color as his face. There had to be at least a hundred children waiting to see Santa. They had already spotted him, and were pointing and cheering.

Nick panicked. It was more than stage fright. He had thought he could handle the occasional kid making a pitch to Santa, but this mob wasn't anything he had bargained for.

"Wave," said Angie, managing to put bite into the word even through her smile.

"I'm not ready for this."

"Of course you are. They're only children."

"Yeah," said Nick. "Have you ever seen anything more frightening?"

"This way, Santa," said Angie, and she put her arm through his. Nick wondered if she felt his trembling. She must, even through all his padding. Nick wanted to pull away, but she was already leading him down the red-carpeted path toward his throne. Through her waving and calling she kept coaching him: "Wave. Smile. Speak."

It was all a blur to Nick. There was another elf besides Angie working the area, and she led him by the hand to the sleigh. She introduced herself, but Nick was too dazed to catch her name. He felt like an actor in the throes of stage fright. What was he supposed to say? What were his lines?

Angie went to bring a little girl forward. The youngster looked to be about four, and half her body seemed to consist of big, blue eyes.

"This is Terry, Santa," she said. "She's been waiting a long time to see you, and she's very anxious to tell you what she wants for Christmas."

The girl and Santa looked at one another. Neither appeared very certain of the other. Angie had told him it was important to repeat the child's name, but for the life of him he couldn't remember it. He thought it was Mary, but it might have been Kerry, or even Geri. Or perhaps it was Terry. That sounded right, but he didn't want to say the wrong name. Santa was supposed to know everything.

He looked at Angie for guidance. She made a little motion with her hands. He copied the gesture, his fingers opening up to signal welcome. That decided the girl. She came forward quickly, placing herself right into his hands, and then he lifted her into his lap.

Nick bit his lip, remembering the last time he had held a little girl in his arms. Remembering the blood. The doctors said she must have lost at least a pint of it before he brought her in. You never know how much that is until it's spilling on you. He didn't like thinking about what had happened. And besides, this was a different little girl.

Suddenly everyone was looking at him and there didn't seem to be a thought in Nick's head. He panicked and turned to Angie. She mouthed, "How old are you?"

He turned back to the girl. "So what's your date of birth, Mary?"

Right away Nick knew he sounded too much like a cop interrogating a suspect, and that was even before the Elf whispered in his ear, "Terry."

Nick tried again: "So how old are you, Terry?"

"Almost five."

"And how's the world treating you?"

The little girl's face reflected her puzzlement. Nick gave much the same look to Angie, who mouthed the words, "Have you been good?"

"So," said Nick, "have you been a good kid?"

"Yes," said Terry.

Nick snuck Angie another look, and she whispered, "Toys."

"I'll bet you're looking for a big haul this Christmas, right Geri?"

"*Terry*," said Angie, "Santa wonders what kind of toys you want."

The girl was prepared for that question. Nick listened to her long answer, which included Brace-a-lots, which were some kind of fancy bracelets, and Bead Seeds, which sounded like they were seeds that grew into beads when you watered them. Or maybe they were beads that looked like seeds. Nick knew enough to do a lot of head nodding. When she was done, he said, "All right, sounds great. Guess I better bring my extra big sleigh for all those toys, Terry."

Nick was proud he finally got the kid's name right. Angie wasn't quite as pleased. "Santa is delighted you came to see him, Terry, but he might not be able to get you everything you asked for. What he wants you to do is try and be extra good between now and Christmas. Do you think you can do that?"

Terry nodded very seriously.

"Santa has something for you, Terry." With her head Angie motioned to a box with the lettering, "For Santa's Good Children." Nick reached inside, pulled out a candy cane, and handed it to the girl.

And then another child was already being escorted up to him. Between helping the children up to Santa, getting smiles, taking pictures, collecting money, and spreading goodwill, the elves were even busier than he was, but Angie still found time to be his personal advisor. She told him not to lift the children up with his arms ("you'll throw out your back"), and was quick with the breath mints ("Santa doesn't have bad breath"), and kept him hydrated, frequently filling his mug with water.

The sweat was pouring off Nick. It was hot, difficult work, and he couldn't believe how much he was perspiring. There was no place for his body to breathe. His head was covered with a wig and cap, his face smothered with a beard, his hands imprisoned in gloves, and his entire chest and stomach were mummified with batting.

The children kept coming. Some were terrified of him, and it took all the coaxing of moms and the elves to get them up in the sleigh, while other kids treated him like their long lost best friend. There were so many kids Nick felt overwhelmed. Everything was so busy and otherworldly it felt like he was in the middle of a Dr. Seuss book. A rhyme started percolating in his head:

*Snotty-nosed kids, most of them sick,*
*Coughing and hacking on poor St. Nick.*
*The little extorters, each with a rant,*
*Demanding, 'I want this, and I want that.'*
*And oh how Santa wishes he heard the word 'please,'*
*Before the elves cued the shot and shouted, 'cheese.'*
*To Santa's lap come screamers, and weepers, and huggers,*
*Where, oh where, are those muggers?*

Nick took a moment to gauge the onlookers. He was hoping to see a few hardened criminals, but there were only smiling adults watching them. It was his bad luck.

"And this is Reed, Santa."

Reed wasn't one of the shy ones. He looked like a happy Jack-o'-lantern. He had orange hair, and a big smile, which showed about as many gaps as it did teeth. He jumped up and down as he approached the sleigh.

"Santa Claus! Santa Claus! Santa Claus!"

He landed in Nick's lap, all adoring eyes, all wiggling enthusiasm. And then his expression changed, becoming frozen, and Nick felt something in his lap.

Something wet.

Reed looked up at Nick. He didn't say "uh-oh." He didn't have to. The boy was holding his breath.

Nick was holding his as well. He'd been peed on. He stifled his urge to toss the kid off of him so he could wipe off his pants. The boy looked terrified, and Nick didn't want to add to his trauma.

"It's all right, Reed," Nick said, his voice soft, talking only to the boy, making it their secret. "I'm used to getting wet at the North Pole."

"There's lots of snow there," the boy said.

"Yeah, lots of snow."

Only Angie seemed to have noticed what occurred. While Nick talked with Reed, Angie whispered to Reed's mother, and handed her a large plastic bag. When Reed got off of the sleigh, Angie put up a sign that read: "Santa Is Feeding His Reindeer." At the bottom of the sign were the words: "He'll Return" and a clock. Angie set it for eleven.

Those waiting in line groaned. Tough, thought Nick. They hadn't gotten peed on. It was a long walk back to the locker room. He covered up his stain with the candy cane bag.

Angie caught up with him halfway there. "I'm sorry," she said.

"Shot in the line of duty," said Nick.

"We have another name for it. We call it, 'Surf's up.' Do you surf?"

"I barely float."

"You're never too old to take up surfing. I started after my daughter Noël was born last year."

The name of her daughter didn't surprise Nick. If she had a son, he was probably named Rudolph. There. Nick had remembered the name of that damn reindeer.

"I'll go get some club soda for the stain," she said, "and you'll be as good as new."

"Don't hurry," Nick said.

# CHAPTER FOUR

*Jolly Old Saint Nicholas*

When his shift finally ended, Nick didn't even have the strength to totally strip out of his Santa outfit. He was sprawled atop a bench in the locker room, jacket and padding off, pants, boot covers and beard still on, when the door opened and Forster walked in. He felt like a heavyweight boxer unable to leave his corner to answer the bell.

At least he had finally stopped sweating. His Santa uniform was saturated with his perspiration. No wonder St. Nick lived in the North Pole. With that kind of outfit, he would have to.

Nick's arms ached, and his back ached. Too much lifting. He had a killer headache and his ears were ringing. Some kids had spoken so softly he'd had to strain to hear them; others had seemingly taken on the challenge of shattering his eardrums. There had been a few screamers terrified of him, kids so frightened you'd think they were being taken to see Old Nick, not St. Nick.

Maybe he should call in sick tomorrow. This job made him feel inept. Like at the end of his shift when that kid had asked him: "Are you the *real* Santa Claus?"

The question kept echoing in his head. The boy had looked him in the eye and Nick hadn't known how to answer. He supposed that was the kind of situation they went over in Santa School.

Of course he had done his best to finesse the question. "Santa has many helpers," he said, but even to Nick those words had sounded lame.

The kid hadn't bought his answer. He knew that Nick had dodged the question. You could tell he wanted to believe in Santa Claus, and that most of all he had wanted to believe Nick was *the* Santa Claus.

And so the boy had asked him again, "Are you the *real* Santa Claus?"

Maybe I should have been honest with him, thought Nick. Told him Santa was a crock. And then I could have disillusioned him on everything from the Easter Bunny to the Bill of Rights. But instead he'd just said, "Yes."

Yes. One small word, and one more lie. Nick was surprised the lie bothered him. It certainly wasn't his first.

Well, if the kid was still hanging around the mall, and if he was at all observant, he'd see that a very different looking Santa was now sitting in the sleigh. Maybe he'd go ask that new Santa what the true story was. That would be fine with Nick. Make some other Santa sweat instead of him.

The second-shift Santa was a lot younger than Nick, a college drama major named Bret, who had evidently seen *Miracle on 34th Street* too many times. Santa Bret had been doing these weird breathing exercises in the locker room, and then had explained to Nick in a voice a lot bigger than his body that he was a method actor who believed in getting into the role.

"When I make my entrance," he said dramatically, "I will not be *playing* Santa Claus, I will *be* Santa Claus."

Nick hoped he'd get peed on.

Forster cleared his throat from the doorway. He knew better than to smile, though it probably took all his willpower not to. Nick was only too aware of how his tiredness was on display, and how ridiculous he looked sitting in his red pantaloons.

"I'm not talking to you," Nick said.

"Angie tells me that you did a bang-up job for your first day, especially considering you didn't have any training."

"If I was talking to you," Nick said, "I'd probably say, 'Who cares?' And then I might say, 'Gee, I'm so honored that I got the Elf seal of approval.' But I'm not talking to you."

"She says the kids took to you."

"Then they had an unusual way of showing it. They came, they saw, and they peed. And they cried and screamed. I'd hate to see what they would have done if they hadn't taken to me."

"Angie says you're a natural."

Nick would have waved off the compliment if his arms weren't so tired. "Consider the source."

"I did."

"Your Angie seems to be a little fanatical about the holidays."

"She feels," said Forster, "that the holidays are the time of year when people should give back to the community."

"So she gives back as an elf? What's her job in the off-season—professional cheerleader?"

"Angie's an accountant the other eleven months of the year. She has her own business, a very successful one that allows her to schedule this time off."

Nick shook his head. Something wasn't right here. "Why?"

"Who knows?"

"Something's got to be behind her Norman Vincent Peale act."

"It's no act."

"Maybe you brought us together thinking I needed a role model for positive thinking."

Forster shook his head. "I wish I was clever enough to engineer your paranoid theories, but the truth is I didn't tell Angie anything about you except that you're a cop. I needed a good pair of eyes, and you're the best."

"Not today. Not ever with this setup. Lady Godiva could have ridden by and I wouldn't have noticed."

"First couple days are always the hardest."

"Tomorrow's my last day, remember?"

Forster shrugged. Nick would have preferred it had he nodded.

"A kid asked me if I was the real Santa Claus," said Nick. "What's the answer to that one, Chief?"

"I suppose it depends on who's doing the answering."

"Is that one of those Zen kinds of answers? Someone who has Santa Claus in their soul *is* Santa Claus, is that it?"

"Something like that."

"I told him I was the real thing. The mall will probably get sued."

"Probably."

"Thing is, if the kid had asked me, 'Are you the *real* Nick Pappas,' I would have had just as much trouble answering."

The two men had a history. Roots. Nick could say things to Forster that he couldn't to anyone else.

"It was like part of me got misplaced sometime, somewhere, and I'm not who I should be. I'm not the real Nick Pappas."

Nick sighed, and shook his head as if trying to clear it. "See what I mean? The real Nick Pappas wouldn't be babbling like this."

"You're wrong. That's what the real Nick Pappas used to do."

"As a partner, I must have been a real pain."

"Some things never change."

"So the Elf told you I wasn't half-bad, huh?"

"Better than half-bad. She told me when she was doing her song and dance this morning she turned around and saw you handing out candy canes and making with the happy feet."

"Now I know you're full of it," said Nick. "I don't dance."

# CHAPTER FIVE

*Toyland*
*November 30*

Exhaustion had taken care of Nick's insomnia. For the first time in over a month he had needed to set his alarm clock, and when he awoke to its buzz, he just lay in bed for a minute listening to it. Maybe it didn't sound as bad as he remembered it.

He ate a hurried breakfast of cereal and was surprised at his appetite. Ever since his suspension, food hadn't appealed to him. He hardly took notice of the gun at the table. It was still sitting there, right next to the sugar. He was just too rushed to give it much mind.

The batting was still wet. He had meant to throw it in a dryer the night before, but hadn't gotten around to it. And the Elf was right about its aroma. It already had a locker room smell, but he wasn't going to sprinkle rosebuds on it, or whatever it was that Angie had suggested. He grabbed a can of deodorant, liberally sprayed it, and then took a few sample sniffs. It seemed okay. He filled a thermos with water, found some old breath mints, and hurried out to his car.

Nick had the eight to four shift. When he arrived at the mall, he was amazed that the parking lot was almost full. Didn't people have anything better to do than shop? As he made his way to the locker room he actually found himself humming along to the holiday Muzak. Brainwashing, he thought, was an insidious thing. Or maybe he was just in a good mood because this was his last day on the job.

Putting the Santa suit on was much easier the second time around. The Elf had been a good teacher. He smoothed his wig and beard with his cap. Halfway through dressing, he gained an audience.

An older black man had silently entered the locker room and was leaning on his mop, a spectator to Nick's transformation. The man wore an industrial outfit, with polyester navy pants and a light-blue shirt embroidered with the name "Henry."

"Maybe I should get me one of them outfits," Henry said with a wink. "Women loves a man in a uniform."

"You got a uniform."

Henry shook his head from side to side in one long, slow movement. He was totally bald, but his head had a shine to it, as if waxed.

"Not like yours, young fellow," he said. Henry's wistful smile showed several gold-plated teeth. "The ladies, I see how they pay to sit in your lap."

"Not my lap. Santa's. There's a difference."

Henry did another round of head-shaking, this time more vigorous. "Didn't you get deputized, young fellow?"

"Deputized?"

"Yeah, Santa deputized you. Made you one of his helpers. You've earned the perks, boy, and perks is perks."

"I suppose so."

"Suppose? S'posed to be the season to be jolly."

Henry sat down on the bench with a satisfied sigh. "And you got a sit-down job too, with banker's hours. Can't beat that. When I retire, I wants to be Santa Claus."

"When are you going to retire?"

"Thinking about four years from now, young fellow. I'll be eighty then. But could be I'll wait until I'm eighty-five."

Nick had the distinct feeling that everyone was "young fellow" to Henry, and that he was of an age where remembering names wasn't one of his priorities. He introduced himself anyway: "Nick Pappas," he said, extending a white-gloved hand.

Henry took the hand. "Henry Ragsdale. Now's Nick your name for real?"

Nick nodded.

"Nick, Saint Nick." Henry looked pleased with himself. "Don't that beat all, we got us a real Saint Nick."

"Better not expect any miracles."

"I'm not expecting no miracles, Saint Nick, but I won't say no to none neither."

"That's two of us."

Nick finished with the final touches on his uniform, and Henry nodded his approval. "Go get 'em, Saint Nick."

"On Dasher, On Dancer," said Nick.

Henry clapped his hands.

There was no Angie waiting to walk with Nick to his post. It felt a little bit like going solo on patrol for the first time. He tried to remember the other reindeers' names. The line, "On Comet, On Cupid" came to him, and he remembered Rudolph, but he blanked on the other names.

*On Dummy*, Nick thought.

For the second day in a row the utility tunnel was deserted. The side lighting on the walls made his shadow huge, big enough for the St. Nick of legend. Like most shadows, it lied. But he had to think big, as big as the shadow. St. Nick was even bigger than that. As a cop, Nick had learned to always act as if he were in total control. Stepping from the tunnel into the spotlight of the mall, he called out, "Merry Christmas!"

The shoppers greeted him with smiles. Fingers pointed his way, and hands started waving.

"Merry Christmas!" Nick called out again. But what he was thinking was "eight hours." In eight hours he could hang up his Santa suit. Soon, it would be all over.

Nick didn't have any candy canes to hand out, so he just offered waves. He was already sweating. Christmas in Southern California was as much an oxymoron as jumbo shrimp. He'd lived in San Diego long enough to know there were more hours of sun breaking through the clouds in November than in any other month of the year. And this November had been particularly warm, with the thermometer consistently hitting the 70s. He wiped his forehead. There should be a different uniform for Southern California Santas—red tank tops, red running shorts, and sandals were in order. And as for the long beard, that definitely didn't work. In SoCal, it would be more in keeping for Santa to have a trimmed goatee.

He shouted out another rousing "Merry Christmas!" and the words were returned to him by all the shoppers in his vicinity. They didn't know, thought Nick, that he was the Emperor with his new clothes. It would serve him right if some little kid pointed out that he was no Santa, no Santa at all.

As he rounded the corner to the North Pole, he was glad to see there wasn't much of a line waiting. Angie was the first to spot him.

"Look! It's Santa Claus! Good morning, Santa."

Some of the kids echoed her words; some clung that much tighter to Mom or Dad. At least no one started crying—yet. Nick tried not to be self-conscious. He knew that all the young eyes were on him as he made his way to the throne.

"Your cookies and milk, Santa Claus," announced an elf, and with a flourish brought him a mug and a plate full of cookies.

In a voice that no one but Nick could hear, she quietly introduced herself as Darcy. Like the other elves that Nick had met, she seemed entirely too young, and too full of energy.

Nick took a sip of his milk and a bite of cookie, and then the show began.

———————✴———————

It wasn't as much of a madhouse as the day before, but it was still busy. Every kid was a different challenge. If Nick didn't get sick it would be a miracle. Half the children seemed to have runny noses and coughs, and they could have used a full-time makeup artist getting them ready for pictures.

"Twins, Santa!" Darcy's enthusiasm sounded a little off, and her smile looked strained. "Meet Sean and Dawn."

"Me first," said Sean.

"No, me."

The twins pushed and shoved; Sean ended up on Nick's right leg, Dawn on his left. The twins wore identical outfits of red short sleeve shirts and green shorts.

"Santa, I want a Barbie for Christmas—"

"You don't need another stupid Barbie. What I want is a—"

"No, me first," said Dawn.

"No, me."

"Ladies first," said Nick.

"She always goes first."

Dawn looked smug. "I was born eighteen minutes before you were."

"Were not."

"Was so."

She made a face at her brother, and then started reciting her list: "I want Playhouse Island . . ."

Dawn ignored Sean's raspberry and kept talking.

". . . and my own iPod so my stupid brother can have the old one and play his stupid songs in his stupid room . . ."

Sean razzed her again, even louder. Nick wished he could do the same to both of them, but he held up his hands.

"I'm disappointed in both of you," he said, his voice severe, his white eyebrows knit. "This is the time of year for goodwill, for kindness. If brothers and sisters can't get along, how can we expect peace on this earth? Santa is going to be watching the two of you between now and Christmas and if your behavior doesn't improve . . ."

Nick let his threat hang in the air. Both twins seemed to take it seriously.

"I'm sorry," said Dawn.

"I'm sorry *too*," said Sean.

"I'm glad to hear that," Nick said. "Now what else is on your list, Dawn?"

In a meek voice, Dawn did her asking. Her brother refrained from interrupting her. Then Sean told Santa what he wanted. When it came time for their picture, the twins smiled for the camera like little angels.

Nick handed each of them a candy cane, feeling pretty good about himself. Almost smug. That was before the twins examined the digital proof.

"I have a bigger smile than you do," said Dawn.

"Do not."

As Darcy helped the twins' mother decide on the appropriate picture package, Nick looked at Angie. Both of them shook their heads. "My headache is bigger than yours," Nick said.

"Is not."

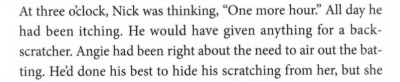

At three o'clock, Nick was thinking, "One more hour." All day he had been itching. He would have given anything for a back-scratcher. Angie had been right about the need to air out the batting. He'd done his best to hide his scratching from her, but she seemed to see everything. It didn't matter. In sixty minutes he'd be free of his Santa hair shirt forever.

As he finished talking with a little boy he felt sorry for—the kid's mother had dressed him up like Little Lord Fauntleroy for his picture with Santa—he scanned the upper levels. Mall patrons were always leaning along the railings, pausing in their shopping to watch Santa. Their smiles weren't only for the children, but for themselves. In their faces, Nick could see their trips down memory lane. But nostalgia didn't seem to be on one viewer's mind.

He was probably twenty-five, with a body that looked as if it had been sculpted in a prison weight room. He had long hair, dark and unkempt, that was at least a week overdue for a shampoo. His eyes were brown and predatory, and he was searching for something: prey.

Nick saw the man's eyes alight on something, and then start tracking it. Nick followed the direction of his gaze and saw a woman loaded down with packages leaving a jewelry store. His suspect continued to follow her with his eyes, and then he pulled out a cell phone and punched in a number.

Nick's every instinct was to follow the guy, but his Santa outfit wouldn't exactly be inconspicuous. He reached into the candy cane bag, digging for the two-way radio and hoping Angie had remembered to pack it. In his haste he spilled half the candy canes into the sleigh. Finally he found the walkie-talkie.

"Dispatch," he said, "North Pole here."

The reply crackled through the speaker. "Go ahead, North Pole."

"I think I got a line on a Grinch."

"I copy."

"He's on the second floor walkway overlooking the sleigh. Suspect is a white male, six foot, with dark hair, around twenty-five. He's wearing jeans and a white T-shirt with no lettering. Suspect is on the horn tracking a red-haired female exiting northwest from Luna Jewelers."

"I copy. Security is on the way. Ten-four."

As Nick clicked off, he looked up and was taken aback by the presence of a delighted-looking boy and his startled parents. Darcy mouthed the word "sorry" to Nick, and then overenthusiastically said, "Hi, Santa, this is Jason."

"That was *so* cool," said Jason.

Nick wondered how long they'd been standing there. "I suppose you heard me talking to my North Pole operator."

The boy nodded.

"Well, Jason, unfortunately, I was discussing the behavior of some boys that aren't good like you. I'll let you in on a little secret; they're going to be getting coal in their stockings."

Jason nodded very seriously.

When Nick finished with Jason there were several other lap-sitters waiting. He wondered if the bad boys had been apprehended. So this is what a retired fire dog feels like, Nick thought—useless. As much as he wanted to deny it, he was a cop to the bone. That's why he couldn't stand the thought of being booted off the force. Even his Union Rep hadn't been blowing his usual smoke the last time they'd talked. He had told Nick that he was working to save his benefits. That wasn't what Nick wanted to hear. It was his job he wanted, not the benefits.

For half an hour the children kept coming, but as soon as there was a lull in activity, Nick surreptitiously picked up the walkie-talkie and called security for an update.

"We tracked the woman to her car and watched her drive off," said the dispatcher. "There was no sign of your suspect following her."

The unsaid insult came through loud and clear: *You wasted our time on a wild goose chase.*

"That guy wasn't here doing Christmas shopping," said Nick. "He was scouting out targets."

The dispatcher clicked off without answering.

The last few minutes of the shift were slow and anticlimactic. Nick was sorry he wasn't leaving the job with one last bust. It surprised him that he cared enough to want to go out with a bang.

It was time for the changing of the guard. Darcy put up the "Santa Is Feeding His Reindeer" sign, and Angie turned the display clock to 4:10.

Angie went off to hand out a few candy canes to children, returning to Nick's side on their walk back to the locker rooms.

"I think your time as a police officer helped to make you a good Santa," she said.

"I'll use you as a reference on my résumé."

Angie seemed to think that was funny and Nick didn't feel the need to add that his Santa days were over. When they reached the utility tunnel, he took off his cap and wiped his forehead. He moved his wig to the side, and fanned his head while waving away steam. As they walked, Angie took off her own cap and used it as a makeshift fan to send a breeze Nick's way.

"I don't think I've ever seen any other Santa sweat as much as you do," she said.

"I'm Greek," Nick said. "Hot blooded, you know. And let me tell you, this costume's designed for sinners, not saints."

Angie looked at his sweat-stained costume. "Maybe you can do me a favor," she said.

"Shoot."

"There's a one-hour cleaners in the mall. It would be a big help if you could drop off your uniform there."

"No problem. I'll do it on my way out."

"I'd appreciate it if you could keep the Santa suit hidden from little eyes."

Nick saluted. "Yes, ma'am," he said. "Don't worry. Santa's secret is safe with me."

# CHAPTER SIX

## For Unto Us a Child Is Born

When Nick walked into the locker room, he found another Santa sitting there. The second-shift Santa was wearing earbuds and moving his head to the beat of the music. His headset muted most, but not all, of the heavy metal sounds.

Nick wondered if it was bad luck for two Santas to be in a room at the same time. But the second-shift Santa apparently didn't believe in some great Brotherhood of Claus, and didn't even bother to acknowledge Nick's presence. He pulled a cigarette from a pack, lit it, and then inhaled deeply.

As he blew out the smoke he said, "The local Gestapo's looking for you."

"What?"

"The big, bad mall sheriff said he wanted you to go to his office."

Nick figured that this other Santa couldn't be older than twenty. Punk Santa, he thought. The kid's eyes were shut again, and he was lost in his heavy metal. Nick walked over to where he was reclining and tapped him on the shoulder. Punk Santa reluctantly removed his earbuds.

"I think Santa's supposed to be back from feeding his reindeer by now," Nick said.

"Yeah, well, I'm waiting to make an entrance."

He went back to his music. Nick yanked the earbuds out of Punk Santa's ears, and then pulled the cigarette from his lips, dropped it to the floor, and ground it into the cement.

"Hey," said Punk Santa, standing up. For a moment Nick thought they might come to blows. Beard to beard, gut to gut, they stared at one another like two aged and costumed Sumo wrestlers. Great, thought Nick. In the spirit of Christmas two Santas were ready to duke it out. But something about Nick's calm, and the way he was holding himself, must have spooked the younger man.

Punk Santa shook his head and sneered. "Fine," he said, his tone mocking, "for the sake of the children I'll lose my tunes and smokes." Then he offered up a last display of sarcasm: "Anything else, grandpa?"

Nick nodded. He tossed him a candy cane and said, "For your breath."

Punk Santa walked over to a garbage can, tossed the candy cane into it, and then sauntered out of the locker room without saying another word.

In some ways Nick knew that he'd picked the fight. Lots of kids that age just postured for the sake of posturing. It was possible the kid would act differently when he was around the children. Maybe he wouldn't be so flippant. Maybe he would even care. Not that it was Nick's business anymore.

He popped off his cap and wig, pulled off his beard, then heaved a sigh of relief. He wondered what Forster wanted him for, and whether it could wait until after he changed. No, he decided. Maybe it had to do with the lowlife he'd spotted.

Forster was in his office doing paperwork. "What's up?" Nick asked.

"Crime," said Forster.

"I'm not surprised. Your dispatcher pretty much blew me off. Did anyone even try and follow up on my potential suspect?"

Forster nodded. "We made sure your suspect wasn't following the woman that came out of the jewelry store."

"He targeted her and then he made a call," Nick said. "Anyone stop to think his partner might have been outside in the parking lot waiting for that woman? Instead of trying to take her down there, and being on candid camera, he might have decided the best thing to do was follow her home. I wouldn't be surprised if he rolled her in her own driveway."

Forster sighed. "I suppose that's possible. Normally we would have done a better job of following up, but right after your call came in we got pulled every which way. We had to call the EMTs for what looked like a heart attack, and we were in the middle of taking down a shoplifter."

"I'm betting the guy I spotted is one of the muggers. I know he's bad news. Don't say I didn't warn you."

"And don't say I'm not listening to your vibe. I was just on the way to the control room to get a printout of your suspect. Care to join me?"

Nick pretended it didn't matter to him, but he followed Forster into the next room. A security guard, another Jarhead, was sitting at a desk studying two monitors with split screens. In Nick's time in the Navy, all Marines had been called "Jarheads," and all sailors had been called "Squids."

"We got CCTV security cameras throughout the mall," said Forster. "Everything you see on the monitors is going on in real time."

The eyes in the sky had views inside and outside the mall. Nick could see the food court, walkways on all three floors, and the parking lot.

"Did you queue up that film I wanted?" Forster asked.

The Jarhead nodded and hit a button. They watched the tape. "There," Nick said, "that's the guy."

They watched as the suspect kept moving his predator eyes. "He's checking out all the security cameras," said Nick. "He knows where every one of them is. And right there he sees our shopper leaving the jewelry store. He's all eyes now. She looks ripe for the picking, and that's why he's calling his partner now. He's got him on speed dial."

"Where did our guy go from here?" asked Forster.

"I tracked him to the bus stop," the guard said. "Since he wasn't going after that woman, I stopped following him."

Nick let out a long sigh. Forster was more diplomatic. "I'd appreciate getting printouts of him from the best video footage you have."

The guard nodded, and the two men left the surveillance room and returned to Forster's office. "I'd like to say it's been fun," said Nick, "but I'd feel a little funny lying while wearing a Santa suit. Anyway, it's all yours."

"Not so fast," said Forster. He handed Nick a piece of paper. "This guy really wants you to call him back."

Nick looked at the name and number on the paper, and didn't recognize either one. "I never heard of him."

"He said you might say that, and told me to tell you that he's one of the other Santas. The actor, he said."

Nick started to crumple up the paper, but Forster raised his hands. "Hey. I took the call. This guy said it was really important, like emergency important."

"In that case, I really don't want to call him back."

"He made me promise that you'd get back to him." Forster pointed to his phone.

With a sigh, Nick sat down. He uncrumpled the paper, and then punched in the numbers. Bret answered on the first ring.

"I really, really need a favor," he said.

"What is it?"

"I'm friends with an intern at Los Niños Hospital. A few weeks ago I told him about my Christmas job as Santa and that got him to talking about how they needed a Santa to come to his ward. So we arranged that tonight would be the night. But my car's broken down in LA and they're not going to be able to fix it in time for me to get back."

"So call your friend and tell him you'll be there tomorrow night."

"It's too late. He can't pull the plug now. Santa's visit is all the kids have been talking about. The staff's even collected presents."

"Then get someone on the staff to do it."

"I've got the spare uniform. I know I shouldn't have taken it, but I did. And besides, they need an outsider. The kids would know if one of the staff dressed up as Santa."

Los Niños. The English translation was "The Children." The very thought of that hospital brought Nick all sorts of bad memories. "I really don't want to do it."

"I was going to get paid two hundred bucks. The money's yours."

"I don't want the money," Nick said. "It's just . . ."

What was *it*? *It* was what had happened. *It* was when his life had gone down the toilet. And he was tired. He had put in his promised two days as Santa. That was enough.

"I didn't tell you one thing," Bret said. "There's a reason this is so important. The kids I'm scheduled to see are sick. Some are real sick; the kind of sick where very few things excite them, but my friend said they're all happy Santa's coming to see them."

Nick didn't want to hear that. It roiled his insides. He knew too much about hurt kids. Today had been a bad day that had gotten progressively worse, but this made everything that had come before seem like a cakewalk. He was being asked to walk into a room full of sick kids and make jolly. That wasn't something he could do. He was sick himself, sick in spirit, sick in thoughts. His reservoir was tapped out, not a drop left.

"There's got to be someone else."

"There isn't. I'll really, really owe you. I'll wash your car, I'll mow your lawn, do anything you say."

Nick wanted to hang up the phone. He wasn't supposed to have been Santa at all. He was supposed to have been catching muggers. That was the kind of work he was good at.

"What time you supposed to be there?"

"Six forty-five," said Bret. "You are a lifesaver, Nick. I will not forget this. I will never forget this."

"Okay."

"Thank you. Thank you. Thank—"

Nick hung up. There were no visions of sugarplums dancing through his head, only visions of sick kids. His stomach hurt. He didn't want to go back there, to the hospital, to what had happened, to the worst day of his life. But that's what he had agreed to do.

"Bad news?" asked Forster.

"Yeah."

# CHAPTER SEVEN

## *What Child Is This?*

When Nick took off his Santa padding in the locker room after his meeting with Forster, he could see why he'd been scratching all day. There was a rash over most of his chest. It was another lousy thing in a lousy day. He remembered how he had sprayed the padding with deodorant that morning. The dampness, spray, and sweat had left him with a red trail of welts, and exposure to the air only made the itching that much worse.

It was already quarter to five. He could run to the cleaners and have a one-hour cleaning done on the Santa suit, and then look for a drugstore with some kind of itching cream. He found a battered cardboard box in the locker room and stuffed the Santa suit and batting inside. I have promises to keep, Nick thought. It was a line Forster had always used when they worked late night patrol together. Forster had said it was from some poem. What was the next line?

"*And miles to go before I sleep,*" he said. Wasn't that the truth.

He added the beard, wig, and accessories to the box. It would make sense to go directly from the cleaners to the hospital. He tucked everything away, making sure it wasn't visible.

Naturally, the dry-cleaning shop was at the opposite end of the mall. The Asian man working the counter accepted the Santa suit without changing his expression or commenting.

"I need it as soon as possible," Nick said.

"One hour?"

He wasn't sure if the man was asking him or telling him. "No more than an hour. Okay?"

He got a nod.

Nick put the padding on the counter. "And can you do something about this? Dry it out, or make it smell better, or whatever?"

The man wrinkled his nose at the soggy mass. He peered at it, and then tentatively touched it like he might the carcass of a dead animal. Mouth closed, he made a universal guttural sound that translated to "not good."

"An hour?" he asked.

It was the same question, but this time it sounded different, as if he was saying a lifetime wouldn't be long enough.

"Yeah," said Nick, "an hour."

He went in search of a drugstore, but couldn't find one. The closest thing was a body and lotion store in the lower-rent district away from the department stores. Most of their stuff was bath beads, and spritzers, and fragrance gels, but there were some salves and creams. They weren't the kind of ointments that advertised "rash relief," but he found one that said it was "cool and soothing," and "promoted healing." The way he was itching, he was willing to try anything.

"Jingle Bells" was playing throughout the mall's loudspeakers. But Nick wasn't laughing all the way; he was itching all the way. He ran down to the locker room, threw off his clothes, and applied the ointment all over. For ten minutes he just sat in his boxers and scratched. The combination of his scratching and the lotion made him feel better, almost normal. The greatest pleasures in life were usually associated with getting over something just so you could feel like your old self again, he thought. Nick wished he could do the same with the rest of his life.

He put his clothes on. His itching didn't start up again, so he took that as a good sign. He looked at his watch. The Santa suit would be ready in half an hour. Nick tried not to dwell on going to that hospital again—Los Niños—but it was impossible. The sick kids weighed on him, made him restless. That annoyed him. He wanted to be miserable on his own terms.

Now that he wasn't scratching, he realized how thirsty he was. He walked over to the mall's Food Pavilion and ordered two extra-large ice teas. Nick gulped down the first and took the other one with him. He stopped to do his sipping while leaning on the second-level railing overlooking the North Pole.

It was a good vantage point to look out for his suspects. Nick studied the mall environs, trying to see as a criminal might. There weren't any visible guards on patrol, and the mall's energy savings meant that lighting was patchy in some areas. Shadows were just what you wanted if you were a bad guy. Forster had once told him that mall management spent seven times more on landscaping than they did on security. Unfortunately, that was evident. And now that he'd put in his two days, it was no longer his problem.

With the clock ticking down, he walked over to the dry cleaners. He expected to be told that the items weren't done, but he discovered the opposite problem. The Santa Claus suit was clean and ready—and hanging all too visibly on the carousel. It was covered in a plastic wrapping, and anyone could see what was under the transparent covering.

"I need the suit covered up," Nick told the counter guy.

"Covered up?"

"Yeah." Nick pantomimed, waving his hands around the Santa suit. "I need you to wrap it up so little kids don't see it."

The man made a sound similar to the one he'd uttered an hour earlier. Nick took it to mean part displeasure and part contemplation.

"Okay," he said. "We wrap."

He shouted to the back in a foreign language, and a woman answered him. The conversation went back and forth until an Asian woman came to the front of the shop. She was small, thin, and frowning. First she looked at the uniform, then she looked at Nick, then she disappeared, but not before saying something to the man. Nick was glad he didn't understand what was being said.

The woman returned with some brown wrapping paper. She tore off three sheets, taping them to hide the Santa suit.

"Okay?" she asked Nick.

Nick thanked her, and got a curt nod back. He had an hour before he was due at the hospital. Putting on the batting and his uniform would take a few minutes, but that would still leave him with plenty of time to get there and get ready.

He heard the crying just as he was exiting the cleaners, heard it well before he saw the upset little girl. She was standing in front of a camera store and had already drawn several concerned bystanders. Punctuating her screams were two syllables she repeated over and over: "Ma-maaaa!"

She was young, maybe five, and looked like the Morton Salt girl in her yellow dress and yellow shoes. But it wasn't salt that was raining. It was the girl's tears, and she wasn't about to be consoled by anyone but "Ma-maaa!" People were trying to calm her, were doing their best to learn her name, but when she opened her mouth it was only to scream her pain.

Nick wasn't good around screaming kids. The sounds seemed to somehow shut off his brain circuitry. But this time he had an idea of how to stop the screaming. He needed a phone booth, the kind Ma Bell used to provide, the kind Superman had always changed in. That was the vision that he had—of Clark Kent going into a phone booth and coming out as Superman.

He ran back to the dry cleaners. "I need to change."

"You need change?"

"Not change money, change clothes."

The man shook his head. Either he didn't understand, or there was no changing room. The girl's screams were even louder. Nick had heard sirens with less volume.

"I need to change my clothes. I'll do it over there." Nick pointed to behind the carousel. The clothes would block him from the public's view, or at least mostly. The man was still shaking his head, but Nick walked behind the counter anyway. The man shouted back to his wife. Her reply sounded incredulous. By the time she came into view Nick already had his shirt and pants off. She started spewing words. The language was unknown to him, but the meaning wasn't.

He threw on the padding, then the coat, then the pants, and cinched them with the belt. The wig and beard and cap got tossed on. And still the little girl's crying went on unabated. As did the woman's speech.

Nick decided to forego the boot covers and gloves. And there wasn't time to apply the white eyebrow stick. He was only a half-dressed Santa, but he hoped it would pass a child's muster. The entire mall had to be hearing the girl's screams, even if they had somehow escaped the attention of her mother.

He hurried out of the store, the Asian woman shouting behind him, the little girl screaming in the distance. It was no contest. Nick ran up to the little girl, and in his jolliest voice yelled, "Now who's that crying?"

He made big with his footsteps, exaggerated them to almost a swagger, and at his approach all the hovering adults said, "Look, it's Santa Claus."

Every head turned, even the girl's. And her mouth, opened wide to scream, opened just a little more, but her crying stopped. The hovering adults were only too happy to step aside, to relinquish all responsibility. They were counting on Santa to make everything perfect.

"Your mommy told me to come get you," Nick said, "but she said that first we could stop and get an ice cream cone. Does that sound good?"

The little girl's upper lip, quivering and covered with snot, raised itself, and in a very little voice she said, "Yes."

Nick offered his hand, and she took it.

# CHAPTER EIGHT

## Silent Night

Nick and the little girl, Erin, were halfway through their ice cream cones when her mother showed up, accompanied by Henry. The woman's face was flushed, and her eyes were red and teary. With a glad cry she scooped Erin up and held her tight. The daughter, now a picture of calm, took her mother's emotional outburst in stride.

"I was just with Santa Claus, Mama," she said, as if that should have explained everything.

The mother turned to Nick. With her panic subsiding, she was rapidly returning to being the picture of a well-heeled professional, one that didn't want to be mistaken for a negligent mother. "As I was telling this gentleman," she said, nodding to Henry, "Erin was right beside me. I was looking at some dresses, and when I turned around she was gone. We were on the first floor. I don't have any idea how she got up here."

She put Erin down, placed her head at her daughter's eye level, and in a stern voice asked: "How *did* you get up here?"

"I don't know," said Erin. The little girl had the decency to appear contrite until she went back to licking her chocolate chip cone.

"I think we need to have a talk, young lady. You better not ever, ever, ever walk away from me again."

She took Erin very firmly by the hand. "Thank you," she said to Nick. "I am so grateful that you looked out for her. Can I at least pay for the ice cream?"

"No," said Nick, "Santa's treat."

If Nick hadn't been in a Santa suit, he might have told Erin's mother his own story of the time he'd turned his back on George for just a moment. They'd been in one of those home improvement stores, and Nick had been checking out some plumbing fixtures when his Georgie-Porgie had vanished. At the time Georgie was only two. Nick had looked right, and then left, and was just about to start yelling when he heard grunting coming from above. To this day Nick didn't know how his youngster had climbed up the shelves. He was sitting atop a toilet display, and his strained face told Nick more than he wanted to know. Nick had scooped up his son and raced out of the store. At the time he'd been mortified. But as Georgie grew up, it became the most repeated story of his childhood. Maybe in years to come Erin would hear about her ice cream with Santa.

Erin's mother thanked him again, and then left with her daughter in tow. With Erin's one free hand she waved to Nick, and called out, "Good-bye Santa Claus."

Nick waved to her until she was out of sight.

"You the hero," said Henry.

"I'll gladly share the glory if you'll do me a big favor."

At least I was smart enough to order vanilla ice cream, thought Nick. He dabbed at his beard with a wet napkin, trying to get the spots out.

He looked at his watch and saw that it was almost five forty-five. He debated whether to change out of his Santa suit and then change into it again at the hospital. He'd be cutting the time close enough as it was, so he decided to leave the uniform on. He knew the mall well enough now to go through the mall tunnels and avoid onlookers.

Besides, it was possible he wouldn't have any choice in the matter. Henry hadn't yet returned with his clothes. Maybe they were being held hostage. He'd sent Henry as his goodwill emissary to try and retrieve the clothing he'd left at the dry cleaners.

It had been Santa to the rescue, Nick thought. Part of him was still surprised at what he'd done. It wasn't like him. It was out of character.

Henry walked into the locker room laughing. "You really gots 'em mad," he said. "Security was up at the cleaners, and they was telling them how this crazy man took off his clothes in the middle of their place."

Nick tried to retain a little dignity: "I undressed behind the carousel."

"That lady," said Henry, laughing all the more. "All she kept saying was, 'That Santa *Craus* a bad man.'"

"You straightened her out?"

"Wouldn't go so far as to say that." Henry grinned. "'Bout the best I could do was get your things back. I'd think about finding a new cleaners if I was you."

He handed Nick two bags, then tried to imitate the outraged woman's voice again: "That Santa *Craus* a bad man."

Nick took the bags and listened to Henry's chuckles echoing through the locker room as he made his exit.

There was a knock at the door followed by Angie's voice: "Nick?"

He was tempted not to answer, but finally said, "Yeah?"

"Do you think I could have a few minutes of your time?"

Nick sighed. "I got an appointment at six forty-five."

"This will only take a few minutes.

"I'm busy. Can I ignore you another time?"

When the Elf didn't answer Nick said, "All right."

"Wonderful!" she said in that too-enthusiastic voice of hers. "I'll be waiting for you in Walt's office."

Nick took his time getting there. Whatever the Elf wanted, he thought, would probably be something he wanted to run from.

Angie was sitting in Forster's seat wearing her oversized smile and holding one of those ridiculous quill pens. There was an ink well in front of her. As Nick took a seat she handed him a handful of letters.

"What are these?" he asked.

"They're letters to Santa. Our tradition is to post the letters on the sleigh, along with your answers to them."

"Why give 'em to me?"

Angie answered as if she was explaining to a child: "Because they're addressed to Santa."

"My Santa days are done," he said.

"You're still wearing the uniform."

"And why does that mean I got to play Dear Abby?"

"You don't even have to write your answers," said Angie. "I'm here to take dictation."

The Elf kept smiling. Nick finally broke down and opened an envelope and then began to read the letter aloud: "Dear Santa, I want a paint set, a makeup kit, and Magic Mansion. My daddy says we should leave you a beer instead of milk. Is he kidding me? Your friend, Brooke."

Now it was Nick who was smiling. He leaned back in his chair. "Dear Brooke," he said.

With ornate calligraphy, Angie started taking down his words.

"No, your daddy is not kidding you," said Nick. "Leave him a tall, cold one. Your friend, Santa."

Angie's pen had stopped moving. Her smile was still in place, but she looked at Nick expectantly.

"What?" Nick said.

Angie didn't answer.

"Dear Brooke," said Nick, "Santa loves cookies and milk. Thank you for thinking of me."

Angie's pen started moving again.

They finished a few more letters, but with each Nick grew antsier. "Listen, I got to leave. You'll have to finish up the last few letters for me."

Angie shook her head. "Those letters were addressed to Santa, not to me."

He would have argued, but time was short. Besides, there was no reasoning with this Elf. "Fine," he said. "I'll take 'em home with me and return them tomorrow with my Santa suit. You can write up my answers with that fancy pen work of yours."

"Thank you so much, Nick," said Angie.

"No problem." She took her job so seriously, as if she was on some kind of mission. Once upon a time he'd felt a similar need to help. But that already seemed like another lifetime.

Nick was five minutes late arriving at Los Niños. In some ways he was glad he was rushed. He didn't have too much time to think about his last visit to the hospital. Still, he hesitated a moment before stepping through the doors, flashing back to how his shirt had been covered in blood, and he had been holding a screaming girl.

He took a deep breath and tried to steady himself. The darkness had allowed him to walk through the hospital parking lot unobserved, but once he stepped into the lobby he'd have to face the Christmas music. He took another deep breath, and then threw the door open. All at once children began calling out his name, and Nick responded with waves and smiles. Several children ran up to him, and he felt like a besieged rock star. That escort, he thought, better be here.

She was. A woman in uniform waved to him, and then approached with an extended hand. Her name tag read "Isabel Castillo, RN."

"Hi, Santa," she said. "My name is Isabel"—she pronounced it *E-za-bel*—"but most people call me Easy. We're so glad you are here. Everyone's waiting for you."

Nick offered a few words for the children in the lobby, said that he'd be looking forward to seeing them on Christmas, and followed Easy to an elevator bank. The hospital's interior designer seemed to operate under the rule that no space could go unadorned. There was such an abundance of colorful murals, paintings, and framed posters that Nick felt as if he was in the San Diego Zoo. There were monkeys swinging in trees, bunnies nestled in tall grass, kittens playing with yarn, and puppies licking children's faces. Balloons and kites were flying everywhere, and suns were on the rise. The music playing from the speakers was faster than a Sousa march and more upbeat than ragtime. And the brighter and faster and cuter everything was, the more it screamed *Hospital!* God, he hated hospitals, especially this one.

The elevator door opened. Easy waited for Nick to get inside. Maybe she sensed how much he wanted to bolt. When the doors closed behind them and they were alone, she said, "We all heard how you're filling in for us, Nick, and we appreciate it. Can I get you anything before you begin your rounds?"

"How about a tranquilizer?"

She laughed. "I suppose you've come to the right place for that, but how about juice, or soda, or some water instead?"

"Anything liquid would be good."

Nick had always gotten along with nurses. Cops usually did. They shared a lot of the same defense mechanisms, had similar armor of bold fronts and black humor. Easy was middle-aged, about five foot two and heavy. Nick wondered what she had weighed before she started working her job, and whether the extra pounds defended her from what she had to deal with every day.

"You mind if we walk up a flight of stairs?" she asked.

"Fine."

The elevator came to a stop. He didn't think they were taking the indirect route for exercise, and Easy didn't keep him guessing about their detour for long. She paused at the foot of the stairwell and took off her thick glasses, ostensibly to wipe them. The nurse had big brown eyes, pretty eyes that he hadn't really seen behind the lenses.

"How much were you told about the patients you'll be visiting?"

"I know they're real sick."

She nodded, but didn't say anything.

Nick took a deep breath. "What I'm guessing is, some of the kids are dying."

He wanted Easy to contradict him, but she didn't. Instead, she just said, "Yes."

And Nick remembered this sick joke he had once heard another cop tell. "So," the cop said, "there's this little boy, and he says to his mother, 'Mommy, Mommy, why do we have a Christmas tree in August?' And she tells him, 'Jimmy, if I've told you once, I've told you a thousand times, you got leukemia.'"

Nick hoped he hadn't laughed, but he didn't remember. God, he hoped he hadn't laughed.

Easy put her glasses back on and the two of them started up the stairs. Pooh characters were dancing on the walls, Winnie, Christopher Robin, Roo, Tigger, and Owl. Even Eeyore was kicking up a hoof—dancing for God's sake.

Hypocrites, Nick wanted to yell, wanted to vent. He had read the Pooh stories to his own children, and he knew that Eeyore was never happy. The hospital could at least be that honest.

They came to a landing. "I'm glad you understand the condition of these children," Easy said, "but that's only part of it. You need to understand what you're going to see. The staff is used to looking at these kids. Outsiders aren't. But you're not an outsider to these children, and you won't have an outsider's excuse for flinching, or looking away. You're Santa Claus, and that means you have to love them without any reservations.

"You'll see amputated limbs and children with tubes running every which way in and out of them. You'll be talking to children with bodies more skeletal than not, with skin stretched so thin you could almost rub it away with an eraser. You'll see bald heads and open wounds. You'll have to deal with children without voices, and make yourself known to children who can no longer see.

"And despite all that, you're going to somehow have to be Santa Claus."

Nurse Castillo stared at him. Her lenses had to be almost half an inch thick. Nick was afraid that with her glasses she could see into his soul. If she could, she'd see nothing was there.

"Some welcoming committee you are."

"Better you turn around now," she said, "than go inside and lose it. These kids have had too many disappointments in their lives. I won't have Santa Claus betray them."

She was being unfair. Nick wanted to tell her that. It wasn't as if he had ever asked to be St. Nick. The job had been thrust upon him unfairly, just as this night had been. And how could he prepare for a hall of horrors? No one could. But much as he wanted to, he couldn't walk away.

"I was a cop," he said, then amended that. "I *am* a cop. I won't lose it."

It was as good a vow as he could come up with. The cop credo. Pretty shaky ground, he thought, but Nurse Castillo, with her X-ray vision, apparently decided it was good enough.

"Eighteen children in the Pediatric Oncology ward," she said. "We'd like you to spend five to ten minutes with each. Most share a room, except for those who have recently had surgery, or who are very sick. I'll tell you a little bit about each child before you talk with them. We have special presents for everyone, gifts we know they wanted, or were picked out especially for them. We'll keep restocking your Santa's bag prior to your visiting each room."

"I didn't bring my bag . . ."

"We've got one."

Out of habit, Nick stopped to pat himself down. It felt as if he was missing something. On the job, he had always reached out and touched his gun before going into a dangerous situation. Not that he'd drawn it more than two or three times all of his years on the force. And he'd only fired it on that one occasion, that one occasion that changed everything. But old habits die hard. He found himself unconsciously reaching to touch his gun because death was near. Different uniform, he remembered. And besides, he no longer had possession of his police firearm. The review board was holding it, along with his badge, pending their final decision on him. Unarmed, he had to go in and see some sick and dying kids. Backup. He needed backup.

"You'll be with me the whole time?"

"Every step of the way."

Nick gave the nod, the one that said, "Let's do it."

They walked up the remaining stairs, and Easy opened the door. The interior designer had evidently just been warming up with the hospital lobby. Stuffed animals lined the entire back wall of the nurse's station, animals of all shapes, sizes, colors, and textures. Several were almost as large as Nick.

Even more plentiful were the holiday trappings. Every available nook and cranny seemed to be stocked with nutcrackers, little drummer boys, and colorful miniature sleighs. A toy train set wound its way through the lobby. Santa was at the locomotive's wheel, leading a caravan of trains laden with trinkets and toys. The trailing caboose flashed red and green lights.

More lies, thought Nick. What were they thinking? Make enough noise, make merry loud enough, and death wouldn't visit?

The sound of clapping made him turn. A handful of nurses, doctors, and techs were standing in the hallway. It took Nick a moment to realize that they were cheering for him. Their applause created a stir throughout the ward. Little faces started to appear, some of them dragging medical equipment behind them. To Nick, they looked like concentration camp victims.

"Don't worry," said Easy, calling out to the children in a very loud voice. "Santa's going to visit everyone here."

"I promise," said Nick.

"See? Now just be patient."

Some of the staff tried to come forward to shake Nick's hand, but Easy shooed them away. "Kids first," she said. "That's Santa's rule."

The children, still lingering, laughed to see the adults being sent off. Their laughter startled Nick. He didn't expect that out of them.

Easy herded him into a lounge area and closed the door behind them. "Your first visit will be to Jessica Brisbane," she said. "Jessica is five years old. She was operated on for thyroid cancer. Last week a tumor, her thyroid gland, and most of Jessica's larynx were removed. Some more surgery is going to be necessary, so at the moment, Jessica has no voice, mechanical or otherwise."

"No voice." Nick considered Jessica's situation, and his own. "Does she read or write?"

Tell me she's incredibly precocious, Nick thought. Let her be a child prodigy who was reading and writing at the age of three. Give me that much slack at least.

"No, but Jessica finds ways to make herself understood."

"Maybe she can teach me," said Nick.

The nurse started dropping wrapped presents into a bag. "Jessica likes to draw, so we have some drawing sets for her. We also have some musical storybooks. All she has to do is push them for sounds."

Another wrapped present went into the bag. "And we found a special music box for her. Jessica loves music."

Easy lifted up the bag and offered it to him. "Are you ready to go?"

Nick accepted the bag. It was the only way he could answer. His throat was dry, and he worked his mouth to try and generate some saliva. Unless he could get some spit going, he and Jessica were going to have a very short conversation.

He thought about his own daughter. Corinne had adored him once. But when things had started going south between him and Teddy, she had become distant. When she'd been a kid you couldn't shut Corinne up. He and Teddy used to call her "Chatty Cathy." How had things gotten to the point where neither he or Corinne now talked much to the other? It wasn't as if they had Jessica's problem. Both of them had voices.

Nick followed Easy into the room, into that place that had him scared to death. He listened to Easy say, "I think you already know we have a very special visitor today, don't you, Jessica?"

Jessica's eyes were bright. She was sitting up on her bed, and had the expression of a child who knows the answer and desperately wants to be called upon. Upon her head was a red scarf that made her pale face appear that much more white and ghostlike. The scarf covered her baldness.

"Merry Christmas, Jessica!" It wasn't his voice, Nick thought. It was more like Angie the Elf's voice. But at least the words came out.

He took a seat in the chair next to her bed. "Well, then," he said.

There was a moment's silence. What was he doing? Waiting for her to answer? He remembered the scene from *Miracle on*

*34th Street* when a Dutch girl was seated on St. Nick's lap. No one expected him to be able to communicate with her, but suddenly he started speaking Dutch. And after the girl went happily on her way, the Saint revealed that he knew the language of all children.

But how would St. Nick have talked to this girl who couldn't speak? He couldn't ask her questions that involved more than a nod or a shake of the head.

Nick reached into his bag. He could start with the presents. Dessert first.

"I brought you some special gifts, Jessica, for a very special little girl. I know right now it's frustrating for you to not be able to speak. That's going to change over time, but talking isn't the only way of communicating. There are other ways."

Nick reached into his bag and felt around, found the right present, and handed it to her.

"This is one way you can express your thoughts," he said, but Jessica wasn't listening. She was already digging into the wrapping and pulling open the coloring book and markers.

Nick handed her another of the drawing sets. "I know you're a very talented artist, Jessica. There's an old saying: A picture paints a thousand words. If you draw the right pictures, people will consider you positively chatty."

There was more frantic tearing, followed by more smiles. Back in the Dark Ages, Nick had been taught in the Police Academy that most communication was non-verbal. On the street he'd learned to trust body language more than words, and he'd communicated back to people in the way he stood, and the way he looked at them, or didn't look at them.

Like the way in which he was sitting away from Jessica, as if she was a stranger. That wasn't how Santa would be sitting, or acting.

Nick handed her another present, one of the sound books. He couldn't hand her gifts all night. They'd be running out soon. There had to be another way to communicate with her. He moved closer to Jessica, then reached out his gloved hand and lightly touched her. There. He had been afraid to do that, as if death was contagious. But wasn't the same contagion in his own soul? He hoped it was a case of two negatives coming together and making a positive.

Jessica smiled at him, and then went back to her storybook, touching the characters for their sounds. Bees buzzed and birds chirped and frogs croaked. It was a jungle out there.

The time with Jessica went faster than Nick could have imagined, and they didn't run out of things to say to one another, even though Nick was the only one doing the talking. When he handed Jessica the last present in the bag she turned it around several times in her hands before carefully removing the wrapping. Her mouth was open, and Nick didn't need to hear any sounds to know how delighted she was. Atop the wind-up music box was a ballerina. Her toes were pointed to the wooden stage, her arms raised over her head. Jessica wound up her prize, then put it on her bed stand, and both of them listened to music from the *Nutcracker Suite*.

Side by side they watched the ballerina dance round and round just for them.

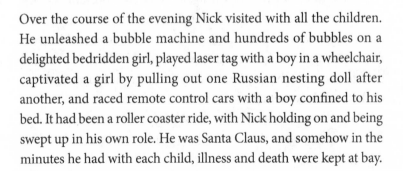

Over the course of the evening Nick visited with all the children. He unleashed a bubble machine and hundreds of bubbles on a delighted bedridden girl, played laser tag with a boy in a wheelchair, captivated a girl by pulling out one Russian nesting doll after another, and raced remote control cars with a boy confined to his bed. It had been a roller coaster ride, with Nick holding on and being swept up in his own role. He was Santa Claus, and somehow in the minutes he had with each child, illness and death were kept at bay.

"One last stop," said Easy.

The change in Easy's tone made Nick take notice. She now looked apprehensive. That surprised him, since only moments before she had been saying that his visit with the kids had exceeded all her expectations. He watched as Nurse Castillo slowly and deliberately dropped the last wrapped presents into Nick's bag.

"Raymond is very sick," she said.

Her eyes sought Nick's out. She was telling Nick the boy was dying.

"His parents live back East. They brought him here hoping for a miracle. There was this new treatment. There's always some new treatment. So far it hasn't taken, though. The hope is that Raymond can get stronger so that the doctors can try again. But he's been getting worse, and he knows it. Very little reaches him now.

"Everyone deals with death differently. I try to not be judgmental. Raymond's situation is made worse by the fact that his parents live three thousand miles away. I'm sure they are stretched to their limits financially. I am sure they bet everything on this miracle cure, and they are not willing to accept that it's a bust hand.

"One parent or the other visits him once a week, and stays for several days. It's an awful schedule, and I know the visits bring them no relief. Raymond's parents believe they have done the right thing by their son. They think they have sacrificed everything just to give him a chance, and they're still putting their hope on that miracle that's not going to happen. Raymond doesn't understand all of that. He only understands that his family is far away. He thinks he's been abandoned, and that he's facing death alone. Don't be surprised if he's not responsive to you."

The adrenaline that had been running through Nick's veins suddenly went dry. Reality surfaced, and Santa's sleigh crashed into it.

"What kind of gifts did you get him?"

"Raymond's always looking out his window. He doesn't seem to miss anything that goes on, so we got him picture books: one on clouds, another on astronomy, and still another on San Diego birds. And we got him a snow dome."

"Snow dome?"

"One of those water globes you shake, and the snow appears as if it's falling. Raymond loves the winter."

The winter back East, thought Nick. A wintry day in San Diego meant putting on a sweater. Few of its residents had gloves, or scarves, or winter coats. Jack Frost didn't live around here.

There was only this last chimney to go down, he thought. If the kid ignored him, it wouldn't be his fault. The happy sounds from the ward emboldened Nick a little. His visit had brought an excitement that had not yet passed. The staff was glad to let the children stay up later than usual; the adults were acting as excited as their charges. Instead of musical chairs it looked like musical rooms, with everyone popping in and out of them.

All except for one room, the darkened room, the room that Easy was leading him to.

"He says lights bother him," she said, "but I think it's more that the darkness suits his mood."

The nurse knocked, and then opened the door. There wasn't any response from the figure on the bed. With her head, Easy motioned for Nick to follow her inside.

"We have a visitor for you, Raymond. He's traveled a great distance to be here."

The room wasn't totally dark. Some of the medical equipment shed light, and overhead it was a starry, starry night: affixed to a mobile were stars, luminous stars that glowed in the dark.

And there was also the white of the boy's eyes, orbs in themselves. Raymond was staring out his window. Nick took a seat in the chair next to his bed and joined him in looking out the window. Neither said anything. They just surveyed the night sky, though there wasn't much to see. The quarter moon was hidden behind dark clouds, its presence hinted at more than seen.

"Not many stars out tonight, are there?" asked Nick, finally breaking the silence.

No answer, nothing to even indicate the boy had heard. The silence in the room grew, broken only by the teakettle sounds of Raymond's labored breathing. The IV tubes running into the boy's arms made him look as if he was trapped in a spider web.

Nick raised his eyes to the mobile and took in the glowing stars. "I'm afraid the best star gazing tonight is right above you."

"They're *fake*."

Raymond's words were whispered, but they hung in the air like a challenge, an accusation.

"Not fake exactly," Nick said. "They represent real stars and planets." He pointed. "I can see Saturn up there with its rings. And there's the Milky Way. And I guess that red-tinged one is Mars. All those places are real."

Raymond's eyes flicked momentarily up to the mobile, then back down, deep into himself. He still hadn't looked at Nick. The boy was painfully thin.

"I brought some presents for you, Raymond."

Going away presents, Nick thought. That's what they were.

But Raymond didn't take the bait. Instead, he said, "My mother took me to see Santa Claus when I was a boy."

*When I was a boy.* The words echoed in Nick's head. Raymond couldn't be more than eight years old. But for all he had been through, he was right: he was no longer a boy.

"Are you that same Santa Claus?"

Raymond looked at Nick, ambushing him with his prematurely old eyes. "No," said Nick, answering even before he could consider the ramifications of what he said.

Out of the frying pan and into the fire: "Are you the *real* Santa Claus?" Raymond asked.

It was the second time in two days Nick had been asked that question, but it felt different this time, felt like a crucible. The eyes in the darkness hung on his answer.

"The world's grown larger," Nick said. "It's more complicated. The job's too big, even for Santa. So he has helpers."

"And you are one of those helpers?"

The day before he'd lied to a healthy boy, had blithely told him that he was the real Santa Claus. But he couldn't do that again, not with this particular boy.

"Yes. But the way it works is that all of Saint Nick's helpers are given part of his spirit. So I don't only speak for myself. Santa Claus talks through me. I know that must be hard to understand, because it's tough enough to explain."

There was a slight rustle of Raymond's covers, his shoulders apparently moving to signify a shrug. "I don't believe in Santa Claus."

Nick matched the boy's shrug. "Before I worked for him, I didn't believe in him either."

"Really?"

"Really."

"He's real?"

"Am I real?"

"Of course."

"There's your answer. Look at your glow-in-the-dark stars. They hint at what's really out there. If you look at me, you'll see that same hint of the real thing, of the real Santa Claus."

Raymond's long look appeared to consider Nick in a different light. The boy's eyes weren't as hostile, or as dubious, but he still didn't look convinced. Nick hoped he had something that would tilt the scales.

"He picked out some presents especially for you, Raymond."

The prospect of gifts didn't excite the boy. "I don't want any presents," said Raymond, his breathing labored. "Give them to someone else."

"Uh-oh."

Nick infused his voice with fear. Raymond turned his head, and Nick could see his surprise. The boy hadn't expected that reaction.

"What's wrong?"

"Nothing." Nick was working without a script. "It's just that I hope I don't get into trouble."

"For what?"

"If I come back with presents, Saint Nick's not going to be happy. That'll put him in a bad mood."

The boy seemed to be considering Nick's dilemma.

"I hope he doesn't blame me," Nick said. "Maybe I can write a note that explains everything, and have you sign it. That might get me off the hook."

"What happens if I don't sign the note?"

"Santa doesn't keep helpers that don't take their responsibilities seriously. They're no longer allowed to wear the uniform."

"But it's not your fault."

"That's not for me to decide."

Raymond's body was failing him, but not his compassion. "Then I'll take the presents."

Nick sounded relieved: "Good."

As if fulfilling a solemn duty, he handed Raymond his first present. The boy slowly pulled apart the wrapping, and then started fingering the pages of his San Diego bird book. Nick handed him another present, and then another. With the unveiling of each gift, the corners of Raymond's mouth turned up more and more, until there was something on his face that almost resembled a smile.

Nick handed him the snow globe last. When the wrapping came off, there was no longer any doubt: Raymond's smile took up most of his face.

He raised the glass world aloft. The quarter moon cooperated, offering enough light for Nick and Raymond to see a winter wonderland. Skaters skimmed across the surface of an iced-over pond, and under a canopy of frosted trees spectators watched from the shoreline. Two dogs were running along the edge of the frozen water.

Like a weight lifter struggling under the load of a heavy dumbbell, Raymond shook the globe with his trembling arm. He pushed out once, twice, gasping first for the effort, and then at what he saw. The landscape was adrift in falling snow.

Nick and the boy both hunched close to the globe, each transfixed by the swirling flakes. It wasn't until every flake had fallen that Raymond dropped his exhausted arm, but even then, he was careful to make sure the globe landed softly atop his chest. There, he nestled it close to his heart.

Since entering the room, Nurse Castillo had stood quietly in the background. Now she motioned to Nick that it was time to leave. Even though he wasn't looking at her, Raymond must have sensed the signal.

"When my mother took me to see Santa, I sat in his lap. I remember that he asked me what I wanted for Christmas. Is that what you do?"

Nick nodded, and then realized the boy's eyes were closed. "Yes."

"You didn't ask me what I wanted."

Nick sensed a trap, but he had to ask anyway: "What do you want for Christmas?"

He was afraid the boy was going to ask him for his health. That had been Nick's fear the entire night, but the children hadn't responded that way. They'd wanted the same kinds of toys healthy kids wanted.

But that wasn't what Raymond wanted.

"I want snow. I want to sit here on Christmas Day, and look out my window, and see snow falling. I want that more than anything else."

# CHAPTER NINE

## All Through the Night

The uniform was off—no beard, wig, red pantaloons, or boots—but it didn't feel as if it was off. That's how it had been for the longest time when Nick was a cop. It hadn't mattered when he wore civilian clothes. He was still a cop.

Nick paced around his apartment. It's over, he told himself. He'd be dropping off his Santa Claus uniform in the morning and that would be the end of it. But he kept thinking about that sick boy who wanted snow. Raymond.

The harder Nick tried to put him out of his mind, the more he kept intruding. Snow. Who'd ask for a crazy kind of Christmas present like that? It was impossible, of course. Nick had lived in San Diego for thirty years and he couldn't remember seeing any snow. There had been one or two flurries, but nothing had ever stuck to the ground. If you traveled a couple of hours away to the mountains, then maybe you'd have a chance of seeing some snow in the middle of winter, but it just didn't happen anywhere along the coast. Raymond might as well have asked for diamonds to fall from the sky.

It wasn't a fair request anyway. It went against the unsaid rules. Santa Claus was in the business of delivering presents, not miracles. That's what he should have told the kid; should have firmly stated that Santa had nothing to do with the weather, but instead he had babbled some nonsense about how he'd take up the matter with Santa and together they would see what could be done.

Snow job, that's what he had given Raymond. Maybe I should have promised to look into world peace while I was at it, thought Nick, and the end of all famine and war.

He threw himself down on the easy chair. He tried to get comfortable, but couldn't. Darn chair. He'd only spent ten bucks for it, but had overpaid. Odd, though, that it had never bothered him before.

He dropped his feet onto the coffee table and shifted around some more in the chair. Nope. It was like that "Princess and the Pea" story. Something was there, even if he couldn't quite feel it, and it was causing a royal pain in his backside.

His shifting feet knocked a few envelopes off the coffee table to the floor. Nick leaned over and picked them up, and remembered the letters to Santa that he'd promised Angie he would finish. He didn't want to face up to them, though, so he grabbed the remote control and turned on the television. When he saw Ebenezer Scrooge looking at Christmas past he turned off the TV and reluctantly reached for the letters.

He selected a piece of paper that had been addressed to Santa Claus in red crayon. The letters were large and shaky. He opened the envelope, and saw that the same crayon had been used to write the letter:

> *Dear Santa Clause.*
> *I want the Delux Doll Hous. And I want skats.*
> *Love.*
> *Janet.*

Janet was an artist who didn't like white space. She had used the crayon to draw pictures all over the page.

Nick opened a second letter that was a by-product of the computer generation. Next thing you know kids would just be e-mailing Santa.

> *Dear Santa Claus,*
> *Last year you gave my brother a football. He won't let*
> *me play with it. I'd like my own football, only better. I*
> *also want a skateboard. And I want a street hockey set.*
> *And boxing gloves.*
> *I will leave you cookies and milk.*
> *Love,*
> *Lisa*

Nick did a double take at the name. He had a feeling Lisa's brother better watch out if she got the boxing gloves. Maybe he didn't let her play with his football because she was too rough on it.

The promise of cookies and milk reminded Nick of when his own children had left out goodies for Santa. He recalled one Christmas when the cookies had sustained him while he'd stayed up all night trying to put together Georgie's tricycle. Teddy had told him he should have paid the extra few bucks to have the store do it, and on Christmas Eve he had made that same discovery for himself. Try as he might, he had never been able to perfectly straighten out the handlebars. They tilted to the right, but Georgie never noticed. He had just kept flying around their driveway, laughing while he pedaled.

Nick had been just as happy the Christmas he'd gotten his own bike. That's what so much of Christmas was about—reliving memories. He had felt so proud atop the bike, so grown-up. His Grandfather Alex—his Papou—had puffed on his pipe while keeping an eye on him. Nick still remembered the old man's smile and his glowing dark eyes. Grandma Theresa—Yiayia he called her—had been too busy to come out and watch. She was in charge of the kitchen, and that meant turning out tables of food, but as busy as she always was, Yiayia never neglected to slip Nick handfuls of of *kourambiethes*, the best sugar cookies in the world. The aroma from her kitchen drew children and adults alike, forcing Yiayia to periodically shoo everyone off, but the onlookers usually only went as far as the dining room table where there was always fresh baked bread and cheeses, and plenty of wine and spirits ready for the sipping. The table was close enough for everyone to be able to smell the lamb roasting, and the souvlaki and spanakopita baking.

Every Christmas it was Nick's duty to taste his grandmother's lemon chicken soup. Yiayia let him stand nearby while she worked her magic with the broth, fresh lemon juice, carrots, egg yolks, rice, and chicken. When the soup was heating and all but done she would stick in a wooden spoon, blow on the broth, and call him over.

"Hurry, Nico, hurry," she would yell, deathly afraid that the soup might boil and the egg yolks curdle.

She would offer him the spoon, and he would sip, and she'd say, "Is it all right, Nico? Is it okay?"

It was never anything less than perfect. Very seriously, he would nod to Yiayia.

"Does it need more pepper, Nico? A pinch of salt? A little lemon?"

He always shook his head, and then she would refill the spoon for him, and he would greedily suck it down. As the taster, it was his privilege to be first. Other children, mostly his cousins, were called upon to sample other dishes, but Nick was always the chosen one for Yiayia's soup.

Christmas wasn't only the food. After eating, and after eating some more, Uncle Stephanos and Uncle Constantine, with just a little encouragement, would bring out their musical instruments,

Stephanos his *santuri*, and Constantine his *bouzouki*, and they would play and everyone would sing.

Nick's own children hadn't had those kinds of ethnic Christmases, even though Teddy was half Greek. Her other half was Swedish. She always argued like her nationalities. Taking Teddy on was like figuring out a Pacific Northwest weather front. She could storm one moment, be cold and icy the next, and then hot as the blazes. He called her a Sweek. When they fought he called her a crazy Sweek.

Teddy had always been in charge of their Christmases. She never served Greek food or drink, and observed very few of the Greek holiday traditions. And since Nick didn't play any musical instruments, and since he sure didn't dance, there was never any Greek music or dancing. But Teddy always made sure the holidays were special. Every year they would go to a performance of the *Nutcracker*. And no matter how tight the budget, Teddy always took the kids down to the shelter, and the family would give what it could. Everyone on the street would get Teddy's Christmas cookies, but what she enjoyed most of all was the holiday music. The kids loved to go out with a group of carolers, singing loudly if not on-key. We had our American Christmases together, Nick thought, whatever that is.

He opened another letter to Santa. On one side of the letter was writing, and on the other was a picture that had been drawn with colored pencils. Nick studied the drawing. Santa Claus was in the middle of the scene, and dwarfed everything around him. He was bigger than the palm trees, and even bigger than a red San Diego Trolley. Several menacing figures were leaning against a mural. They had the look of gangbangers. It was clear they were up to no good, but they were keeping their distance from the huge Santa Claus. Across from them were what looked like carolers, but they weren't the Elizabethan type. Their music wasn't quite staving off the darkness.

There was something about the picture that was familiar. And there was something that was a bit off-putting. This wasn't a Christmas drawing of some country landscape; this was an urban Christmas. The drawing wasn't awash in bright sunshine; it was darker. And the palm trees weren't Christmas pines; their fronds looked like daggers.

Nick turned the drawing over and scanned the note. At first glance there wasn't anything that made this note stand out from the others, nothing to warn him about the heartbreak inside.

> *Dear Santa,*
>
> *You didn't come visit me last year. I guess you couldn't find us because we were moving around.*
>
> *My mommy says you might not make it this year either, especially if we have to go back in the car. It's slow at work, she says. That's why her hours have been cut. She says you visit so many other boys and girls that you can't get to everyone, but I hope you do find us. I really want a pink purse and a stuffed animal. My favorite stuffed animal would be a gorilla. I would also like some books of my own. I read all of the Magic Trunk Tales and I love the Four Seasons fantasy novels.*
>
> *Please come visit me this year Santa.*
>
> *Love,*
>
> *Laura*

Nick dropped the page and let it sit in his lap for a minute. He finally picked it up again with the edge of his fingertips, as if he were handling evidence, and read it a second time.

No return address. No last name. The writer knew cursive. Her letters were large, but well formed, the product of a young hand. There were no misspellings. She'd taken pains to make the letter as perfect as it could be.

*Laura.* Nick couldn't remember talking to any Laura, but then he had seen so many children. And it was possible the letter had been dropped off during one of the other two Santas' shifts.

He turned the letter over and once more studied the drawing. Santa Claus was the bright spot in a threatening world. The page had been neatly torn out of a composition pad.

Maybe the letter was a phony. People got their jollies in an awful lot of strange ways. Someone might have decided to dummy up a letter just for kicks. Now that he thought about it, the handwriting looked a little too good, and the vocabulary too large, and the sentiment too much, for a young kid. Everything was designed to pull at the heartstrings. And most kids couldn't draw that well.

The letter was a phony, thought Nick. Or was it?

He remembered he had been seven or eight when he had stopped believing that there was a Santa Claus. Most of his friends had expressed their doubts about then. And this new generation was anything but naive. They seemed to be Doubting Thomases right out of the womb.

Could a seven- or eight-year-old create such a letter? It was possible, he supposed. Or maybe the kid was younger, and her mother had helped her to write it. Maybe the mother wanted to believe in Santa Claus as much as her daughter.

Nick dropped the letter again. That's what happens when you open Pandora's Box, he thought. The letters hadn't been meant for him. He should have just let well enough alone. The problem with Christmas was that it was just another day and yet it brought all these expectations with it. To his thinking, the heartache and disappointment surpassed the joy.

The phone rang, and Nick's first thought was, *Trouble comes in threes*. He'd seen Raymond, gotten Laura's note, and now there was this call. He didn't have to answer the phone, but he couldn't ignore it.

Forster must not have liked his growl. "Why is it that you always sound like a pit bull with an attitude?"

"What do you want?"

"It's not what I want. Angie wanted to call you herself, but I said you didn't like your number handed out. So she asked me to run her request by you, and then have you call her back."

"What request?"

"She had your replacement all set for tomorrow. There was no problem with that. But something came up tonight. The second-shift Santa messed up."

Nick remembered the punk he had argued with in the locker room and wasn't surprised. "What happened?"

"Seems there was this little boy sitting on his lap, and our Santa asked what he wanted for Christmas, and the kid said, 'I want a baby brother.' Our Santa gave the boy's mother a good once over, and then announced, quite pointedly, 'Have your mom come around when my shift ends tonight, and I'll see what I can do about it.' Mom wasn't pleased."

"I'm not filling in. That's what she wants, isn't it?"

"That was my impression."

"It's not my fault someone hired a rotten apple."

"Don't blame the messenger, Nico."

"I did my promised two days."

"Don't tell me, tell Angie. She has a line on a few candidates, but she needs to interview them first."

"This is crazy," Nick said. "That Santa suit is like some kind of tar baby. I keep trying to get rid of it and it keeps sticking to me. If I were superstitious . . ."

"What?"

"Nothing. I'm not superstitious."

Nick believed that people who wanted to find omens found them. It was as simple as that. They believed because they wanted to believe. That wasn't something he wanted, or was willing, to do.

"So, can I give Angie your num—"

"No." The last thing Nick wanted was the head Elf calling him at home.

"Then you call her. She's waiting on your answer."

"Are you supposed to be softening me up for her? Playing the good cop?"

"I'm not playing anything, Nick. I'm too busy to be playing anything. I'm calling you from work, and my office is getting more crowded by the moment. In fact, a couple of San Diego's finest just walked in."

"Why? What happened?"

"Our bad boys struck here less than an hour ago."

# CHAPTER TEN

*Hark! The Herald Angels Sing*
*December 1*

When Angie picked up the phone, Nick heard the sounds of her little girl in the background. What was her kid's name? Noël, he remembered.

"Sorry to be calling so late," he said.

"I'm glad you called."

Hearing how the muggers had messed up a shopper had changed matters for Nick. They had preyed on a woman whose car was on the outskirts of the parking lot, had pulled up alongside her and struck her from behind by flinging open their car's passenger door. They had followed up with a few savage kicks and then had stolen her purse and packages. Those scumbags needed to be nailed.

"Forster tells me you're in need of a Santa, and he apparently still wants me working undercover."

"Welcome back, Saint Nick," said Angie, sounding entirely too cheerful.

"Just so you know, when we catch the bad guys I'm hanging up the Santa suit."

Angie laughed. "See you tomorrow, Nick."

She hung up before Nick could ask her what was so funny.

———— ✳ ————

In between lap-sitters, Nick was trying to concentrate on his *real* job of looking out for bad guys. Naturally, last night's assault had happened in an area where there was no video surveillance. Forster wasn't sure if the bad guys had disabled the parking lot bullet camera, or if it had gone on the fritz. The victim had only seen the backs of the two assailants as they had run off, laughing. It galled Nick that they had been laughing. He couldn't wait to nail those two.

Angie was busy at work taping up the letters to Santa. Nick had given her all the letters except for Laura's. He had wanted to throw the letter away, but hadn't been able to bring himself to do that. As much as he didn't want to, he felt personally involved. The kid needed help—no kid deserved a miserable Christmas— and it was as if she had asked it of him. Nick decided now that the best way to rid himself of Laura's letter was to give it to Angie. Maybe Pollyanna would have a good idea of how to deal with it.

The letter was in his pocket, but Angie interrupted his intentions once more. Instead of him passing her a letter, she gave him one.

"Another note left in Santa's mailbox," she said.

"Wonderful," said Nick.

He opened it up, and was relieved Laura hadn't written again. It was just a letter from a kid wanting presents.

"Dear Santa," read Nick, "I really, really, really want a skateboard. I want the one with lightning wheels. Yours truly, Ryan. P.S. I am the Ryan with red hair."

Since it was quiet at the workshop, Angie must have decided it was a good time to tackle correspondence. She had her quill pen at the ready and looked at Nick expectantly: "Any thoughts, Santa?"

Nick shrugged, and then said, "Dear Ryan, red is my favorite color. Ho, ho, ho, Santa."

"That's perfect!" clapped Angie, and started writing.

He waited until she finished. That's when Nick said, "I got a letter here that I don't have the perfect answer to. In fact I don't know what to say at all. Maybe you've got some ideas."

Nick handed over Laura's letter. As Angie read it, her smile wavered slightly, but never completely disappeared.

"So?" asked Nick.

"The obstacle is the path," announced Angie.

"What's that supposed to mean?"

"If we close our eyes and concentrate," she said, "we might be able to visualize a solution together."

"Why don't we just clap our hands for Tinker Bell?"

"It's easy to be a skeptic, Nick."

Angie closed her eyes. Nick rolled his. With her eyes still closed, Angie whispered, "Do you see anything?"

"Yeah," Nick said, "I see me passing you Laura's note and saying, 'Lots of luck.'"

Angie opened her eyes and regarded him. "The letter came to you, Nick. I think there was a reason for that."

"The letter came to me because you insisted I take it."

Angie didn't argue. With her infuriating smile she just waited him out, until, with a loud sigh, Nick reluctantly closed his eyes.

In a calm voice she advised, "Breathe in and out."

"Is there any other way?" asked Nick.

Still, he tried to humor her, but after only a few seconds opened his eyes. Someone was shining a light. He lifted up a shading hand.

"What's that light?" he asked.

"Follow it!" advised Angie.

The light was coming from a camera. A woman was holding a mike. "There's a TV reporter," he said.

Angie's eyes were still closed. "That's wonderful, Nick. You've tapped into the magic."

"Open your eyes, Angie. We got company."

The reporter was approaching the sleigh, one hand patting her highlighted hair to make sure it was in place. Nick gauged her to be mid-forties. She was wearing a designer suit of Christmas colors, but he assumed it was an empty suit. In his experience, most local TV reporters were as bubbly as champagne, and usually about as substantial as cotton candy.

The woman extended a hand to Angie. "Good afternoon," she said, "I'm Charlotte Davis with News Three San Diego."

"I'm Angie with the North Pole," the Elf said. "You look so radiant in white!"

For just a moment, the reporter's smile failed her. "But I'm not wearing white."

"Not at the moment," said Angie.

Nick hid his laugh behind his hand. It was nice seeing someone else on the receiving end of Angie's non sequiturs.

"Anyway," said Charlotte, recovering her smile, "I'm here to do a piece that we're calling 'My Visit with Santa.'"

"We were expecting you," said Angie.

"You were?" said the puzzled reporter.

"We were visualizing a solution and you appeared," said Angie.

Charlotte studied their faces. "Did my anchor put you up to this? He's always pulling pranks."

A smiling Angie shook her head, and Charlotte grimaced, then pulled out a steno pad and pointedly turned to Nick. "Spell your name for me, would you, Santa?"

Nick, with exaggerated clarity, spelled, "S-A-N-T-A."

The reporter tapped her steno pad with suppressed annoyance. "Your real name, please."

When Nick didn't answer, Angie did: "He's Nick."

"Nick what?" asked Charlotte.

"He's Saint Nick."

By this time the reporter had lost her smile. "I don't think my news director is going to buy that one."

Nick had been afraid to offer his name because of his recent notoriety, but he saw the opportunity to remain anonymous for another reason. "When I'm sitting in the sleigh, Santa Claus *is* my real name."

Charlotte raised her hands in surrender. "Yes, Virginia, there is a Santa Claus. Far be it from me to be the instrument for corrupting the belief system of minors. You can be the one and only Santa Claus."

She turned to her cameraman who had been busy setting up. "You ready with the shot?"

He gave his thumbs-up, and Charlotte turned back. "Okay," she said, "the way we'll do this is you'll treat me like any youngster coming to see Santa. So I'll need everyone to act normal and pretend the camera isn't here."

The presence of the camera had brought a growing crowd of onlookers over to the sleigh. Everyone but Nick looked excited to be part of the local news.

The reporter pulled out a compact, examined her makeup and hair, and then motioned to her cameraman that she was ready. When the camera light turned on, she became animated, her voice higher and more enthusiastic.

"Here at the Plaza Center it's beginning to look a lot like Christmas. And you know what that means. Yes, Santa Claus has come to town!"

She waved at Nick and shouted, "Hi, Santa!"

Nick offered a half-hearted wave back.

Charlotte's voice dropped to a confessional tone. "Now I must admit I'm a bit nervous about going to see Santa. It's been a long time since I last saw him, and I'm worried about what he might ask me, like whether I've been a good girl or not. Truth to tell, I'm feeling a little bit *Claus*-trophobic, but it's time to put aside those fears."

Angie approached Charlotte, and asked if she was ready to go and see Santa.

"My moment of truth," said Charlotte with mock-nervousness.

"Don't be scared," said Angie. "Going to see Santa is fun."

It was a good thing the camera wasn't on Nick. All the treacle was making him scowl. As Angie and Charlotte approached the sleigh, the reporter exaggerated her mannerisms; she chewed her nails and made her steps tentative.

"Santa, this is Charlotte," said Angie.

In a little voice the reporter said, "Hi, Santa."

Charlotte signaled to the cameraman, and he cut the lights. Her cutesy voice completely vanished. "You get all that?"

"It looks good," he said.

There were even more onlookers now. The upper walkways were crowded with lookie-loos. A distraction like this would be prime cover for the muggers, but Nick didn't even try to look for the bad guys. There were just too many people.

"All right," Charlotte said to the cameraman, "we're going to need a close-up on me sitting in Santa's lap. Shoot it so that I'm looking up into Santa's face like I'm some kind of munchkin or something."

As the cameraman worked to get the shot, Charlotte turned to Nick. "If it's okay with you, *Saint Nick*," she said, not sparing any sarcasm, "I'd like you to refer to me as young lady while I'm sitting in your lap. Then do the usual: ask me what I want for Christmas. That work for you?"

Nick tried to hide his smile. "As long as I'm not chewing gum while I'm talking, I should be able to manage that."

This time it was Charlotte's turn to hide her smile. She approached the sleigh, and turned to the cameraman. The lights were already on and he signaled for her to proceed. She took a tentative step up to the sleigh and Nick reached out a white-gloved hand.

"Come aboard, young lady," he said, "ho, ho, ho."

Charlotte turned to the camera and said, sotto voce, "Being called young lady already makes this a great visit! I can't wait for Santa to ask me what I want for Christmas."

She settled into Nick's lap, and he asked, "Have you been a good girl, Charlotte?"

"Mostly," squeaked the reporter, although her body language seemed to suggest otherwise.

"And what do you want for Christmas?" asked Nick.

"Well, you know what they say, Santa, diamonds are a girl's best friend."

Using her eyes, Charlotte signaled the cameraman, and the lights went out. "My Christmas wish," she called, "is that we don't have to re-shoot."

"Amen to that," said Nick.

"I'm checking it . . ." said the cameraman. "Looks okay."

"How's the audio?" she asked.

"Perfect."

Charlotte pulled a pair of glasses from the inside of her blazer, consulted her notes, and turned to Nick. "Word on the streets is that you're the man to go to for a candy cane," she said.

Nick answered so that only she could hear, "Yeah, I'm a regular sugar daddy."

He handed her a candy cane, and she removed the wrapping. Once more she consulted her compact mirror, but this time she smeared her red lipstick to make it look like she had been hard at work on the candy cane.

After a signal, the camera lights went on again. Charlotte stopped licking the candy cane and looked guilty as if she had been caught doing something she shouldn't. "Oops," she said, "I know I've had a great time here. How many men do you know who ask you for a gift list? This is Charlotte Davis, sitting in Santa's lap at Plaza Center." She stopped talking to the camera and turned back to Nick. "And you know what else I want, Santa?" she asked.

As soon as the camera lights went off, Charlotte got to her feet. Angie came forward, and with folded hands looked from Nick to the reporter. "I love weddings!" she announced.

Charlotte turned to Nick. "Am I missing something?"

"It's an elf kind of thing," Nick said.

"You sure my anchor didn't put you up to this?"

The Elf shook her head. "Laura put us up to this."

"Laura?" asked Charlotte.

Angie looked at Nick meaningfully. Maybe there was a method to the Elf's madness, he thought. He nodded to her, and she handed the reporter the letter.

"If you're a real reporter," Nick said, "you'll find Laura. That's the Christmas story you should be doing."

Charlotte took the note, and slid it into her purse without looking at it. "We need to get to another location," she said, "but I'll read this later. If there's a story here I'll pass it on to our assignment editor."

Sure. Out of sight, out of mind, thought Nick. They had tried, he told himself. The note wasn't his problem anymore. But he couldn't leave it at that. Barbie Newscaster had turned her back to him, and was busy texting.

Suddenly Nick was angry. Angry that cops and reporters too often only paid attention after a crime had been committed. Laura had suffered last year, but this time they could stop it from happening again.

"Why don't you put that phone away?"

Charlotte glanced toward him. She looked surprised, but something in his tone made her stop texting and turn.

The onlookers had drifted away, and the cameraman was talking with the elves. It was just the two of them.

"That note was from a little girl who wrote saying Santa didn't visit her last year," Nick said. "And she's worried Santa might not stop this year either."

Charlotte didn't say anything.

"The note was signed 'Laura.' There's no return address, and there's no telephone number. There's a drawing on the note that shows a trolley station. This mall can be accessed from the trolley, and bus lines. That's probably how Laura got here. If you want, I can probably identify that trolley stop near to where she lives. That might narrow down your search."

"I haven't committed to a search," Charlotte protested. "I haven't committed to anything. I haven't even read the note."

"What's stopping you?"

Her face reddened. "A killer schedule is what is stopping me. Like I said, I have to get to another story."

"If you got time to text," said Nick, "you got time to read Laura's note."

The two of them had a stare down; Charlotte blinked before Santa did. She reached into her purse and retrieved the folded note with a sigh. Nick watched her as she read. Like all cops, Nick knew how to look for tells. He saw the stillness overcome her. When she finished reading, she turned the letter over and stared at the drawing.

Finally, she turned her gaze back to Nick. She was in, Nick realized. Only a cop would have noticed the slight dampness in her eyes. He wondered what she saw in his.

"Santa?" interrupted Angie. "There's someone to see you. This is Jayla!"

Nick turned his attention to a little girl with elaborately braided cornrows who was playing peek-a-boo from behind her mother's leg, her large, brown eyes appearing and then disappearing.

"Jayla?" said Nick. "Why, I remember that name from my good girl list."

As Nick sat down in the sleigh, he watched Charlotte take one more look at Laura's note before carefully sliding it into her purse and walking away.

# CHAPTER ELEVEN

*Angels We Have Heard on High*
*December 2*

"Winter Wonderland" was playing on all the mall's intercoms. The music buzzed in Nick's ear like a nettlesome mosquito, but he couldn't just shoo it away. The song was wrong for San Diego, the same way most holiday songs were wrong: it was December, but it was still seventy degrees outside. Yet every year Southern Californians acted as if they were part of a great big costume party.

Let them eat fruitcake, thought Nick.

His discontent had built throughout the shift. For once, it wasn't the work. It had been relatively quiet, with no incidents. There was no sign of the muggers. Maybe it was just the heat of the day, and his hot uniform, speaking to him.

Darcy seemed to be tuned into the same heat wave. "The weather report said we'd be having a Santa Ana condition all week," she said as "Frosty the Snowman" started up. "Hardly seems fair for Santa Claus to have to deal with Santa Ana."

Warm, dry desert winds blew in from the east and the heat often lingered for days at a time during Southern California winters. It was a good thing the mall was air-conditioned. Otherwise Frosty wouldn't even be slush. He'd be a puddle.

Nick usually didn't pay any attention to the weather. It was that kid's fault he was taking notice. Raymond had asked him for snow.

Why couldn't the kid have been reasonable instead of asking for the impossible?

Because he's dying, Nick thought, that's why.

"Frosty" finished, but the musical delusion didn't. Bing Crosby started crooning, "I'm dreaming of a white Christmas." Snow and more snow; Nick was being forced to listen to the one-track weather channel.

"Christmas music," said Nick, "or instruments of torture?"

Angie was humming along with Bing, of course. "Something wrong?" she asked.

"Lots of things," he said.

Now she looked concerned. That was even worse than her fatuous smiling. "Anything in particular?"

Nick knew he shouldn't have said anything. But talking would at least drown out the lyrics to "White Christmas." "This kid I know is real sick."

"One of the children at the hospital?"

"How did you know about that?"

"Bret told me how you saved the day."

"I didn't do anything heroic. I was the Santa du jour. And it wasn't like I didn't get paid."

"Bret said you were a big hit with the children."

"Bret wasn't there, so don't believe everything you hear."

"So what didn't I hear?"

"That I tried to act like a big shot, and that I let this kid named Raymond think I was tight with the real Santa Claus. I don't even know how it happened, but he's expecting me to work things out with Santa so that it snows on Christmas Day."

"Snow?" asked Angie.

Nick laughed, or he tried to. "The kid's not from around here. He's from back East. His parents brought him here hoping for a miracle cure that's not going to happen. His system is all messed up, and he's probably got cool on his brain. He's had all sorts of chemo, and they have him on these meds, and I know he's sick of being so sick. I guess that's why a pile of snow probably sounds so good to him."

For once Angie wasn't smiling. "I'm sorry, Nick."

"You and me both," he said.

———❈———

At the end of his shift, Nick didn't feel the usual relief from shedding his Santa garments. Even when the uniform came off it felt as if it was still clinging to him. It was like being a cop, but worse. People expect a lot of cops, but at least they don't expect a miracle worker. When he wore an SDPD uniform no one asked him to make things right, or expected him to bring presents, or make snow.

Nick went to Forster's office so that he could feel like a cop again. Forster was just finishing up a call as Nick sat down.

"What's up?" said Nick.

"My blood pressure," said Forster.

Forster prided himself on being a comedian, along with every cop in the country.

"You got anything new on our muggers?"

"You want the good news or bad news?"

"Bad," said Nick.

"Right choice," he said, "because it's all bad news. They're driving a Ford truck, but since there are about fifteen million of those on the road that doesn't help much. And although we picked up a license plate number nice and clear, that didn't help because it was stolen."

"They'll slip up. They always do."

"Yeah, maybe they'll leave a trail of tinsel for us to follow."

"Don't forget to look for coal as well."

"Santa knows best."

"Since that's the case," said Nick, "I'm going to need your help on another mystery I'm working here. I guess you could call it a missing person's case."

———— ✳ ————

When Nick left Forster's office he went in search of an open desk with a phone. Forster had told him they would piece together all the visitors to Santa's Mailbox on the twenty-eighth and twenty-ninth in the hopes they could get a visual on Laura, but he said it might take a few days.

Two doors down from Forster he found what he was looking for. His kids had grown up with cell phones glued to their ears and thought their dad was crazy for no longer having one. He picked up the phone, got an outside line, and dialed the hospital. He knew the number by heart. After the incident that led to his suspension, he'd called it so many times that he'd memorized it. Nick asked for Nurse Castillo, but when she got on the line he found himself tongue-tied.

"This is Nick Pappas," he finally said. "We met the night before last. I'm the guy . . ."

"You're Saint Nick."

"Yeah."

In his mind Nick had rehearsed what he was going to say, but now the script seemed stupid. "Listen, I was wondering if I could come over to the hospital."

"Wearing your Santa suit, or in civilian clothes?"

"I'll be in my street clothes. What I really want to do is talk to Raymond."

"It's past visiting hours."

"Oh."

"But we can make an exception for a saint."

———※———

Even going as himself, Nick hadn't wanted to visit Raymond empty-handed. He had run into a department store and grabbed the first item that had caught his eye. It was late to have buyer's remorse, but as he stood at the threshold to Raymond's room he wondered whether he had chosen well.

Nurse Castillo walked him to the entrance of that dark door again. "If he's asleep," she whispered, "it would be best not to wake him."

"Yeah, no problem," he said.

It would be easier that way, Nick thought. He could just leave a little note, and then escape like some thief into the night.

They walked into the darkened room. Over Raymond's bed, his mobile of stars twinkled. On his bed stand was the snow globe. Nick followed behind Easy. She walked silently; Nick, even on tiptoes, wasn't nearly as quiet. But it didn't matter. Raymond was awake.

"You have a visitor, Raymond. You might not recognize him . . ."

"I recognize him."

There wasn't much apparent welcome in his recognition.

Easy examined her watch. "I can only let you stay fifteen minutes."

"No problem," said Nick. He wondered if it would be the longest fifteen minutes of his life.

The nurse gave Raymond a little pat, and then offered Nick a reassuring smile before walking out of the room.

Nick had things to say, but he didn't know what to say. "Okay if I sit?"

Raymond shrugged, and Nick took that as consent. Fourteen minutes and thirty seconds and counting, thought Nick. He took a seat and looked around. The room was as depressing as it had been during his last visit. Next to the chair was an IV stand with some bags feeding into Raymond. Nick wondered if the kid was ever free of the stand. To him it seemed the opposite of an umbilical cord.

"I'm surprised you knew who I was."

"Eyes," Raymond said.

"Eyes?"

"I could tell who you were by your eyes."

Most people wouldn't have seen that. They would have been stopped by the beard, or wig, or uniform that Nick had been wearing the day before last, and wouldn't have been able to see beyond those things. The kid was a good observer.

"On the job, that's one of the things I try and take in," said Nick. "My other job, that is."

"You're a policeman, aren't you?" asked Raymond.

Nick started. "How did you know that?"

"I remember seeing you on the news a few times. You always looked upset."

Nick winced. None of his conversations with this kid ever seemed to be easy. "Yeah," he said. "There was this—situation. Some people think I discharged my firearm inappropriately. What that means is that I'm in limbo until this thing called a review board decides whether I can be a cop again."

"What happened?"

The kid was always asking the questions that Nick hoped he wouldn't ask. But it was the same question Nick had kept asking himself.

He shifted in his chair, knew there was no way he would ever get comfortable, and finally faced the boy's questioning eyes. It wasn't an appropriate story to tell a youngster, but there was no way to sugarcoat it.

"I was off duty. It was late. I had been out playing cards with some pals and I stopped to get a burger. While walking up to the door I saw a line of people facing the wall with their hands up. And just then, the door got thrown open and this guy came running out. He had a gun in his hand. I drew my gun and I identified myself as a police officer."

*"Police. Halt! Drop your gun! Throw it away from you!"*

*The kid almost fell over. He looked young enough to be in high school. Too young to be doing what he was doing. He was tall and thin and pale. With a gun aimed at him, he was that much more pale, a ghost. The kid dropped the sack he was holding, and the bills fell to the ground. His eyes were huge. They looked like they were ready to pop out.*

*"Throw the gun away from you! Throw it down! Now! Do it now!"*

*Nick had dropped into a shooter's stance. His gun was centered on the kid's chest.*

*The kid's jaw fell first, and then his gun.*

*"On the ground. Now! Now! Face down! Hands at your side!"*

*The kid complied. And that's where it should have ended.*

*The gunshots came from behind Nick. He threw himself on the cement walkway, didn't roll like they do on TV, but landed with a belly flop. The wind was knocked out of him. Another shot was fired. Nick thought he saw where it was coming from. Fighting for breath, he raised his right arm and fired back.*

*Kick, kick, kick. He felt the impact on his own hands. The bucking. Over twenty years on the force and he'd never fired in the line of duty before. His bullets hit metal and glass and concrete.*

*"I give up. I give up."*

*The voice didn't come from where Nick expected it. The shooter was several cars over from where Nick had returned fire.*

*The shooter got out of the car. His gun was still in his hands. Another kid. This one with a military haircut and big, red pimples that looked that much redder on a very white face.*

97

*"Throw your gun toward me! Now! Now!"*

*He did as told. Nick was shaking, partly out of fear, partly out of adrenaline, but mostly from anger.*

*"Down on the ground! Face on the ground!"*

*The shooter complied. It was only when Nick was handcuffing him that he heard the sounds. The noise had probably been there all along, but between the gunshots, the screaming, and his fighting for breath, he hadn't heard the shrill cries. Now he did.*

*A child was crying. A child was screaming.*

*And the cries were coming from where Nick had fired his gun.*

"For a moment I was thinking I'm the luckiest guy on earth, stopping both robbers, not getting shot, but then I heard this terrible sound. The way the ballistic guys figured it, one of my rounds ricocheted off the asphalt, and a poor little three-year-old girl took the bullet in her leg. You see, she'd been asleep, so her parents had left her in a car seat while they went to put in their takeout order. They could see the car from the restaurant, so they figured there was no harm in leaving her for just a minute."

*He'd tried to stop the bleeding, but as he applied pressure all he could think was, "I did this." For someone so small, there was so much blood.*

*He wrapped a towel around her leg. She never stopped crying, and every one of her screams reddened the towel that much more.*

*Her cries of pain and the frenzy of the panicked parents made him feel helpless. "I'm a police officer," Nick shouted. He made the announcement to reassure the parents, and maybe to reassure himself.*

*"Chrissie!" The mother kept screaming her name. "Chrissie!"*

*The father: "Where's the ambulance? Has someone called for an ambulance?"*

*"Chrissie!"*

*The parents didn't know what had happened. They only saw their screaming and bleeding daughter. Nick was as scared as they were.*

*"Chrissie!"*

*"Where's the ambulance?"*

*Nick's years of experience meant nothing. He wasn't prepared for what had happened. He knew the paramedics were on the way, but he decided he couldn't wait for them. He had to try and right his wrong.*

*Over all the screaming, he yelled, "I'm taking her in."*

*He fled an unsecured crime scene. The only thing he did right was cuff both of the suspects. He grabbed the car seat, and the child in it. Nick didn't even take the parents with him. He just drove, drove as if death were on his heels.*

*He didn't have a siren. Nick was in his own car, but he kept thinking he was in his patrol car with the siren blaring because Chrissie's screams were louder than his siren, so loud he was sure the whole world could hear.*

Just the memory of the event sent Nick's heart racing. His hands were sweaty and he felt clammy. He took a few deep breaths. "She lived, but she was hurt pretty bad." Nick exhaled hard. "I drove her to this very hospital."

It had happened only a month ago, hard as that was for Nick to believe. For a while it had looked as if they were going to have to amputate the girl's leg from the knee down. They'd operated on it three times since the shooting, and there would be more operations in the future, but she was all right now, thank God.

"It wasn't your fault."

Raymond's words didn't make Nick feel any better. What kind of a man would try and get sympathy from a terminally ill child?

"There are other people deciding that."

"So that's why you became one of Santa's helpers?"

Maybe that's what it did boil down to: "Yeah."

The boy nodded. Apparently Raymond could accept Nick's career change much more easily than Nick could.

"Is the girl all right now?"

"They tell me she's getting better."

The parents hadn't let him see her. That had made it worse for Nick. Of course they were probably operating on a lawyer's advice, just as he was. He didn't blame them, but he wished that they had let him see her. Not that he could have explained anything to her. She was too young. But at least he could have said he was sorry. He would have said that to the whole world, but his lawyer had advised him to not make any public or private apologies.

Nick changed the subject. "Hey," he said, "Easy's time clock is running, and I want to talk to you before she bounces me out of here."

"Talk about what?"

"Talk about my not doing a very good job of explaining some things. I guess I'm a better cop than I am a Santa's helper, but that's probably not saying much. I came over to straighten out a misunderstanding. And I brought you a present. I didn't have time to wrap it, though."

Nick lifted up a shopping bag, and pulled out a square-shaped box that was large but thin. The box was light enough so that Nick tried spinning it on his finger, but he was no Harlem Globetrotter.

"Catch," Nick said, but he faked the toss and then reached around the IV stand and gently placed the box on Raymond's chest.

Raymond picked it up. In the darkness he seemed to be having trouble figuring out what it was.

"It's nothing," said Nick. "It's just one of those Advent calendars. I remember my boy and girl used to love them. Every Christmas I had to get two of them so they wouldn't fight over who got the treat."

Raymond was still looking at the calendar with a puzzled expression.

"You ever see one of these before?"

The boy shook his head.

"I'll show you."

Nick removed the calendar's cellophane wrapping and then used his finger to point. "You see, you got to look for the numbers. There are twenty-four of them, one through twenty-four, counting the days until Christmas.. And behind all those numbers are little doors waiting to be opened. Find the number, open the door, and get a treat. Some Advent calendars are really elaborate. They got neat little prizes in them. But this one's only got chocolate. You like chocolate?"

"I like chocolate."

"That's what I figured."

The festive calendar seemed to cast a glow in the dark room. It showed a winter scene, Santa Claus delivering presents under an outdoor Christmas tree that was elaborately decorated. Around the tree, an assortment of animals waited. Raymond put his hand on the calendar and touched that world.

"You know the date today?" Nick asked.

Raymond shook his head.

"It's December the second. That means you have to find yesterday's number, and today's number. So look for numbers one and two, and then open the flaps."

"There's one." Raymond pointed to the number. It was in the middle of one of the tree's ornaments.

"Push in on that perforated line," said Nick. "Get a fingernail in there. That's it."

The flap opened and Raymond scooped out a miniature chocolate ornament. He looked at it for several seconds before popping it in his mouth.

"Now find number two."

"It's not there."

"It's there. You just got to look."

The number was camouflaged amidst the brightly wrapped presents under the tree, but eventually Raymond located it. He thumbed open the tab and revealed a miniature chocolate. Smiling, he lifted the box up to Nick.

"It's for you," Nick said.

Raymond shook his head. "We'll share."

The boy's arms were already trembling from the exertion. Nick decided not to argue. Maybe the kid shouldn't be having too many sweets anyway. He reached for the chocolate, and popped it into his mouth.

Raymond struggled to lower the box to his chest. He looked like a weight lifter laboring to get through his last repetition. The box dwarfed his thin chest.

"Good chocolate," said Nick.

The boy barely nodded. He reached over to his bed stand and fumbled for something.

"You need help with something?"

Raymond shook his head. He put his hands around a water cup and drank. When he finished he said, "It's hot."

Nick nodded, even though he didn't think it was hot. If anything, the room was cold.

"Really hot," the boy said.

Nick reached over and touched Raymond's forehead, and then his cheek. The boy was burning up.

"You have a fever," Nick said. "I better go get somebody."

Raymond didn't seem to hear. His eyes were closed. "Did you have your talk with Santa Claus?"

His words sounded disconnected, the output of a fevered mind. Nick didn't answer.

"It's so hot," said Raymond.

"I'm going to get a doctor."

"Did you tell Santa to bring me snow? That will cool me down. Snow . . ."

"I need someone to help in here!" Nick yelled. "I need someone right now!"

# CHAPTER TWELVE

*Go Tell It on the Mountain*
*December 3*

Nick slept fitfully. Instead of visions of sugarplums dancing through his head, he kept thinking about the sick kid. The sun wasn't even yet up when he called the hospital.

"How's the kid doing?" Nick asked.

"It's been a long night for Raymond," Easy said. "They had to intubate him."

In his mind's eye Nick pictured the boy with a tube down his throat, and he winced. It took all of his willpower to ask, "Can I see him later?"

"He's probably still going to have the tube in him," said Easy, "and he won't be able to talk."

It was a good excuse to avoid seeing the kid. But Nick said, "Talking is overrated. When you see him, say I'll be coming to visit later."

Nick was doing his final Santa touch-ups when he heard the sweeping of Henry's broom. The janitor came into view and stopped his sweeping to signal "A-OK" with his thumb and fore-finger to Nick.

"Looking good, Saint Nick," he said. "You a regular celebrity."

"Is that so?"

Henry nodded. "Saw you on the news last night."

For a moment Nick thought there must have been yet one more story on the trigger-happy cop.

"That reporter looked mighty cozy sitting in your lap," added Henry.

Nick let out a pent-up breath. "It must have been an optical illusion," he said, with maybe just a touch of regret in his voice.

"Didn't look like no optical illusion," said Henry, and then continued with his cleaning.

Remembering Charlotte brought on a twinge of guilt. Nick wondered if it had been a mistake to give the reporter Laura's letter. He should have secured the evidence, but he hadn't. What if she tossed the note? These days it seemed all the news stations only wanted to do happy news. He'd made a copy, but wished he had the original. If the reporter was a flake, he might still be able to do something. According to a calendar posted in the administrative offices, there were still twenty-one shopping days until Christmas.

Strange, he thought, how Christmas was now defined by how many shopping days lead up to it.

He made his way through the mall to his sleigh, and saw Angie waving to him as he turned the corner. The head Elf seemed to have eyes in the back of her pointy hat. "Hi, Santa!" she called. When he drew closer she enthusiastically whispered, "You looked great on the news!"

Over the course of the day Nick heard that repeatedly. It seemed as if everyone had seen the spot except for Nick. He heard from Forster, and shopkeepers, and even parents. They commented on how cute the feature was, which made Nick glad he hadn't seen it.

There was a steady stream of children all day, and whenever it was slow Nick scanned the balcony and surrounding area for the two predators he called the Grinches. So far his Grinches were no-shows.

His shift was coming to an end when he heard a nearby commotion of excited voices. People were pointing and commenting on a confident, athletic-looking man in an expensive suit holding hands with a little girl. Someone thrust a piece of paper and a pen into the man's free hand, and he quickly signed his signature.

"What's going on?" asked Angie.

"Downtown Danny Brown is what's going on," said Nick.

"Who's Downtown Danny Brown?" she asked.

Nick gave her an incredulous look. "What planet are you from?"

Angie didn't have time to answer the question. Danny Brown was on his way to Santa's sleigh, and so was the growing throng behind him. On the gridiron, Brown was the quarterback for the San Diego Sea Lions. He was used to leading huge men onto a field of battle, but as they drew nearer to the sleigh it was clear that he was having trouble directing a daughter who couldn't weigh more than fifty pounds.

"Come on, Savannah," implored Brown. "You know you want to see Santa."

The girl balked. Nick had seen this dilemma countless times; she desperately wanted to see Santa, and yet she was afraid. The girl was looking at Nick from behind one of her father's large legs. She had big blue eyes that took up half her face, and there were blue and gold ribbons in her long, sandy-brown hair; colors for the Sea Lions.

"Come with me, Daddy," she said.

The crowd behind them laughed. Now it was Brown's turn to look reluctant. The quarterback's body language said it all: seeing Santa wasn't something macho athletes did.

"I'll be right near you, Savannah. Just go on up."

But still she clung to his leg. "Come with me, Daddy."

The audience yelled their encouragement, and Brown shrugged. Savannah came out from behind her father's legs and started tugging at his hand. It was an unfair tug-of-war: the little girl won easily, and her father accompanied her up to Nick's sleigh.

"Sit down on that knee, daddy, and I'll sit on this knee."

"I don't think Santa's leg can support . . ."

"Sit down," said Nick. His shift was almost over and Raymond would be expecting him.

The crowd echoed Nick's invitation. Shrugging, and then mugging, Brown settled on Nick's right knee. With her father so near, Savannah wasn't afraid any longer. She turned to Nick and became positively chatty, and over the course of the next few minutes was very specific about what she wanted for Christmas.

"Okay," Nick finally said, deciding her list was long enough as is. "You want an ant farm, a talking Mother Goose, some dance slippers, a puppet set, a dollhouse, a volcano kit, some play horses, and a corral to put the horses in."

"A palomino and a mustang."

"Right. Are you sure you don't want a football?"

She shook her head very firmly.

"Ask her Daddy what he wants, Santa!" yelled someone in the crowd. The notion was seconded, and then some.

"It's your turn, Danny," said Nick. "Have you been a good boy?"

"I sure have."

"And what do you want for Christmas?"

Brown spoke loudly enough for everyone to hear: "I'd like an early Christmas present, Santa. We play Kansas City on Sunday, and we really need a win."

The onlookers cheered. Cameras had appeared and pictures were being snapped.

"Okay," said Nick, "since you've been good, I'll give you the early Christmas present you want: a gift-wrapped win over KC."

Nick's pronouncement drew the largest cheers yet.

"That's going to surprise the odds-makers, Santa," said a smiling Danny.

"Never bet against Christmas," advised Nick.

"I sure won't."

The quarterback picked up his daughter. She wasn't that much bigger than a football. He held her gently, but firmly. Nick could tell she was one thing in his life he would never fumble.

For once, no one was watching Santa. All eyes were on Danny Brown. Pieces of paper were being thrust at him as Angie put up the "Santa Is Feeding His Reindeer" sign. Nick expected to slip away unnoticed, but one person fell in next to him.

"I thought it was against the rules for Santa to promise a particular gift."

"Sue me," said Nick.

At least this time the reporter hadn't brought her cameraman.

"I'd rather interview you," Charlotte said.

"You already did," said Nick.

"No I didn't, *Mr. Pappas.*"

He walked faster. "I got nothing to say," he said. His secret was out.

"This isn't about your *situation*," she said, trotting to keep up. "It's about Laura."

Nick slowed down a little, but he was sure his face reflected his uncertainty. He didn't trust the media.

"I want to discuss her letter with you. I've barely been able to sleep since reading it," Charlotte confessed.

Maybe she was on the up and up. "Join the crowd," said Nick.

"If you want me to try and find Laura you're going to have to help me, and that means we have to talk."

"I don't know," said Nick.

Charlotte smiled. "If the only way I can get you to speak with me is by sitting in your lap, don't think I won't resort to that."

"Quit with the threats," said Nick, doing his best to hide a grin. He thought a moment. "Your only interest is talking about that letter?"

"That's right."

"I got to meet with someone now," he said, "but I'll be free around eight if that works for you."

"Why don't we eat while we talk?" said Charlotte.

It had been a long time since Nick had dined with a woman. "Sure," he said.

Easy wasn't working at the hospital that night, but she'd made arrangements to let Nick in to see Raymond. The boy was still intubated and Nick decided to make light of his condition.

"Some people will do anything to get out of talking with me," said Nick.

He patted Raymond on the arm, and the boy's eyes smiled back at him. Raymond reached for the Advent calendar and extended it to Nick.

"No way," said Nick. "I'm not finding today's door for you. That's your job."

Raymond scanned the calendar, and then jabbed triumphantly at the number three. He pointed to Nick and motioned that he eat.

"Why don't we save it for when they pull that tube out of you?" Nick asked.

The boy shook his head.

"Always did have a weakness for sweets," said Nick, patting his stomach. "Santa and I have that in common."

He removed the chocolate, and then bit into it. With his hands and eyes the boy asked Nick how he liked it. "Tastes great," said Nick. He didn't tell Raymond his chocolates could never be anything other than bittersweet.

Nick finished up by licking his fingers. Raymond seemed amused by the display.

"Guess who visited me at my sleigh today?" Nick asked. "I'll give you a few hints."

Nick thought about his first clue for a moment. "He's a professional athlete, and he wears the number twelve."

Raymond pantomimed the catching of a baseball, the shooting of a basketball, and the tossing of a football. Nick stood up, responded with the motion of a caught football, the upraised hands of a score, and his spiking the imaginary ball on the ground, but his theatrics were all but ignored by Raymond. The boy was looking around for something, and found it. He started tapping the bed table insistently, and then ran his finger along it. After a few seconds Nick figured out what he was saying.

"Brown," said Nick, recognizing that the boy was pointing at the table's color. "That's right. Downtown Danny Brown came to the mall with his daughter."

Raymond nodded triumphantly.

"Danny only asked for one thing," said Nick. "He wanted an early Christmas present of a win over Kansas City on Sunday. I'm probably going to be in Santa's doghouse for saying he could have it. None of Santa's helpers are supposed to promise any gifts. Only Santa can do that."

Raymond seemed to get great pleasure out of rubbing his index fingers together in a motion that all but said, "Naughty, naughty."

"Yeah," agreed Nick, "I'm not much of a Santa's helper."

Raymond shook his head in disagreement. "Thanks for that vote of confidence," said Nick.

He thought about bringing up Raymond's request for snow, but it didn't seem the right time.

"Afraid I can't stay too long tonight," Nick said. "Since Easy's not working I can't abuse visiting hours, and besides, I got to go meet a woman for dinner."

Raymond made a sound and Nick said, "It's not like that. This lady's a TV reporter. You see, Santa got this letter from a girl named Laura, and Christmas kind of passed her by last year, so this reporter and I want to help the girl. Anyway, for a reporter she seems okay."

Raymond tapped his heart and pointed at Nick.

"You trying to say I like her?" said Nick. "Anyone ever tell you that you talk too much, kid?"

# CHAPTER THIRTEEN

*The Holly and the Joy*

It had been years since Nick last visited Old Town. It was one of those spots that most locals had conceded to the tourists, even though the area laid claim to many of San Diego's historical roots. The old mission was there, and the Casa de Estudillo, and the Whaley House and other attractions, but Old Town was mostly a string of restaurants and *mercados* designed to gather in the tourists.

Nick had forgotten how attractive Old Town was. The area was dressed for the holidays, but not overdressed. Most of the white-washed buildings were adorned by strands of white icicle lights. *Luminarias*, lit candles inside paper bags, lined walkways and offered their soft glow to passersby. The luminarias had a warming radiance, not emitting light as much as serenity. Against the wind and the darkness the candles burned on.

For the fourth time Nick brushed at his shirt, trying to pat down the wrinkles. Before entering the open-air restaurant, he sucked in his gut. No need, he thought, to look like Santa off the job. Charlotte was standing at the hostess stand. She examined him for a moment before looking away. Nick was secretly pleased she didn't recognize him.

Charlotte looked up again at Nick's approach, and this time she did recognize him. She took her time taking in his features, and when she finished offered up a little smile.

"You clean up pretty good," she said.

"You say that to all the Santas in town?"

"Charlotte," she said, extending her hand.

"Nick," he said.

They were seated at a table that was half in the shadows, and half out. It was December, but the garden area was still vibrant with colors, and the aromatic scent of jasmine filled the air. A stand of ivy made it feel like a private setting, while a heat lamp eliminated the slight chill in the air. Atmospheric lights were strung overhead, and the candle on their table flickered seductively. Nick hadn't thought he was that hungry, but that was before he was seduced by the restaurant's aromatic offerings. With so many wonderful scents, and too many menu choices, Nick ended up ordering the chile relleno plate. Charlotte finally decided on the fish tacos.

With their orders behind them, Charlotte pulled Laura's letter out of her purse. She unfolded the notebook paper, and carefully placed it so that it wouldn't get soiled or wet. Then she looked at Nick and asked, "How did you end up getting this letter?"

Nick told her what little he knew of its history.

"So it could have been dropped off any time after Santa's mailbox was put up?"

Nick nodded.

"How many other letters were in the mailbox when it was first emptied?"

"About a dozen, I think. Angie collected them. She's the head elf."

"Do you still have those letters?"

"They're all posted on Santa's sleigh."

"Have you talked with anyone working the Santa display to see if they remember Laura?"

"No . . . I . . . No." Nick had been tempted to explain how he was only a temporary Santa, and how he'd had other pressing concerns, but that would have taken too long, and maybe told her more about him than he wanted to reveal. "I have asked the security director to pull footage of anyone leaving a letter in Santa's mailbox, though."

"Good idea," said Charlotte. "But you're saying that you don't personally remember a girl named Laura?"

He shook his head, but then added, "That's not to say she couldn't have sat in my lap. When it's busy, everything sort of becomes a blur."

She nodded, and then reached for the note. "Do you think this letter is legitimate?"

"Yeah, even though I wish it wasn't."

"Why is that?"

"Now I feel like I know Laura. I don't like it that she's scared. It sounds as if she is in danger of being evicted. And I hate the idea of her not waking up to any Christmas presents."

Nick was surprised at how much he was talking, but his honesty seemed to be contagious.

"I know what you mean," said Charlotte. She sighed. "When I said I was having trouble sleeping because of that letter, I wasn't kidding. It brought back a lot of memories. In many ways I *was* that girl, and I'm afraid there's a part of me that always will be."

"You were poor?" asked Nick.

Charlotte nodded. "I remember one Christmas when my mother and I were living in a car, just like Laura might be. Santa didn't visit me either."

"Not exactly a Hallmark moment," said Nick.

"Not exactly."

The two of them were quiet for a minute. Charlotte finally said, "Laura," and shook her head. "Even the name's enigmatic. It's an every-girl name. She could be any race or color."

"It's an every-girl name without a last name."

Charlotte nodded. "It was quite the challenge you and your elf friend threw me. Find the needle in the haystack."

"You struck us as a person who doesn't give up easily."

"I don't."

Charlotte took a tortilla chip, and dipped it in the salsa. She came away with a full reservoir of the salsa, which she downed in one bite. Nick had already tried the spicy salsa. Either Charlotte liked it hot, or she was too preoccupied to notice.

"I've already started looking for Laura," she said. "There are a lot of cracks little girls can fall through, but I'm familiar with those cracks. I've already contacted all elementary schools within a fifteen mile radius of the mall."

"Aren't the schools bound by confidentiality laws?"

Charlotte grabbed another chip, and scooped up more salsa. She did like it hot.

"Confidentiality laws don't exclude teachers talking with any of their students named Laura who might have written the letter, and encouraging her to call me."

Nick tried to keep his doubts off his face. Apparently he didn't succeed.

"What?"

"I'm curious why Laura's mother didn't contact some of the toy drives around town, or charitable institutions, to make sure her daughter got some presents."

"Maybe she did. Last year the charitable agencies ran out of presents for children."

Nick nodded thoughtfully.

"Or," said Charlotte, "it could be her mother doesn't speak English, and was afraid to contact anyone for help. She might be undocumented. Or maybe she's just too proud to accept charity. Finding Laura is already proving hard enough, but if her mother doesn't want her to be found that's when this hunt gets real difficult."

"You always full of such cheery thoughts?"

"You're the one who gave me the letter."

"'Tis the season to be guilty," said Nick.

They both laughed.

"Why don't you put Laura's letter on the air?" asked Nick. "Someone might recognize her that way."

"That could work," she said, "but what if she doesn't want to be made into a spectacle?"

Nick opened his mouth to say that he wished the media had been as considerate about him, but then closed it.

"Before I go that route," Charlotte said, "I want to see if I can find her. It might not be easy, though, especially if Laura and her mother are in hiding from something or someone. Maybe the two of them escaped an abusive household, or maybe the mother is mentally ill, and suspicious of everyone, or maybe they're not legal citizens."

Nick nodded. There were times on his job when he needed to track down a reluctant witness, or a suspect; if someone was of a mind to disappear they usually found a way.

"I hope you still want to help me with this," Charlotte said.

Nick nodded. "Every year Metropolitan Transit sponsors a holiday entertainment series. There are usually only two trolley stations where entertainers perform, at Euclid Avenue or at Sixty-Second Street. I am pretty sure Laura's drawing is a composite of both stations. She must have seen carolers performing. And it just so happens there's a bus that leaves from the Sixty-Second Street station that goes to Plaza Center. I'd like to canvas those neighborhoods around Southeast San Diego, go to youth centers and the like, and ask around."

"We'll both start there," said Charlotte, "but if we don't have any luck in the next few days we'll need to cast a wider net. And the best way I can think of to involve the public is to interview you on air."

"Whoa," said Nick, raising his hands. "Why involve me in your story? You got the letter. That's the story."

"Every story has to be personalized. The letter was delivered to you. Without Laura, you're the only other face to this story."

"So talk with one of the other mall Santas. It's not like the letter was addressed to me personally."

Charlotte shook her head. "I can't play fast and loose with the facts, and I can't change the chronology of what happened."

"So that's it."

"What is *it*?"

"You can drop the friendly act."

"What act are you talking about?"

"You pretended to be interested in Laura, but all you wanted to do was get your shot at me on camera."

Red spots appeared in Charlotte's cheeks. "You figured it out, Sherlock. But why is it that I didn't ambush you on camera at the mall? Before my story aired I knew who you were. I wasn't about to let you get away with giving me a first name, so I called up the mall manager and he had human resources provide me with your name. The moment I heard it, I knew who you were."

Nick digested the information, and then said, "Amazing."

"What?"

"That you didn't use that information."

"I was tempted. It could have been played up big: suspended cop involved in a shooting now working as Santa at Plaza Center. I could have asked you if you were packing. I could have painted the story with all sorts of sensationalistic elements."

"So why didn't you?"

"Because the story was about my visit to Santa, and not about the little girl you accidentally shot. And the story I'm working on now is about Laura, not you."

"How could it not be about me? According to your peers, I am not Santa. I'm Satan."

"You haven't exactly been forthcoming. Since the shooting, you've been the invisible man. I've been following the story."

"You've been following the lie. It was *reported* that on the night of the shooting I'd been playing cards and drinking until late. That was printed in black and white, and aired on radio and television. And the stories kept getting worse. Anonymous sources kept popping up. They said I had a gambling problem. They claimed I was a rogue cop and loose cannon. I've seen serial murderers get better press than what I got."

"You never denied anything."

"You're right. On advice of counsel, I never said anything, but I know there were plenty of people willing to speak up for me, trying to speak up even, but you guys weren't interested in getting to the truth. It's true I was at that card game until late, but what's not true are all those stories about how I was boozing it up, and that I lost heavily, and how I left so depressed. I lost six bucks. The stakes we play, if I'd lost every hand I wouldn't have been down more than twenty-five bucks. And my so-called gambling habit consists of that weekly poker game. That's it. As for my heavy drinking, I had one beer the whole night. That's my usual. I've never had a taste for booze. Some of the other guys get juiced at the games. That's not me. Everyone who was there, everyone I've ever played with, could tell you that. I walked into that situation stone cold sober."

"I believe you."

Nick's mouth was open. He was ready to argue. He was ready to rail. What he wasn't ready for was her support. Embarrassed, looking away, he said, "You're in pretty small company then."

"If I have to interview you, you could wear the Santa suit."

"I don't know."

"And I don't know how else I can finesse the story if we don't find Laura. Without you in the picture, there would be too many gaps among the five Ws."

"I guess we need to find Laura then."

"I can't invest the time and effort without your promise that you'll go on camera if we hit a dead end."

Nick didn't answer right away. After the media's hatchet job on him, he wasn't sure if he could ever trust any reporter.

"You'd have to use my name?" asked Nick. "I couldn't be an anonymous Santa Claus?"

"I'm afraid not," she said, but then Charlotte's hands started moving, almost as if she was weaving an invisible fabric. "There might be another way," she said. "What do your friends call you?"

"The guys on the force call me Zorba, or Z, or Nick, or Nick the Greek."

"But your first name is Nicholas?"

Nick nodded. "Nicholas Alexander Pappas," he said.

"We could identify you as Nicholas Alexander Pappas. With you in your Santa suit, I doubt anyone will make the connection."

Nick thought about it. Finally he shrugged. "I'll do it as a last resort."

# CHAPTER FOURTEEN

*While Shepherds Watched Their Flocks*
*December 4*

Nick arrived home too charged up to sleep. He and Charlotte had talked until they were the only ones left out on the patio. The staff had finally turned off the heat lamps or else they might still be talking. Though it was late, Nick wasn't anywhere near ready to sleep. He sat in his easy chair and tuned into the replay of the local news, but mostly what he did was mentally replay the dinner conversation. Suddenly the sound from the set caught his attention, something about Downtown Danny Brown.

"We have exclusive video footage," said the sportscaster, his voice far too enthusiastic to sound credible, "of a secret weapon the Sea Lions will be employing for this Sunday's big game with Kansas City."

Santa Claus suddenly appeared on the television; Nick started when he realized he was the one dressed in the Santa suit. Danny Brown was on one of his knees, his daughter Savannah on the other.

"Danny Brown is apparently willing to do anything to get a win," said the sportscaster. "This home video was taken at the Plaza Center."

Nick heard himself asking Brown, "Have you been a good boy?"

And then he listened to the quarterback's answer, and what was worse, heard this bogus Santa promise a gift-wrapped win over KC.

The sportscaster stuck a thumb in the air. "Hear that, sports fans?" he asked. "The Big Claus has promised our Sea Lions a vic this Sunday."

Not the Big Claus, thought Nick, stabbing the remote until the picture disappeared. More like the Big Mouth.

---

The next afternoon an amused-looking Forster was waiting for Nick as he stepped out of the locker room. He greeted Nick with a whistle of approval.

"What?" Nick asked, suspicious of his former partner's smile.

"That Santa suit's a flashy number," Forster said, leaning against the wall.

"What are you babbling about?" asked Nick.

"It looks like a dance outfit to me."

"Santa doesn't dance, and neither do I."

"Of course you dance. You're Greek."

"What's Greek to me is dancing."

"C'mon, Nico, I bet you get happy feet every time you put that suit on."

"Yeah, twenty pounds of costume makes me feel like a real Fred Astaire."

It was easy for the two men to slip into the banter that had been a constant during their years together on the force, but Forster was there for more than social reasons. He had lost his smile.

"Afraid I didn't come over to discuss your dance card," he said. "This morning I got a call from the security director over at Fashion Valley. It looks like our boys have expanded their operation. They did a crash and dash in the parking lot, used a moving truck to flatten a thirty-year-old male and grab what he was carrying.

The way the victim figures it, they had to have been scouting him while he was buying his fiance a rock at the jewelry store. He was lucky he escaped with only heavy bruises and scrapes."

"What are we going to do about it?"

"I'm increasing foot patrols."

"I keep thinking we're missing something. These guys somehow have had the advantage over us. They know the lay of the land. I'm wondering if that means they have some inside help."

"If the fix is in, it's not coming from security. I'd vouch for my whole crew."

"Maybe they've just been lucky so far," said Nick. "But it's time we went on the offensive. We know our bad guys are targeting jewelry stores and high-ticket items. We need to be identifying our muggers before they identify targets."

"I've already put out that memo to our eyes in the skies."

"Maybe we should set up some decoys in the parking lot. We can make it look like they're easy pickings walking around carrying a big haul."

"I've been trying to float that suggestion to management."

"And?"

"And they hope our muggers are happy at their new mall and don't come back. In other words, you're still our one and only secret weapon."

---·❄·---

It wasn't only the two-legged that sat on Nick's lap that day.

"Oh, how cute!" said Angie, petting and cooing over the dog. "What's his name?"

"Beauregard," said the proud owner of the basset hound. "He's here to have his picture taken with Santa."

Nick wasn't keen on the idea of the dog being in his lap. He didn't want fur on his Santa suit, and he sure didn't want fleas.

Beauregard didn't look very happy at the idea either, but they seemed to be the only two who had reservations. Everyone else was delighted with the idea. With some coaxing, Angie settled the dog into Nick's lap. Man and dog exchanged a glance; Nick hoped he didn't look as miserable as Beauregard but he wouldn't have wanted to bet.

The owner and Angie stood side by side making sounds to try to get Beauregard animated. Nick kept a strained smile on his face until Darcy snapped the shot. Instead of taking the dog from his lap, Angie and the owner went to the digital display to examine the results.

The owner shook her head. "That shot really doesn't capture the essence of Beauregard," she said. "He looks dispirited."

Angie nodded and said, "He doesn't look happy."

At the best of times Nick wondered if the dog *could* look happy. Beauregard had droopy, bloodshot eyes, and jowls that sloped downward. The dog's long ears seemed to weigh down his head. How did they expect a basset hound to look joyous?

"I have an idea!" said Angie. She clapped her hands. Nick tried to think if he knew anyone else who clapped their hands when they were happy.

Angie's head was deep into what she called her "Christmas bag." It was a handbag, but Santa's toy bag wasn't much smaller. Encouraging sounds came from within the bag, and Angie emerged with not only a doggie treat, but some bouncy reindeer antlers. Only Angie would have those kinds of items in a handbag. She had reindeer pins that flashed, jewelry that played holiday tunes, bells, and even chestnuts. She was the Christmas Elf with the Boy Scout motto: Be Prepared. While Beauregard munched on his treat, Angie did the doggie makeover.

When she finished with the dog's transformation, Angie stepped back and whistled softly. Beauregard perked up, and Darcy got the shot. Moments later everyone was looking at the digital display.

"Perfect!" said the owner. "Why, he looks better than Rudolph!"

Nick thought the dog looked more like a jackalope—a taxidermist's union of a jackrabbit with horns—than he did a reindeer, but in the picture Beauregard did look like a happy jackalope.

As their shift was ending Angie approached Nick. She had let Darcy leave early, so no one else was around.

"How is Raymond?" Angie asked.

Nick didn't think he had told her the boy's name, but then again, maybe he had. "He was feeling better yesterday. I'll be stopping by to see him later."

"Take him a candy cane," said Angie.

The Elf seemed to think candy canes could solve all the ills in the world. "Sure," he said.

Angie surprised Nick by holding out two closed hands. "Pick a hand," she said, "any hand."

To humor her, Nick tapped her right hand. She opened it up, and he saw a folded scrap of paper. Nick lifted it out of her hand and began to unfold it. The process took longer than he expected; what appeared to be a scrap of paper eventually unfolded into a full page of Angie's unmistakable calligraphy. With her usual flourishes, and some new touches, including snowflakes, she had written the words "Igloo Ice" and a telephone number.

"What's this?" Nick asked.

"They're a company in town that makes snow scenes," Angie said.

"Snow scenes?"

"They make snow, Nick."

She extended her other hand toward him; Nick took the hint and tapped it as well. In one motion Angie opened her hand and then blew. Snowflakes suddenly dropped out of the air, covering

Nick's face and beard. How in the world? The flakes dissolved on his face and left a wet trail. He caught a flake on his finger, and watched it disappear in front of his eyes.

He wondered how the snowflakes hadn't melted in Angie's hand, but like any good magician she hadn't hung around to answer questions. She was skipping away, singing, "Glad tidings of great joy I bring, to you and all mankind."

Snow, thought Nick. Raymond's Christmas wish had seemed the most impossible of pipe dreams before, something so far removed from San Diego's climate that Nick had never even considered his request.

Nick finally recognized the Christmas carol playing over the mall's music system. The tempo to "While Shepherds Watched Their Flocks" was more upbeat than he was used to hearing, but that was the way with most Yule songs these days.

His daughter Corinne had been about Raymond's age when she and her Sunday school classmates had practiced that song. One of the kids had taught them alternate lyrics, much to the displeasure of the choir director. Nick remembered how Corinne had thought the new lyrics were so funny. His little girl had sung to him while sitting in his lap. She said it was the version all the kids wanted to sing. It took Nick a minute, but finally he remembered the first lyric.

*While shepherds washed their socks by night, and hung them on the line, the angel of the Lord came down and said, "Those socks are mine."*

On the day of the recital Nick remembered there had been a bit of tension. Would the kids sing the funny lyrics they liked, or would they go with the traditional lyrics? With big smiles they made their choir director happy, but it was clear what they were really thinking as they sang.

Nick found himself smiling, remembering Corinne's big smile as she stood in front of the church singing.

The mall's loudspeakers started playing a new song, and Nick's thoughts returned to Raymond, and snow. He took what he heard as a good omen. Dean Martin was singing, "Let It Snow!"

# CHAPTER FIFTEEN

*Away in a Manger*
*December 5*

Where had all the payphones gone, Nick wondered? It had taken him fifteen minutes to find one that worked. The day before, he had told Charlotte he currently didn't have a cell phone, and she'd been shocked. If he'd told her he had two heads, she probably wouldn't have looked as surprised.

"You must be the only person on the planet without a cell phone," she said.

"I had one," he said, "but I lost it a few months ago and decided it wasn't worth replacing."

"That means you can't text or tweet."

"Anyone who would want to get my texts or tweets, I wouldn't want to know."

She thought he was being funny, and had laughed.

Charlotte answered on the second ring. Nick was glad he didn't have to leave a message. He never quite knew what to say and hated leaving messages. Maybe that was why he didn't even have a message machine. That would be something else Charlotte would find hard to believe.

"This is Nick," he said. For a moment he considered saying he'd had a good time last night, but he was still coming to terms with the reportorial divide and wasn't convinced she could be trusted.

126

Instead, he said, "I spent my morning on the Laura trail. It's like I thought: the drawings tell us she knows the Euclid Avenue and Sixty-Second Street Trolley Stations. That's the area we need to focus on."

"Maybe I could make a few discreet flyers and post them at those stations."

"That's kind of what I was thinking."

"I know a few relief agencies in that area," said Charlotte. "Tomorrow I'll bring Laura's note and suss them out."

"Suss?"

"I once had an English news director and that was his favorite word. In British parlance it means to investigate."

"I'll spare you police parlance."

"Why is that?"

"Because most of it violates obscenity laws," he said. In a British accent Nick added, "Anyway, while you suss the relief agencies, I'll suss the recreation centers and the Boys and Girls Club."

"I'm regretting using that word already."

"I was kind of hoping you would."

"You're not the only one who's been working the case," she said. "This morning I put in some calls to the new underground railroad, but my contacts didn't remember a girl named Laura. They promised to make some calls on my behalf, though."

"What is the new underground railroad?"

"Women assisting other women in getting away from abusive husbands," said Charlotte. "Often families are involved. The mother and her children get relocated to safe houses. But based upon the people I talked to today, I'm fairly sure if Laura and her mother escaped from an abusive household, they did it on their own."

Nick heard something in Charlotte's voice. These trips down memory lane weren't easy for her.

"And when I get a minute I plan to start calling schools in and around Southeast San Diego," she continued. "I know one administrator who might be able to help."

"We'll find her," said Nick, trying to sound confident.

"Thanks for spending time looking," she said.

"It made me feel like a cop again. I didn't realize how much I missed that."

In the background Nick could hear how busy Charlotte's workplace was. The news was getting ready to go on air. It probably wasn't a good time for her to be talking with him, even though she hadn't said anything to make him think that.

"So," said Nick, "tomorrow I'll call some contacts at Child Protective Services."

"That sounds great," said Charlotte. "And I'll spend the morning talking with some church relief agencies that help undocumented workers."

It was the children of immigrants, Nick thought, who often spoke for their parents. On many occasions Nick had done his field interviews with children translating for their mother or father.

"Lots of immigrants around here," said Nick. "They come from around the globe. There are storefront signs in languages I can only guess at. From what I can tell these people have two things in common: many are poor, and all of them are suspicious of cops."

"How do they know you're a cop?"

"It must be the doughnut in my hand."

In the background he heard someone say, "Charlotte, we need you in editing."

Nick didn't wait for her to tell him she had to run. "Better hang up before the talk box asks for more money."

"Call me when you can," she said.

"Sure," said Nick.

He slowly hung up the pay phone. Did she mean call him later? He wondered if their relationship extended further than the hunt for Laura. When they had dinner, he had sensed there was something between them, but maybe he had just been reading things into the conversation. To be safe, he figured he would wait until tomorrow to call her. His search for Laura would at least give him a reason.

Nick invested some more change in the pay phone, dialing up the number for Igloo Ice. He had their number memorized; it was the third time he had called that day.

"Is Manuel Cruz in?" he asked.

"Mr. Cruz is out in the field," said the receptionist.

"Is Mr. Cruz ever in?" asked Nick.

"This is a very busy time of the year for him," the woman said. "I can connect you with his voice mail."

"I've already left two messages. Does anyone else there schedule snow scenes?"

"No, I'm sorry. Only Mr. Cruz does that."

"Maybe third time will be a charm," said Nick. "Let me try his voice mail again."

The toy train, with Santa acting as its conductor, was going round and round the lobby of the Pediatric Oncology ward. Nick stood at the reception desk, not quite comprehending what he was being told.

"I'm sorry, Nick," said Easy. "This afternoon Raymond became sick and he needed to be taken to the ICU. It was more precautionary than anything else."

"But he seemed fine yesterday," said Nick. "I mean not fine, but as fine as could be expected."

Easy nodded without making any comment, but her eyes were saying something.

"I told him I'd be coming by," said Nick. "I don't want him to think I pulled a no-show or anything."

"I'll make sure he knows you stopped by."

"I appreciate it."

Nick began to turn around, but then did an about-face and looked at the nurse again. "Can you do me a favor, Easy? I've got something in the works and I need to take a look at Raymond's room."

Easy left him at the threshold of the door, saying she'd be back in a few minutes. The lights were on in Raymond's room. Nick knew that was a sure sign the boy wasn't home.

The room felt cold and empty. The bed was made, and there was a strong disinfectant smell lingering in the air. Nick wondered if the room was already being prepared for someone else.

He sat on Raymond's bed and looked at the ceiling. The mobile turned slow circles, but with the lights on, the stars and planets looked lifeless and cast no glow. Not stars you could wish upon, Nick thought. Though Raymond had lived in the room for two months, his stay was marked by very few personal items. There was only one framed picture. Nick reached for it. Raymond had been at least two years younger when the picture was taken. The younger Raymond had rosy cheeks and a child's eyes. He was sandwiched between two older children, and behind them were two smiling adults. Siblings and parents, Nick decided, noticing the resemblance. It was a winter shot. All the children were standing on a sled. Raymond would have looked at that picture countless times. He would have remembered the good old days, and dreamed of how things had been. Maybe that's why he wanted it to snow so much. Maybe he thought that snow could bring back that little boy in the photograph.

Nick replaced the picture on the bed stand. It was sharing the space with the Advent calendar. Nick examined the calendar, scanning for the opened flaps. Before he had taken sick, Raymond must have opened that day's door.

He remembered his reason for coming to the room, and walked over to the lone window and looked out. The boy liked to look up in the clouds, but Nick turned his head downwards to the ground four stories below. It was by no stretch of the imagination a scenic view, not one of San Diego's memorable beach vistas. On the horizon was Interstate 805. The closer view took in the parking lot, but directly below Raymond's room was a grassy area interspersed with pine trees that stretched from the building to the sidewalks.

There, thought Nick. It would work just fine right there.

The door to the room opened and Easy walked in. She saw Nick peering through the window to the ground below. He motioned with his hand. She came over and looked to where Nick pointed at the patch of grass.

"I don't see anything," she said.

"You will. That's where Raymond's going to get his Christmas wish."

"What wish is that?"

"The snow he asked for," said Nick. "Raymond wanted Santa Claus to deliver him snow on Christmas Day, and that's what going to happen."

Nick was too busy checking out the view to gauge Easy's expression. "There's an ice company in town that does these snow scenes, and it seems to me that the lawn down there is just begging for a blizzard."

This time Nick looked at Easy. Although she was smiling, he sensed her enthusiasm was tempered. "It's a great idea, Nick."

Nick said the word she hadn't: "But?"

"*But*, I am not sure about your timeframe."

"What do you mean?"

"Raymond's entire immune system is compromised. His cancer has metastasized. We're fighting it every inch of the way, and there's always a chance for some sort of remission, but I'd think about having that snow delivered soon."

Nick suddenly realized what Easy was telling him. "You don't think Raymond will live to see Christmas?"

Easy sighed and said, "The cancer . . ."

She shook her head and didn't say anything else. She didn't have to.

Nick found himself driving back to the Plaza Center. He hated not being able to do anything about Raymond's situation. When his kids had been growing up, Nick had never felt worse than when they were sick and miserable. As a parent, he would have rather taken on their illness than see them suffer. It was the same thing with playground politics. Nick wanted to confront whoever was giving his kids a hard time. Since he couldn't help Raymond, he could at least focus his attention on two bullies.

He parked at the outer lot, and slowly worked his way around the mall. Sharks can sniff blood from miles away. Human predators were like that, too—they could sense weakness.

Nick didn't see any sign of his bad guys, but inside the mall he kept up his surveillance, continuing to walk and observe even when nothing stirred his antennae. When he was ready to give up for the night, he strolled behind the scenes and ended up at the security offices. Forster was working late.

"I hope you're getting overtime," said Nick.

"The security director says it's not in the budget."

"There are a few things that should be in the budget. Some copcycles would be good, especially in the parking lots."

"Asked for and denied," said Forster. "But I did call in some favors at SDPD and was promised they'd be sending around more flattops to patrol the area."

"That's a start. We could use some stealth patrol cars without the telltale lights to creep up on our creeps."

"They couldn't hurt," said Forster. "Hey, I got something for you."

"Why do I get a tug in my prostate when I hear those words coming out of your mouth?"

"I guess your guilty conscience has a funny way of showing itself."

Forster handed him a folder. Inside it were pictures taken from CCTV footage. Nick started thumbing through the printouts. The quality of the pictures was so-so. Most showed boys and girls placing letters in Santa's Mailbox.

"Angie helped me match up the letters with the senders," said Forster. "She studied all those notes you got hanging on the sleigh. We're pretty sure Laura didn't deliver her own letter."

"Who did?"

Forster tapped one of the printouts. "We think it's this lady. There are a few shots of her from different cameras."

Nick thumbed through the pictures and shook his head. "I've had DMV pictures that looked better."

"We figure her for about twenty, maybe five foot four, probably a buck twenty, with dark hair."

"You can't even tell her race from these pictures."

"She's dark complexioned if she's white; she's light complexioned if she's black."

"Or she could be a Latina or Filipina."

"There is that."

"She's not Laura's mom."

"How do you know that?"

"I'd bet this one has never had any kids. She's not much more than a kid herself. I'm thinking she's some friend or neighbor that Laura asked to deliver her note. She might even be Laura's babysitter."

"How did Laura know that Santa had a mailbox?"

"She could have seen it last year or this year."

"So you're still without a face to your letter."

"Don't I know it."

"Where do you go from here?"

"I look for the postscript."

"You do what?"

"I find the postscript on Laura's letter."

"She probably doesn't even know what a p.s. is."

"That doesn't mean she didn't leave one."

Forster nodded approvingly, and said, "The frog is back."

"What frog?"

"One of Aesop's Fables tells about a frog that fell into this half-filled pail of milk. And the pail's too big for this frog to jump out, so it looks like he's going to drown, but the frog keeps moving his legs, and moving them—almost dancing, if you will—really putting on the twinkle toes just like you. And then the magic happens: all of the frog's kicking churns the milk into butter, and the frog escapes drowning. The moral of the fable is to never give up. That's how you used to think. You've become the old you, Nico."

Nick looked unimpressed. "The next time you make me Kermit in one of your fables," he said, "at least have the princess kiss me."

"That's too far-fetched of a story."

"You're a riot, Wally. Aesop was Greek. I'm Greek. I am sure we got a lot in common. But Aesop was no cop. And in my fable I want to not only be kissed by the princess, but I also want to find the missing girl, and dispatch the bad guys.

"But as for your dance sequence, forget it. Never going to happen."

# CHAPTER SIXTEEN

*Twelve Days of Christmas*
*December 6*

Nick awakened in the morning with a head of steam. There were Laura leads to pursue, but his first order of business was to see to Raymond's Christmas wish. Nick called Igloo Ice. This time he wasn't going to be put off.

"I'm sorry, Mr. Pappas," the receptionist said. "Mr. Cruz has already left the office, but he did say he would be returning calls later today."

"That's not good enough," said Nick. "I am not going to be in later today. I need to talk with him now."

"He doesn't usually like me to give out his mobile phone number . . ."

"I'd be very grateful," said Nick.

Nick took down the number and called it. After three rings he heard a man shout, "This is Cruz." There was a reason for the shouting. In the background it sounded like a forest was being clear-cut.

"This is Nick Pappas."

"Who?"

"Nick Pappas, the guy who kept calling you yesterday."

"What do you want?"

"I want to book a snow scene."

"What date are you thinking about?"

"Does tomorrow work for you?"

Nick heard something besides the sounds of heavy machinery, and then realized it was laughter. When Cruz stopped laughing he finally said, "Two weeks from tomorrow works for me."

"You got to be kidding."

Cruz just said, "You want to book it or not?"

"That's the earliest date available?"

"That's what I told you," said Cruz. "How big an area you talking about?"

Nick considered the size of the lawn. "It's about a hundred feet by a hundred feet."

"That will cost you two grand," said Cruz, "and that's just for the snow. What you get is two to four inches of snow and that's it. We got packages we can throw in, moving figures, lights, sleighs, things like that, but they're extra."

"I just want the snow," said Nick.

The background noise had let up, but Cruz didn't immediately notice and continued yelling into the phone. "We need a five hundred dollar deposit. You'll need to bring it by the office by the end of the week. And we get the balance when we deliver the goods."

Nick heard the whooshing and whistling of air, and knew Cruz was waving his hand and the phone in it. He heard him yell, "Hey, quit watching Shamu and get back to work."

The noise started up again, and Nick decided he'd had enough of shouting. "Are you working Sea World?"

"Yeah, it's frozen fish week."

At Sea World Nick didn't have to ask where Cruz and his men were working. He just followed the sounds and found them filling a slope with snow. It was no wonder the crew had been distracted. The slope overlooked the aquarium that housed Shamu the killer whale. Nick watched the orca swimming. It had been at least a decade since he'd seen Shamu jump out of the water and kiss someone. For some reason he thought about Charlotte.

He made a straight line for a short and stocky man who looked like he was in charge of the operation. Huge blocks of ice were being fed into a grinder, and a stream of white snow was being shot into the air out of a tube. The man was using his hands to signal the direction of one of the blowers.

"Manuel Cruz?" shouted Nick.

"Who wants to know?" asked the man.

"I'm Nick Pappas. We talked on the phone a little while ago."

Cruz led Nick far enough away from the operation so that it wouldn't be such a trial to talk. "So what can I do for you?" he asked.

"I want to book that snow scene we talked about, but I am still hoping we I can push the date up."

Cruz was already shaking his head. "After here we go to Legoland, the Zoo Safari Park, the Prado, and more private parties than we can handle."

"If it means paying extra . . ." started Nick.

The other man didn't let him finish. "We're backed up and booked up. I've had broken equipment, and men out sick. I'm running double shifts just to catch up enough to say we're behind schedule."

"Is there any way I could rent the equipment?"

"This isn't like making a snow cone, man. For your snow scene we're going to have to send out two large trucks and four men. Now, excuse me, but I got to get back to work."

"Okay," said Nick, "let's book it for the twenty-first."

He didn't like the late date, but maybe it would work. Maybe Raymond would still be alive. Maybe something would happen.

"But if someone cancels," said Nick, "I'd like to be bumped up. You keep a waiting list?"

"Mention it at the office when you give your deposit."

Cruz was already walking away. "Hold on," Nick shouted.

"What?" Cruz said, not hiding his impatience.

Nick struggled between the words and his anger. He wasn't good at asking anyone for help, at least not for himself. His pride had always gotten in the way. But he needed this man's help.

"This isn't about me. There's this real sick kid who asked Santa Claus for it to snow on Christmas. Only thing is, the kid's probably not going to live that long. That's why I want the snow as soon as possible. I want him to be able to see the snow from his hospital room."

Cruz stared at Nick but said nothing. His look made Nick feel stupid. He had humbled himself, something he never did, and felt dirty for having done it. That's what happens when you lick someone's boot, Nick thought. You get kicked in the teeth.

Nick turned around abruptly and started marching away, and then heard one word over the sounds of the grinding and blowing: "Hey!"

He came to a stop and looked back at Cruz, who was now walking toward him. Face to face, Cruz took a measure of Nick's eyes and asked, "Are you for real?"

Nick's throat constricted, and the words came out in a hiss: "You think I'd make up a story like that?"

"Some people will do anything—"

"Not me. You want the kid's name? His doctor's name? You want his prognosis in writing?"

Cruz was shaking his head back and forth. "I got kids of my own. They're healthy, thank God."

Nick heard his indecision, but what he heard mostly was the sound of snow. Heavy snow. Snow was supposed to be silent, but not this snow. He listened as ice was crushed and ground.

"Maybe I can do it on the morning of the eleventh. It would have to be early. Sunrise. You can hear how noisy this whole operation is. You'd have to get permission from the hospital."

"I'll get it."

# CHAPTER SEVENTEEN

*For Here We Come A-Caroling*
*December 7*

"It's too slow," said Angie.

"No, it's not," said Nick.

Whenever Angie thought it was too slow in the North Pole she always found ways to gather a crowd.

"Maybe the two of you could help me," said Nick.

"What do you need?" asked Darcy.

"Santa is sort of tied to the sleigh," said Nick. "But you two elves can go wherever you want. You can be my eyes."

Darcy looked ready to cooperate. She was a freshman at San Diego State, and being an elf was her first *real* job, if you could call that a real job.

"What are we supposed to be looking for?"

"Santa wants us to be undercover elves," said Angie.

"Our bad boys would never suspect an elf. You could be the perfect observer."

"Don't listen to him," said Angie.

"You can make your surveillance into a game," said Nick. "I had all sorts of games I used to play when I was working surveillance, and those games made me notice more than I would have otherwise. For example, we could play Carnie Barker. When you do that you guess the weight, height, and age of the suspect. What our bad boy can't disguise is his height and weight. We got a general description of those."

"We already have a very important role to play," said Angie, taking Darcy by the arm. "We are not going to play carnival."

"It's not carnival," replied Nick. "It's the guessing game they have at a carnival. The pitchman yells that he can guess your weight, or age."

Angie wasn't listening. "I think it's time for a song and dance. That's what Christmas elves do, not carnival."

Angie and Darcy started skipping around and singing, "*Here we come a-caroling, among the leaves so green! Here we come a-wandering, so fair to be seen! Love and joy come to you, and to you glad Christmas too, and God bless you and send you a Happy New Year, and God send you a Happy New Year.*"

Nick muttered, "And God send me some peace and quiet."

Shoppers gathered to watch, and Angie decided to do standup. "What do elves learn in school?" she asked. When no one answered, Angie said, "The elf-abet."

The groans didn't stop her. "What Christmas carol is a favorite of parents?" she asked. Again, the crowd was stumped. "Silent Night," announced Angie.

Nick nodded. He could endorse those sentiments. Unfortunately, the shoppers were getting into the Christmas spirit and most of them applauded.

"Don't encourage her!" shouted Nick.

People laughed, thinking Santa was part of the act.

"Does anyone know the difference between the Christmas alphabet and the regular alphabet?" asked Angie.

Nick wondered where she came up with all these things. Or maybe the better question was: Why did she come up with all these things?

"In the Christmas alphabet," said Angie, "there is no L."

Nick groaned. He wasn't alone. But there were smiles on every face. Angie's spirit was infectious.

"Who can tell me where the mistletoe went to become rich and famous?" asked Angie.

Once more she stumped the crowd. And then she sang the answer like Ethel Merman at the Oscars, "Holly-wood!"

While people cheered Angie pointed at Nick and asked, "Okay, it's not Christmas until you go visit Santa! It's time to go see Santa."

Angie was playing carnival even if she didn't know it, thought Nick. Pitchmen could have learned from her. Parents and their kids started to line up.

Nick's shift was almost over when an attractive woman not wearing the usual Christmas ensemble entered the North Pole enclosure. Her long legs were accentuated by black stockings and finely polished stiletto heels. The woman didn't hesitate on her approach to Nick's lap.

"My annual tradition," she announced to Darcy. "I'd like my picture taken with Santa."

Darcy giggled. "And I'm sure Santa wants his picture taken with you."

Angie tried to escort the woman to Santa's sleigh, but found herself waved away. "There's no need," the woman announced. "I know my way."

She made her way up the steps with apparent ease, and with a few twists and turns settled very comfortably into Nick's lap. "Hi Santa," she said in a coquettish voice, and then nestled her face into Nick's beard. He got a heady dose of her perfume. Some onlookers stopped to enjoy the show. Women frequently sat in Santa's lap, but most didn't make spectacles of themselves. Their usual Christmas wish was for jewelry, or a luxury car, or a boyfriend or husband. They usually jumped on and then off of Santa's lap. This woman was making herself at home and Nick felt uncomfortable at the familiarity she was radiating.

"Did you miss me, Santa?" she asked in a breathless voice.

"Why, yes, I did, young lady," said Nick.

"Young lady?" The woman pretended to pout. "You don't remember Kathleen? You said you'd never forget me, Santa. Don't you remember last Christmas Eve? The eggnog? The open fire?"

"Santa visits many, many homes."

"But the way you filled my stocking, Santa, made me think I was something special."

Kathleen was seated sidesaddle on Nick's lap. She swiveled her hips and nestled a little closer to him, if that was possible. Nick could feel himself turning red. He sat up very straight, forcing Kathleen's pose to be less suggestive.

"You're violating a clause in my contract," said Nick.

"What clause is that?" she asked.

"Mrs. Claus," said Nick.

His remark drew laughter from those who were watching, and seemed to put Kathleen off-stride for a moment. Nick tried to return to a more standard and accepted script.

"So have you been a good girl this year, Kathleen?"

"Not when I could help it," she said.

"Well, Santa only brings gifts to those who have been good."

"That hasn't been my experience," said Kathleen.

The woman turned to Darcy and said, "I'm ready for my close-up, Ms. DeMille."

She pressed a long, red fingernail under Nick's chin, and moved his face toward hers. "Pucker up," she said, and leaned in.

At the last moment Nick turned his cheek so that Kathleen ended up planting most of her kiss on Nick's beard, but she didn't seem to notice. Her eyes and smiles were directed at the camera.

After the flash went off, Kathleen stood up. "Same time next year, Santa?" she asked. "It's been a *real* pleasure."

Nick suspected his face was redder than his hat.

While Kathleen was buying her picture from Darcy, Angie came over and started dabbing at Nick's beard with a kerchief. "What are you doing?" he asked

"I'm getting rid of the lipstick on your beard."

"Santa the chick magnet," he said.

Angie stopped her dabbing and stepped back, examining the damage. "It needs a little more soda water," she announced, and went over to her oversized bag and poured some on the kerchief.

"Anything you don't have in that bag?" Nick asked.

"That bag has been three years in the making," she said. "Every year I've been adding to it."

"Is three years how long you've been an elf?"

Angie dabbed and nodded. She stepped back, surveyed his beard once more, and seemed satisfied that all the lipstick had been vanquished.

"Thanks," said Nick, and then remembered what he'd been meaning to tell her. "And thanks also for your snow idea."

"Is it going to be a white Christmas for Raymond?" Angie asked.

"That's the plan," said Nick.

"It's a good plan."

"He hasn't been doing too well, but his mother is in town today and tomorrow. Maybe that will help."

"Nothing like family," said Angie.

She suddenly snapped her fingers, as if remembering something, and went over to her bag. After rummaging around for a minute, she extracted a copy of a familiar letter, her quill pen, and some ink, and brought the whole lot over to Nick.

"We still haven't answered Laura's letter," Angie said.

"That's because we haven't found Laura," said Nick.

"I think we should answer her letter anyway."

"What good would that do?"

"You ever hear how a butterfly flapping its wings in Brazil can set off a chain of events that ends with a twister in Kansas?"

"Yeah, I've heard something like that."

"Then imagine positive energy the same way. Good thoughts can travel over mountains, and under oceans, and reverberate and change things for the better in ways we can't even imagine."

Nick felt his eyes glazing over. As if some butterfly flapping its wings was going to help find Laura, or bring snow to Raymond.

"I'm not into that new age stuff," said Nick.

"Who said anything about new age? I'm just asking you to write back to Laura."

"And maybe we can put that letter in a bottle, throw it in the ocean, and hope a butterfly will beat its wings so that the bottle gets delivered by a bottle-nosed dolphin while Laura's walking on the beach. I'm a cop, Angie. I want to find Laura my way, not by hocus-pocus. I intend to answer her letter in person."

Angie smiled. "That's it, then."

"What's it?"

Angie was already writing. "Dear Laura," she said, "I intend to answer your letter in person. Love, Santa."

"You're one of a kind, Angie," said Nick.

She went to her bag, found some tape, and then posted the letter on the sleigh. Her smile never left her face. Nick wished he had her faith.

# CHAPTER EIGHTEEN

*Up on the Housetop*
*December 8*

Because Nick had Santa duty later in the morning, he and Charlotte met early for what she termed an "aerobic meeting." Nick would have liked it better had she called it a date.

They walked along the La Jolla Cove, taking in the rocks and the surf while chatting. Shore birds floated overhead, and in the distance they could hear the calls of sea lions. The weather was perfect; probably seventy on the nose, and the gentle ocean breeze cooled them as they walked. Scuba divers made their way past the surf line, and there were even swimmers braving the brisk water.

"What if Laura is a nickname?" said Charlotte, "Or what if it's not her real name? I suppose she could be Lauren, or Laurel, or Loretta."

"Or she might go by her middle name," said Nick.

"The schools might not have looked for that," Charlotte said. "Or Laura might be homeschooled. And I never thought of checking into private schools. It doesn't matter that she doesn't have money. Some give scholarships."

"I have an idea," said Nick. "We know Laura's a reader. I was thinking about canvassing the libraries in Southeast San Diego. Since it's likely she has no money to buy books, it stands to reason that she's getting books from the library."

Charlotte nodded. "That's a good idea. The only problem is we're running out of time. Christmas is only seventeen days away, Nick."

They stopped at the sea wall overlooking Children's Cove. Most locals now called it Sea Lion Cove, as it had been taken over by the mammals. Some of the sea lions and seals could be seen in the water, but most were content to bask in the sun along the beach.

"With time running out," said Charlotte, "I'd like to interview you for the Laura story. My producer and I are talking about using it as a springboard into a series called *The Children Christmas Forgot*."

Nick had hoped it wouldn't come to this; part of him was still suspicious that she'd been stringing him along just to make sure he cooperated with her story. She sensed his reticence.

"It's not going to be easy for me either," she said. "I'm going to talk about how it was for me growing up. That's something I've never done."

"Your viewers are going to admire you for having come so far."

"I wouldn't count on that. Do you know how hard it is to be a forty-something female broadcaster? The only thing tougher is to be a fifty-something female broadcaster, and that's not far away. We're supposed to be all smiles without the laugh lines. I'm the only broadcaster my age who hasn't had cosmetic surgery, and that includes the men."

"Hey," said Nick, "I've been meaning to ask you something: Does my Santa suit make me look fat?"

Charlotte laughed, but then gave Nick a sideways glance. "That's not going to work."

"What's not going to work?"

"You're not going to get out of your interview that way. You promised."

Nick sighed. "So when do you want to do it?"

"The sooner we put the story on the air, the better our chances of finding Laura."

He couldn't find fault with anything she said, but the thought of appearing in front of a camera was still daunting.

"All right, I do it in my Santa uniform, and I'm identified as Nicholas Alexander Pappas."

"That's what we agreed on."

A seal raised its head up out of the water and seemed to look directly at Nick. "Christmas seal," he said.

Charlotte followed the direction of his gaze, and laughed.

Nick thought about his schedule. Los Niños Hospital had agreed to allow the snow delivery on the eleventh. It would be best to get the interview out of the way before then. "Let's do it the day after tomorrow," he said, "and in the meantime I'm going to do everything I can to find Laura so as to get out of it."

The Sunday shopping crowds were busy, and so was the North Pole. Every so often Nick heard shouting in the distance, but he couldn't figure out what was getting people excited. After about the third such explosion he remembered the Sea Lions were playing. He had been so busy he had forgotten his promise to Danny Brown. By the sound of it, maybe Santa Claus was keeping his word.

It was late afternoon before he was able to take a break. He downed three bottles of water in the locker room, and was still thirsty. At the water cooler he refilled the bottles. Forster joined him there. His partner's face was drawn.

"Don't tell me the Sea Lions lost," said Nick.

Forster was a big football fan, and for a moment he had something to smile about. "They didn't lose; they won big, as in thirty-five to seven with Danny Brown throwing for over four hundred yards."

"Then why the long face?"

"Our bad boys just snatched two purses. They're back."

Nick felt as if he had let his friend down. It had been busy, but his vibes must have failed him. He had never picked up on the presence of the suspects.

"The women were both about forty," said Forster. "They were walking toward their car and the next thing they knew their purses were snatched."

"With easy pickings our guys will be back."

"I know."

"You get footage from the cameras in the parking lots?"

"They were wearing hats and big sunglasses. And they took off in a Camry with stolen plates."

"When my shift's over," said Nick, "let's do a stakeout."

It was like old times. After an hour in the Food Pavilion, Nick and Forster moved outdoors to a spot that allowed them a good vantage point.

"Our bad guys usually operate out here," said Nick. "What do you think about getting some off-duty cops to dress up as Salvation Army Santas?"

"I like the idea. But I just don't have the budget."

"What if we paid the cops through whatever they collect in their drums?"

"You're saying we should take the donations and put them into the security budget?"

"Why not?"

"It's illegal. It's unethical. And I'd hate to think of the fallout if our shoppers found out."

"To catch these guys we got to think out of the box."

Forster started laughing.

"What now?" said Nick.

"Marco," said Forster.

"It worked didn't it?"

Forster and Nick had been working patrol when they'd gotten a call about a break-in in Mission Beach. A witness had seen two kids prying open a door to get into the Plunge, a huge swimming pool located in Belmont Park.

The two officers had found the broken door, and had gone inside. It was dark, and they didn't know where the lights were. They had shined their flashlights inside the cavernous space, but had seen nothing. The reflection of light off the water had made the place that much eerier.

"Police!" Forster had yelled. "Come out with your hands up!"

No one had come out; no one had responded. It was unclear if their suspects were still there. Even if they were, there were a million places to hide. While Forster stood guard at the door, Nick had checked the two locker rooms. When he returned empty-handed, Forster had suggested they leave.

They'd walked toward the exit, and that's when Nick stopped. He cupped his hands together, and in a playful voice shouted, "Marco!"

And without thinking, one of the suspects had yelled back, "Polo!"

"Remember how mad that one kid was at his friend? 'Why couldn't you have kept your mouth shut? Why did you yell, *Polo*?'"

Nick grinned. "That was a good bust, but let's not forget that you were the one who caught the Hamburglar."

The two of them had responded to a call from a woman who said someone had stolen the meat from her freezer. When they arrived at the scene of the crime they were met by a husband and wife. It was the wife who did all the talking. According to her, someone had rifled their freezer. The missing items included two pounds of bacon, some rib-eye steaks, pork chops, and two packages of ground chuck.

"Talk about an easy call," said Forster. "While the wife was ranting and raving, her husband was looking everywhere around the room except at his wife and us. When I got him by himself all I had to say was, 'I think you got something to tell me.'"

"I'm surprised she never smelled the food cooking when he went to get his midnight snacks."

"He meant to replace all the meat before she noticed," said Forster. "They had gone in on a diet together, and he was ashamed to tell her how he had been cheating. Even when she was calling the police, he couldn't bring himself to confess."

As they continued their stakeout, the two men reminisced about the past and whiled away the time listening to sports radio. The big story of the day was the Sea Lions victory over Kansas City. Over the course of three hours Nick heard the same locker room interview of Downtown Danny Brown five times. Each time it aired, Forster enjoyed it more.

"So," said the sportscaster, "some people are saying this game ball should go to Santa Claus. Tell us about your visit to Saint Nick."

"Well," said Brown, "I took my daughter to see him, and after she got done with her list, I ended up asking Santa for something myself."

"You asked for a victory, I understand. It was a Christmas present the Sea Lions desperately needed."

"Yeah, we really did."

"You had a career day."

"I went in there really loose. Seeing Santa put things in perspective. Football really is a kid's game, and that's easy to forget.

When you're little, all you care about is having fun. That's what I tried to bring to the field today."

"Whatever you did, it worked. You kept the playoff hopes alive. I hope Santa has some more presents in store for you the next few weeks. Are you going to visit the Big Guy again?"

"I might do that, but is it fair to ask Santa for another present?"

"I don't know if it's fair or not, but we could sure use some help against Denver. It's another big game."

"From here on in, they're all big games."

Nick was glad the stores were closing. He wouldn't have to hear the interview again.

"That's enough clichés for the night," said Nick. "It doesn't look like our Grinches are showing up again."

Forster wasn't going to let him off the hook that easily. He held an imaginary microphone out to Nick and spoke with a big voice. "Here I am with today's MVP Santa Claus, who had a *huge* game."

"I couldn't have done it without the reindeer," said Nick.

"What about Mrs. Claus?"

"She's a real gamer."

"Any comment about the elves?"

"They came to play."

"How are you going to approach the big game?"

"It will be one chimney at a time."

"And there you have it," said Forster. "We've heard from the man, the myth, the legend. There only remains one thing for this interview to be complete: the Nick Pappas obligatory victory dance."

"I don't dance," said Nick.

# CHAPTER NINETEEN

*Auld Lang Syne*
*December 9*

*"Please come visit me this year, Santa."*

Nick held a copy of Laura's letter in his hand. He knew its closing line only too well.

He started his prospecting at Valencia Park/Malcolm X Library and Performing Arts Center on Market Street. Nick had heard the locals refer to the buildings as "X." As he stepped inside the library, Nick wished he had some official standing. He walked over to the information desk and the woman sitting behind it smiled.

"May I help you?" she asked.

The librarian looked like she was in her late forties. She had long salt-and-pepper hair and, on her cotton print dress, she wore a name tag that said "Dawn Lambert" and a button that read "Reading Tolkien Can Be Hobbit Forming." Her eyes were the blue seen in marbles, her irises almost opaque.

"I have some questions for you," Nick said, "but they're probably going to sound odd."

"Odd questions are my favorite kind," Dawn said.

"I work at Plaza Center," said Nick. "Recently we received this letter."

He handed the librarian a copy of Laura's letter. As Dawn began to read, her lips pursed thoughtfully, and Nick heard her utter a sympathetic "oh." When she finished reading, her eyes asked Nick to elaborate.

"I was the one who received the original of that letter," said Nick. "I'm one of the Santa Clauses at the mall. When I'm off duty, I go by the name of Nick Pappas."

"It's nice to meet you, Mr. Pappas," she said. "Is this when you're going to start asking me those odd questions?"

Nick nodded. "Laura's note tells us a lot of things, but not her last name or address. That's where I am hoping you can help."

"How?"

"It's clear Laura loves to read. Since she doesn't have money, I'm assuming she gets her books through the library. Her letter tells us some of the books she likes. If you can get me a history on who's checked those books out in the last year, I can cross-index the names."

Dawn was shaking her head even before Nick finished. "I'm sorry, but I can't do that. The city and county systems don't have the capacity to do a history on any title. We can only access what's been checked in or checked out."

"No records?"

"No records."

"No names?"

"I am afraid not, and even if I was able to get names I couldn't give them to you anyway. That would violate confidentiality."

Nick nodded, though it wasn't what he wanted to hear. There had to be some back door. "How old do you have to be to get a library card?"

"If you can sign your own name, and you have parental permission, you qualify."

Laura could certainly sign her name. "Do most children under the age of ten have their own library cards?"

Dawn shook her head: "As a rule, parents check out the books for that age group. Minors are supposed to be accompanied by an adult."

Nick could feel another door closing. He had been hoping that Laura was dealing directly with the librarians.

"What would you do if you were me?" Nick asked. "You know the system."

Dawn opened her mouth, and then closed it. She looked torn between wanting to help, and being afraid to.

"You can talk off the record," Nick said. "This isn't going to backfire on you. I keep thinking about that last line of her note. *Please come visit me this year, Santa.* That's what Laura wrote, and that's what I'm trying to do."

Still, Dawn hesitated. "Why did you pick this library?"

"Take a look at her drawing," said Nick. "It looks like a picture of the Sixty-Second Street Station. This library is the closest to that."

Dawn's scales of justice finally tipped. "I can make a copy of this letter and send it to all the city and county librarians. The only undercover work we usually do pertains to book covers, but I expect this letter will prompt any number of watchful eyes."

The idea of a group of librarians acting like spies prompted both Nick and Dawn to smile.

"Can you also include my name and telephone number and explain I'm looking for her?"

"I'll do that," Dawn said.

Nick scratched out his home number and passed it over to '
"Any other suggestions?" he asked.

"I'll make some calls for you," she said. "Fellow lib
might tell me things they wouldn't tell you."

"Thanks for helping," he said.

Nick could see that Dawn was still chewing her l
ing. "Was there something else?" he asked.

C
to

"I have an idea," she said. Whatever that idea was, she didn't offer specifics. "But it's going to take me a few days to make it operational."

Nick didn't mention that a few days were all they had.

———※———

I feel light. That was Nick's thought at the end of the workday. The feeling wasn't uncommon after a Santa shift—it was always a relief to be delivered from the unwieldy uniform and the padding heavy with his sweat, but it wasn't only the freedom from his Santa suit that made Nick feel as he did. For the longest time he had considered hope to be the domain of fools, but now he saw how it could be the foundation of dreams.

Maybe he didn't have to die a cop. It surprised him how much he liked working with kids. What was to stop him from working in a school as an aide? And it was past time for him to start a garden again. It didn't matter that he lived in an apartment. All he needed was a few planters. By growing tomatoes, basil, eggplant, and peppers he had the foundation for some great meals. And with those ingredients, was it so impossible to think he might cook again for someone special?

There was an extra lift in Nick's step. He had finalized arrangements with Cruz for the snow scene, and couldn't wait to see Raymond's reaction to it. The boy seemed to be doing better, or at least had sounded that way when Nick talked with him on the phone earlier in the day. Maybe spending time with his mother had given him a lift. The snow might be something else Raymond could build on.

Nick was also hopeful on the Laura front. He was convinced that he and Charlotte were getting closer to finding Laura. Tomorrow he had to go through with that television interview, though. Charlotte had offered to take him out to lunch afterwards, but he told her he had Santa duty.

"Rain check, then," she had said.

"Snow check," Nick told her, but hadn't elaborated.

He was whistling as he walked out to the parking lot. The December weather was warm, and the night was clear. Ahead of him, he saw an old woman overburdened with shopping bags. With just a few steps he caught up with her.

"Help you with the packages, ma'am?"

She gave Nick a quick look, and decided he wasn't a threat. Nick wasn't as certain about her. Up close, he could see how very much she was hauling. Her hair was white and she was probably in her early eighties. But her eyebrows were dark. Like her eyebrows, her spirit came across as youthful.

"That's very kind of you," she said. "I don't understand why malls don't provide shopping carts."

The woman slowly began transferring her shopping bags over to Nick. His empty hands caught her attention. "You didn't find what you were looking for?" she asked.

"Nope," he said, "I struck out."

"Perhaps you'll wish I was a little more unlucky with my shopping."

Nick laughed. She definitely wasn't traveling light.

"I have a lot of people to shop for," she said. "That's what comes of having three daughters and six grandchildren."

Nick took the last of her packages. "I think you got everyone taken care of tonight."

"Oh, not everyone, but I made a good start."

She started chatting about her family. The presents, she said, were mostly for the "out of towners" and would need to be mailed. She was glad that half her family was in the San Diego area, as she could hand deliver those.

Nick walked at her slow pace. She said her car wasn't far off, but she had only a general idea of where it was parked. Nick didn't care; he wasn't in a rush. He was listening to a story about one of her grandsons when the shadow descended on them.

A truck was slowly approaching. Nick felt himself tensing as it pulled up to them. The truck was a gunmetal-black color with tinted windows that were too dark for Nick to see inside. The vehicle seemed to hover over them before slowly passing by. Music was playing in the cab, a loud bass. The truck's brake lights weren't working, making it appear that much darker. At the intersection of the lot, it came to a stop.

Nick was no longer listening to the old woman's story. He couldn't bottle up the street cop in him any longer. All his attention was fixed on the truck. It was just sitting there, waiting.

"Hello?" she said. "Excuse me, young man. Here's the car."

The truck finally moved, slowly making a left turn. There was a flash of a match, and in that moment Nick found himself looking into two sets of predator eyes. Then, with an insolent roar, the truck moved off.

For a moment Nick considered grabbing the old lady's keys. But he couldn't risk what might happen during an unauthorized car chase. Besides, no crime had been committed, and he couldn't even be sure these were his bad guys.

Nick stood there fuming. He couldn't make out a license plate number, and wondered if it had been removed. And he couldn't run after them. If they were his bad boys, he didn't want to show himself to them.

"Young man?" asked the old woman, "young man?"

The truck was making its way toward an exit. The duo wasn't coming back, at least not tonight. Nick had gotten between the hunters and their prey, and they were going off to look for other game.

Nick started stowing the presents in the trunk.

"Thank you so much."

"You're welcome," Nick said, and then added, "Make sure you lock your doors and drive carefully."

"Oh, I will."

Nick waited for her to get in the car and start the engine before walking off. His steps were heavier, and his breath was strained. The encounter with the truck and its occupants had a toxic effect. His brief flirtation with happiness felt as if it had been sucked out of him, and his old companion, gloom, returned.

# CHAPTER TWENTY

*In the Bleak Midwinter*
*December 10*

Under the hot lights of the camera Nick felt the perspiration dripping off his forehead. The interview hadn't even begun and yet he was feeling like he was being readied for the grill. Charlotte kept trying to put him at ease, which only made Nick more nervous.

His fears were unfounded, of course. Charlotte had already gone over what they were to discuss. She would ask him questions about Laura's letter, and then he was going to read it. There wouldn't be any questions about the shooting.

"Ready, Nick?"

"Shoot my good side," Nick told her.

"Which side is that?"

"I was hoping you could tell me."

Charlotte laughed, signaled to the cameraman, and then started asking questions.

———❋———

Nick was relieved when the shoot was done. Maybe some viewer would lead them to Laura. Christmas Eve was only two weeks off; time was getting short.

Charlotte had also interviewed Angie. They'd taken footage of the letters hanging from the sleigh, and Angie had emphasized how Santa answered every letter personally. Nick was afraid that might bring a new flurry of letters to his mailbox. He hoped he wouldn't get another letter from someone like Laura.

After Charlotte and her cameraman left, the rest of the day was quiet. At the conclusion of his shift Nick told Angie that Bret was going to be filling in for him the next day.

"I have it on good authority that it's going to snow tomorrow," he told her.

"Oh, Nick," she said, "that's wonderful."

"Yeah, I'm looking forward to it."

"I think you've arrived," Angie said.

"What do you mean?"

"There are three stages of man," said Angie. "Think of them as a progression. The first stage is when you believe in Santa Claus. The second stage is not believing in Santa Claus. And the third stage is becoming Santa Claus. You've reached that third stage, Nick."

"Don't tell anyone," he said.

"Oh, your secret is safe with me."

———※———

When Nick arrived at the hospital he went over the next day's arrangements with Easy. She was working a twelve-hour shift and would be around in the morning when the snow started flying.

"The snow crew is going to be working at dawn," said Nick. "I want Raymond to toss the first snowball."

"I'll bring him down as soon as they start," Easy promised.

"I don't think we'll be able to surprise him. He's probably going to hear them making the snow. It's a pretty noisy operation."

"I'll make a point of being in his room when the noise starts," Easy said. "I can say construction is going on, and then ask Raymond if he wants me to wheel him down to see. That will make for a good excuse."

"That sounds great," said Nick.

"I'm glad you're doing this," she said. "Raymond's been subdued since his mom left."

"He's probably tired," said Nick.

"Probably," said Easy, although she didn't sound convinced.

"Don't worry, I won't stay long."

When Nick walked into the room and saw Raymond's dull eyes, he knew it was more than a case of the boy being tired. As sick as he'd been before, the boy's eyes had always been bright and piercing, but now Nick was looking at eyes that seemed to have a layer of film on them.

"How you doing?" he asked.

The boy barely shrugged.

One of Raymond's favorite toys was his Woody doll from the movie *Toy Story*. The cowboy sheriff was sprawled on the floor and Nick picked him up. He pulled the string and Woody said, "I'll make a cowboy out of you yet."

Raymond's mouth twitched in a grin. Nick pulled again, and Woody said, "Yee haw, cowboy."

On the third pull Woody said, "Hey, this town ain't big enough for the two of us."

Or this world, thought Nick with a suppressed sigh.

He set the doll on the nightstand, and then reached for the Advent calendar. In his days away from Raymond the boy had kept up with opening the doors, but he hadn't turned that day's flap.

"Chocolate waiting for you," said Nick, "behind door number ten."

Nick held the calendar for Raymond to scan. The boy seemed to have trouble focusing, but at last scratched a feeble finger at the number ten. It was clear he was only making the effort for Nick, and when the flap turned Raymond dropped his hand.

"I'm not hungry," he said. "You have it."

"Keep it for a midnight snack," said Nick.

"Don't want it," said Raymond. Speaking seemed to be an effort, but he did sigh out one word: "You."

Nick took him up on the invitation, pulled out the chocolate, and swallowed it.

"Good?" asked Raymond.

"Good," lied Nick. The chocolate stuck in his throat like a bitter pill that didn't want to go down.

"Are you sure you don't want me to get Easy, or a doctor?"

"Just tired," said Raymond.

"Get some sleep then."

The boy gave a small nod.

"I'll see you tomorrow," said Nick.

"Bye," Raymond whispered.

The boy closed his eyes. It was a relief to Nick. He didn't like admitting it to himself, but looking at those dull eyes had unnerved him.

Tomorrow, Nick thought as he made his way silently from the room, the snow will fall and my commitment will be done. Maybe the snow will be just the thing to revive him.

# CHAPTER TWENTY-ONE

*O Come, O Come, Emmanuel*
*December 11*

The phone rang just after midnight. Nick was wide awake, but he still didn't rush to answer it. He hated late night phone calls. Nothing good ever came from them, and he was hoping someone had misdialed. After five rings that hope vanished and he picked up the receiver.

"Mr. Pappas? This is Isabel—Easy—from the hospital."

No, thought Nick. Don't say it.

"I'm sorry to be calling so late . . ."

She paused long enough for Nick to offer some forgiving nicety, but he didn't do that.

". . . but I thought you should know about Raymond. We had to rush him to the ICU."

"How bad is he?"

"He's in critical condition. The doctors have put him on life support, and he's not conscious."

Nick didn't say anything.

"I thought you should know with the snow people coming out in the morning. Maybe you could still . . ." She almost said the word *cancel* but instead said ". . . get them to come another day."

Nick pondered his options. There didn't seem to be a good one among them.

"Where's the ICU located," he asked, "and does it have a view to that grassy area?"

"It's on the third floor. From the south window you can see down to the grass."

"Okay."

"Okay?"

"Let it snow."

———— ✳ ————

In the middle of the night Nick gave up trying to sleep and went downstairs. He sat at the kitchen table and stared at the gun. The revolver was in the same spot where he had left it, but for the first time in almost two weeks he took notice of it. He felt like he was back where he had started, and knew that wasn't a good place to be.

Anger always darkened his mood. The more he tried to keep things inside, the more they had a way of spilling out, like some personal forest fire that blackened his world. But he was tired of keeping his anger bottled up; he wanted to lash out at something, anything. God, he decided, was a big enough target.

He lifted his eyes up from the gun, but not very far up. "I tried to do something right, God, and where has it gotten me?"

His words became louder: "Are you looking to trade, God? Do you need a life so much that you're going to take this kid's? Why don't you take mine instead, then? How about it, me for him? Why don't you just reach down with one of those divine fingers of yours and cure his ills? I'm offering myself as payment. I know it's not much to put on the table, but how about it?"

Nick started rapping his knuckles on the table, and kept rapping them.

"You keep throwing children in my path, God, and it is one bad story after another. I shoot to protect my life, and I almost take a little girl's life. I play Santa Claus, and you make me an angel of death. I get a plea for help, but it's an anonymous plea. Are you trying to drive me crazy, God? You got all these people yelling, 'help, help,' but you've rigged everything so that I can't."

Nick's rapping grew louder.

"You'd think taking away my career would be payment enough, but I guess not. No, I needed to suffer some more."

Nick stopped rapping. He looked at his hands. His knuckles were white and skinned, as if he had been in a fight. I was in a fight, Nick thought, and I lost again.

"Were you listening, God?" he asked, and then he shook his head.

"I didn't think so."

———※———

Nick left his apartment at 4:00 a.m. It was too early and too dark to be going anywhere, but he was tired of talking to himself.

The roads were deserted, and he made it over to Los Niños faster than he would have wanted. He considered going to some fast-food place for coffee, but decided against it. With his luck, he was afraid he would walk into another armed robbery, and besides, he really didn't want coffee. He just wanted to get things over with.

Nick sat in his car for ten minutes before finally getting out. He was wearing a sweater, but he didn't need one. The coastal clouds had never lifted, and the weather had remained unnaturally warm. The temperature was hovering at around sixty, and it was only going to get warmer. Cruz had told him he could expect the snow scene to last anywhere from a day to three days depending on use and the weather. The cold front Nick had wanted was just another hope denied.

The hospital was locked to visitors, but Nick already knew the off-hours routine. He entered through emergency services, and signed in with a moody guard who'd not said three words to him during all his other visits. Easy had put his name on the after-hours list; the guard motioned with his head for Nick to pass.

Everything was quiet, save for the piped-in music. For Nick, there was no reprieve from the Christmas hit parade, even at four in the morning. The songs seemed to be following him everywhere. "O Holy Night" was playing.

Oh, holy not, he thought.

Nick walked over to the elevators, but hesitated before getting in. He was afraid of going up to the ICU and being told that Raymond was dead. Nick hated feeling so helpless, so weak. Whenever someone said to him, "I've got good news for you, and I've got bad news," Nick always wanted to hear the bad first. Death, snow, and cold feet, he thought. He crossed the elevator threshold and pushed a button.

On the third floor the lights were dimmer, or maybe that was just his imagination. The floor appeared very quiet. The door into the ICU was locked, and there was no one at the duty station, just a buzzer for paging a nurse. Nick wasn't in any rush to talk with anyone. He sat down and waited for someone to appear. Eventually someone always did.

Twenty minutes passed before a woman opened the door. Her head reared back in surprise when she saw Nick, but the movement looked more defensive than vulnerable, reminding him of a snake ready to strike. She was a tall, black woman with short hair and a severe expression.

"What do you want?"

The way she was looking at him, Nick figured she had him gauged as an undesirable, and maybe she was right. He hadn't shaved, and his dark circles were probably a mile long.

"I'm a friend of Raymond's," he said. "A few hours back Nurse Castillo called me. I know I can't see him, but I just wanted to know how he's doing."

"You're the cop, aren't you?"

For a moment, Nick wondered whether he'd met this nurse when he had brought Chrissie in. But that wasn't it. Easy knew he was a cop and would have told her.

"Yes." One more half lie to add to the rest.

"Your friend's not doing very well. He is not conscious and he's not breathing on his own."

Nick nodded to show that he'd heard.

"Are you still going to be trucking that snow in?"

Easy must have told everyone about the snow as well. Nick was glad she had spared him the explanation. "It's still coming," he said. "If by some chance Raymond's well enough to look out the window, I'd appreciate it if you, or whoever's working, could take him over there so that he could see the snow."

"We got the word on that already," she said, and smiled gently. "If he opens his eyes, we'll make sure he sees it."

"Thank you."

"I'm from Philadelphia myself. I spent enough winters there that I thought I'd never want to see snow again. But your snow's got everyone around here excited, even me."

The Igloo Ice work crew arrived at 6:30 a.m., none too soon for Nick. He'd been pacing around for over an hour, and had been forced to explain his movements to two different security guards.

Manuel Cruz had a cold, which was contributing to his deep voice. Between his coughing, sneezing, incessant yawning, and talking, his mouth always seemed to be open.

"Thought my crew was going to mutiny when I scheduled this job," said Cruz, "but then I told them about that kid."

There were three other workers, all Hispanic. They spoke Spanish with one another. Cruz collected the rest of the money Nick owed, and then simultaneously carried on English and Spanish conversations; he alternately talked with Nick, and directed his crew. His hands seemed to speak a third language, pointing, signaling, gesturing. Under his guidance, the equipment was positioned.

"So how's the boy doing?"

"Bad." Nick didn't want to say more. He didn't want Cruz and his crew to know their work was likely to amount to no more than a futile gesture.

"Maybe this will cheer him up."

"Maybe."

Nick lightly touched an ice block being fed down a rail. It was about five feet long and two feet wide.

"We call that a rail car," said Cruz. "Each of those blocks of ice weighs three hundred pounds."

The ice looked like some distant relation of snow. Cruz seemed to read Nick's doubts. "Don't worry. The crusher's going to make that ice all powdery. It's going to look like snow, and feel like snow, 'cept it's a little more coarse. Next best thing to Mother Nature, man."

The crusher started up. It was loud, and that was even before any grinding had begun. The first rail car was fed into the crusher, and then it started snowing. Flakes didn't fall, and the process was about as serene as a brigade of leaf blowers, but the end product looked like the real thing. The crushed ice sprayed out of a tube, and soon the green grass began to disappear under a blanket of white. As the crusher crushed, and the blower blew, winter came alive.

Nick was surprised at how quickly the snow was laid down. In mere minutes, the entire lawn was covered. Nick surveyed his white elephant, his folly, but he wasn't the only one looking. All the hospital windows with a view of the snow were fogging up with little faces staring down. The blinds had been opened, and spectators were watching, but from what Nick could see Raymond wasn't among them.

"Pretty, isn't it?" asked Cruz, opening his hands to the snow.

Nick nodded.

"I always feel like one of those pastry chefs, you know, making something that looks so good, but something that's going to disappear just like that." He snapped his fingers.

"Ephemeral," said Nick, "all too ephemeral."

Forster had taught him that word. Nick had been swatting at some insects one day and Forster had said he should ignore them. "Those are mayflies," he had told him. "Their lives are so ephemeral they won't live out the day."

Nick had never forgotten that word. It was hard for him to imagine something being born, flying, dancing, mating, and dying in a single day.

"It's going to be a hot one," said Cruz, wiping his brow. "The snow might not even last the day, especially if it gets a lot of use."

A single day, thought Nick. Like the mayflies.

"We could rope the area off if you want. I get the feeling you're going to have a lot of company soon."

"No."

Cruz made a circle with his index finger to his crew. It was time to wrap things up.

"Some people make a real ceremony out of the snow," Cruz said. "They stick a couple of bottles of champagne in it, ice 'em up, and then pop the corks. Other people like to throw the first snowball. They make a big production out of it, like they're out at the stadium and they're throwing that opening pitch."

Nick made no move to make a snowball, and the closest thing he had to champagne was a warm Coke in his car. He looked from the snow up to the third floor windows.

"Is that where he is?" Cruz asked.

"Yeah."

"Is he going to be coming down?"

"He's too sick."

The work crew had finished, leaving the snow pristine and untouched. The pine trees were frosted, and the bordering bushes wore little white caps. San Diego wasn't any place for snow, but it still looked beautiful, at least for the moment.

Cruz tilted his head to the snow. "Go ahead and touch it."

Nick reached down, picked up a handful, and made a ball of it. It had been a long time since he had touched snow. One winter's day he'd driven his family to the mountain town of Julian so they could all see the white stuff. They had driven for two hours just to freeze their hands for a few minutes. It was the kind of thing families did.

He examined the snow, looked at it a little too long, as if he was reading tea leaves. What did he expect to see anyway? It was white and it was cold, but he had known that even before picking it up. He crushed the snowball into dust. He was reminded of one of Raymond's snow globes.

Behind him, Nick heard a familiar voice reciting a poem about some snowball that a kid took to bed with him, and how not surprisingly it wet the bed. Standing there in full elf regalia was Angie.

"What are you doing here?" Nick asked.

"I'm doing what comes naturally to an elf," she said, reaching for some snow and then tossing it into the air. "I'm playing in the snow."

They heard children approaching, their voices high-pitched and excited. The Pied Piper was calling to them. The staff had bundled them up under robes and gowns and hospital blankets, but the kids were throwing the coverings aside. In the midst of the snow, their illnesses were forgotten.

"You want me to keep 'em off?" Cruz asked.

Nick shook his head. Angie stepped out to greet the kids and shouted, "It's snow time!"

It was clear that many of the children had never seen snow before, but that didn't stop a snow fight from breaking out within seconds of their arrival. More and more children were running to get to the snow, and with them came their laughter and shouts.

"We got to roll, man," said Cruz. "Look at those kids. You did a good thing."

"Yeah, I'm a regular Santa Claus."

Angie was helping the children make a snowman. "To make a winter friend," she said, "bring a carrot and some coal . . ."

In her hands, the carrot and coal magically appeared.

". . . then gather up your friends, and roll together snow."

The children followed her instructions, and Angie kept her young charges laughing with jokes. "You know what snowmen eat for breakfast?" she asked. Little heads shook from side to side, and then Angie announced, "Snowflakes!"

Nick had hoped the coastal fog would last for the morning, but it lifted early and the full rays of the sun began to bear down on the snow. Angie came and joined him, and they watched the children play. The snowman was already looking the worse for wear.

"Your snowman could use some sunblock," said Nick.

He wasn't the only one who noticed the state of the snowman. "Frosty's melting," a little girl told Angie.

The Elf bent down to the girl's level and said, "Snowmen have warm hearts so they never stay around very long. But you know what? When a snowman melts away, a snow angel goes to heaven that same day."

"Really?" asked the girl.

"Really," said Angie, clapping her hands. "Let's make snow angels!"

The two of them lay down in the snow and moved their arms and legs back and forth. When they jumped up they laughed to see the snow angels left in their wake.

"Join us, Nick!" Angie yelled. "Come make an angel!"

He shook his head. "I don't have an angel in me."

Angie brushed herself off and joined him. "I wish I could stay, but I have to get to work."

"It's a good time to leave. You'll miss the mushy part."

"The mushy part is my favorite," she said, and looked at him as though she felt his hurt, but didn't know how to reach it. "Snow melts, Nick, but not love."

The Elf might be crazy, Nick thought, but it was a good crazy. He reached out and gently brushed some snow from her shoulder. "Wouldn't want you giving anyone the cold shoulder," he said.

She smiled at him, and then skipped off singing a poem about a pet snowball. Her absence immediately darkened Nick's mood. He stared at the impression Angie and the girl had left behind. The snow was only a few inches deep, and some of the grass was already beginning to show. The snow angels wouldn't be long for this earth.

As the hours passed, Nick began to hate the sun. It was relentless and unforgiving, and under its rays the snow retreated. Nick kept telling himself he was going to leave, but it was always "another five minutes." By mid-afternoon all the children had abandoned the snow. There were only three small islands of snow left, patches that were rapidly shrinking. Nick's shadow loomed over the largest of the patches. Together, he thought, we'll melt.

He reached out to the snow closest to him, and kept his fingers buried in it until they were numb. So this, he said to himself, is what a cold day in hell feels like. Nick removed his fingers, but didn't bring them to his lips. He was thirsty, but didn't want to drink. Finding no comfort was part of his vigil.

Nick kept telling himself *don't look up, don't look up*, but he kept sneaking peeks at the ICU windows. There were no longer any spectators at those windows, or at any windows. The sight of a few pockets of slush didn't interest anyone except Nick, and even he wasn't sure what was keeping him there. He had known for hours that Raymond wasn't going to be rising from his sick-bed to see the remains of the snow. Even if he awakened now, Nick doubted the nurses would subject him to such an anti-climactic sight.

For the first time in his life, he wondered if he was losing it. His face was stiff and sunburned, his one-day growth of beard was scratchy, and his lips were chapped—all a result of spending a day watching the snow melt. For an encore, maybe he could watch the grass grow, or some paint dry.

It was a beautiful day, and somehow that made it all the worse. Nick's lack of sleep caught up with him in the late afternoon. He sat down on the grass, unmindful of the dampness that seeped into his clothing, and he dozed off. When he awakened, it was dark.

He looked at his watch: seven o'clock. Passersby must have assumed he was another homeless person. While Nick had slept, the snow had melted all the more. Now there was only one small patch that remained.

His mind felt a little less fuzzy, but that didn't make Nick feel any better. He was glad of the darkness. The shadows shielded him from being on display. He felt ashamed for having wasted the day, for having wallowed in his own mixed-up, sentimental sorrow.

Put the blame on mayflies, he thought, and melting snow.

Nick gathered up the little snow that remained and made a miniature snowman. It was probably the smallest and most pitiful looking snowman ever created. He stood to leave, but then recon-sidered. It won't be long now, Nick thought, just a few minutes. He was right. His snowman began disintegrating, hemorrhaging everywhere.

When Nick could no longer distinguish the snowman's foundation from its stomach, or the stomach from its head, he gathered the slush together and squeezed and squeezed until he had a wet ice ball in his hands.

The moon loomed large overhead. Nick took aim and threw, but he missed.

# CHAPTER TWENTY-TWO

*Watchman, Tell Us of the Night*

The idea struck Nick as he was driving home. Under normal circumstances he would have considered the plan too rash and dangerous, but not now. He considered going to his apartment to get his gun, but decided he didn't want the baggage that came with it. Nick was willing to accept the consequences of its absence. More than willing, he thought, even if it was suicide mission. He could leave his troubles behind in a blaze of glory and not have to face up to the disappointments in his life.

He told himself that wasn't it. He'd been hired to do a job, and this was a way to see it through. Besides, being killed in the line of duty sounded a lot better than killing yourself, didn't it?

He arrived at the mall a half hour before most stores were shutting down. It was late enough that he had no trouble finding open spaces, but he purposely parked well away from the stores. He opened his trunk, pulled out a tire iron, and slid it inside his pants.

As Nick walked toward the mall, the refrain from the loudspeakers seemed to play in chorus with the drums pounding in his head: Pa rum pum pum pum, Pa rum pum pum pum, Pa rum pum pum pum.

Me and my iron thumb, he whispered.

Nick tried to tune out the music, but the loudspeakers wouldn't let him. A new song started playing. The tune was familiar, but it took him a long time before he could place it. It wasn't one of the more popular Christmas songs, but Nick remembered it from his youth. Finally he came up with its title: "Watchman, Tell Us of the Night." Tonight, Nick thought, I am the Watchman.

There had been a man at his church who had sung "Watchman" every year during the Christmas pageant. He had an incredible bass voice that could make the stained-glass windows shake. When the chorus asked him what was going on in the world on the advent of Christmas Day, he would answer in stentorian voice. Nick finally matched the lyrics to the tune:

*Watchman, tell us of the night,*
*For the morning seems to dawn.*
*Traveler, darkness takes its flight,*
*Doubt and terror are withdrawn.*

Tonight this was his song, Nick thought. It was time for doubt and terror to be withdrawn.

Nick took the back way into the mall. Because he didn't want to be seen by anyone he knew, he avoided the North Pole display. The locker room was unoccupied, and he quickly collected what he needed. Behind the privacy of a bathroom stall, he put on his white Santa wig. Then he pulled out the padding, but instead of positioning it around his chest and stomach he planted it along his upper back. He hoped a crooked old man would attract crooked crooks.

Before going out to the mall, Nick had stopped at the recycling center where glass, metal, and paper were sorted. Nick rummaged through the paper goods and came away with some wrapped boxes and bags.

With the bags in hand, Nick started shuffling around the mall. He stopped at several expensive stores and tried to look as conspicuous as possible. The clerks, weary of facing shoppers all day, and wanting only to close up, accommodated Nick's request for additional shopping bags without demur, and he began to look weighed down with packages. He wanted the bull's-eye mark to be complete, and his victim status advertised in everything but neon. If anyone was scouting for a mark, he was going to give them an eyeful. Nick paused every so often at store windows. What he kept seeing was an elderly man weighed down with expensive gifts. In all his stops, though, he never noticed anyone else looking at him as a target.

During his years on the force Nick had worked stakeouts and decoys, but always as backup. He'd never played the role of victim. His job was to be part of the mop-up team. Here, he was alone. His only weapon was the hidden tire iron. Nick didn't care.

He was the Watchman.

His head was pounding. At first he thought it was only the long ingrained habit of living that made him afraid—self-preservation coming to the fore—but it wasn't that exactly. Nick was suddenly certain that he didn't want to die. It was a welcome epiphany. In some ways it felt as if a terrible fever had broken. But he didn't accept that as license to walk away from what he felt he had to do.

It was time for darkness to take its flight.

Outside the mall, Nick stopped to take a few deep breaths. He wasn't breathing hard as some acting technique, wasn't doing it as part of his old-man disguise. He was scared. Though he'd seen nothing to indicate he was being targeted, his heart was racing and his breath was short. There was no sign of the two muggers, or their truck, but his inner alarm was sounding, and then some.

*Watchman, tell us of the night.*

As much as he wanted to look around, Nick kept his head down. He started walking again, forcing himself to go slowly.

Adrenaline pumped through his body, making his guise that much more difficult to maintain.

A car passed, and then another. The parking lot was still one-third full. Nick wondered if there was too much activity for the muggers. They had been brazen enough before, but maybe they were getting cautious in their old age, or at least with their old targets.

Nick trudged along, keeping to his turtle pace. The parking lot was adequately lit, but there were pockets of darkness between the street lamps. Nick was in one of those troughs of shadows when he heard the car approach.

It wasn't the truck—he made sure of that out of the corner of his eye—but the driver was speeding, rapidly closing the distance between them. A hundred feet. Fifty. And then Nick knew this was it. They probably only brought the truck out for special occasions. This car was less noticeable, and the better assault vehicle. Nick turned his head. The passenger door was opening, about to be swung at him.

Nick fell to his right. He didn't throw himself, but toppled just out of the way of the door. It was the lucky maneuver of an old man.

The car braked to a sudden stop and one of the men leaped out. There were three of them, Nick realized, not two. Those weren't good odds. The thief glanced around to see that no one was looking, then closed in on his victim. The unmoving old man lay in the midst of scattered packages.

Watchman, thought Nick, it's time to make darkness take its flight. Slowly, he rose to his feet.

# CHAPTER TWENTY-THREE

*Good King Wenceslas*
*December 12*

Henry was the first to spot Nick when he arrived at the mall early. Beyond some scratches on his face and hands, Nick didn't look too much the worse for wear. "Is it true, Saint Nick, you took on four muggers last night and sent 'em all to the hospital?"

"Don't believe everything you hear," said Nick. "You see Angie? I need to talk to her."

"Saw her headed over to the security office just a minute ago."

"Thanks," said Nick. He needed to talk to Forster too. If he was lucky he could catch them both at the same time.

"They's saying when the police arrived you was singing Christmas carols at the top of your lungs."

"Does that sound like something I'd do?" Nick asked.

Henry regarded him with a questioning eye. "Can't say for sure."

Nick gave him a thumbs-up and headed toward the security office. He tried to ignore his aches and pains. Most of what he was feeling was from acting out the fall as the car door had opened toward him. When the first mugger had approached, Nick had pretended he was hurt and yelled, "My leg, my leg."

He had prepared for two bad guys, but found himself facing three. The muggers hadn't just been lucky. For a time they'd had someone working the inside—Punk Santa had been their accomplice.

Somehow this made Nick more furious. They ignored him, and started grabbing for the scattered packages. That was their mistake. They never noticed Nick sneaking up behind them.

"Drop to the ground. I'm making a citizen's arrest."

You would think the tire iron he was holding might have discouraged them, but the mugger with all the ink on his arms just laughed.

"I'm so scared, old man. Anyone ever tell you, don't bring a knife to a gun fight?"

As the bad boy reached inside his waist pocket, Nick ran at him and swung the tire iron. The mugger fell down, holding his arm and screaming. Nick threw himself on the man, and relieved him of his gun.

"Down!" he yelled to Punk Santa, leveling the weapon.

The kid made the right choice. With a whimper he dropped to the ground.

The third mugger took off at a run. It was a footrace Nick knew he couldn't win, so he didn't attempt pursuit. Instead, he jumped up, took aim, and hurled the tire iron at the fleeing man. The missile flew low and true, striking the man in the back of his right calf and tripping him up. He did a face-plant on the asphalt.

Although he hadn't brought handcuffs, Nick quickly improvised, removing the ribbon from the packages he had been carrying around. He tied the men's wrists and ankles. It looked like a perfect gift-wrapping job—or almost perfect. Nick reached down among the spilled packages, found three colored bows, and affixed them to the tops of the crooks' heads.

"Merry Christmas," he said.

Now, as he walked into security, a feeling of déjà vu came over him. This was where his Santa adventure had begun. And this was where his stint as Santa Cop would end. Even Angie was there, waiting for Forster to get off the phone. The mall grapevine was apparently working faster than the speed of sound, because she said, "I heard you fought five muggers last night and then tied them up with Christmas lights."

Forster never gave her a chance to finish. "Bingo," he said, hanging up the phone. "They're nailed. Four of our victims have already picked them out of a lineup. Their lawyer is screaming about entrapment, and vigilantism, and a few other breaches of the Constitution, but the bust is going to hold. Oh, by the way, Nico, the guy whose arm you broke is threatening to sue you."

"I knew I should have let him shoot me."

"Is Nick in trouble?" asked Angie.

Forster shook his head. "Their lawyer is just angling for the best plea bargain possible. Two of our muggers have already done time and have records. As for our bad Santa, surprise, surprise, he's the brother of one of our nasty boys. In the assault car was plenty of incriminating evidence. Our guys were stupid enough to be carrying some of the spoils from their robberies. Add to that, the gun is hot, so SDPD has plenty to charge them on. As far as the police are concerned, Nick was just doing some Christmas shopping."

"The cops knew me," said Nick, "and I didn't see any need to mention that I've been moonlighting as Santa. That's not the kind of PR Santa needs."

"I don't know about that," said Forster. "Kids might really work on being good if they know Santa has some punishment in mind other than coal."

"Anyway," said Nick, "no one knows it was Santa Claus that clocked these guys, and no one need know, especially now that my job is done."

He turned to Angie. "I brought the batting along, and the wig too, but I'm afraid it got a little dirty. I got some grease on it last night."

"No problem," said Angie. "I've got a solvent that will work wonders for you."

Nick shook his head. "Not for me. For someone else. I was hired to get the muggers. I did. End of story."

He wasn't the only one versed in head shaking. Angie outdid him with her version. "No, it's not."

Nick looked perplexed. "You were here when I was hired. You know the job I was asked to perform. Now it's done."

"Your real job has just begun, Nick Pappas," said Angie. "While you were out playing cops and robbers last night, some of us were working."

At Nick's puzzled expression, Angie turned to Forster. "He doesn't know, does he?"

"Guess not," said Forster.

"Know what?" asked Nick.

"Maybe we should show him," said Angie.

Forster nodded. "Maybe we should."

———— ❋ ————

The two of them refused to answer Nick's questions as they led him out to the North Pole. At first he didn't notice that anything was different, but then he saw a roped-off section that was filled with toys and gifts. There were hundreds of toys, maybe thousands. The roped area could barely contain all the presents. Some of the packages were wrapped, and Angie found a present with a tag on it and handed it to Nick. He read the lettering: "For Laura, or a Child Like Her."

"They started arriving right after Charlotte's story aired at five o'clock," said Angie, "and they haven't stopped."

"We received so many gifts," said Forster, "that we started running out of floor space, and had to figure out how to distribute them."

"They ran the story again this morning," said Angie, "and the phone has been ringing off the hook."

Forster was nodding. "Angie's arranged for some trucks so that we can deliver the toys."

"And I'm sending out a Santa with each truck," said Angie. "That means not only can't you quit, but you're going to have to start working some double shifts."

Nick opened his mouth, and then shut it, unsure of what to say. It was great that Charlotte's story had generated such a positive response, but he had been hired to do undercover.

"I'm not trying to put you out," he said, "but I did my job."

Angie shook her head. "Your job's just started. It was you who started this sleigh rolling. You can't pull back now, Santa."

"You'd be leaving us high and dry, Nick," said Forster.

Tag-team wrestling, thought Nick. No, worse. They were playing good cop/bad cop. He had never thought he would see the day when an Elf could be playing the bad cop.

"If you want to give your notice that's fine," said Angie, "but since we're short-handed, I'll need you to do the right thing and give me two weeks."

Nick did the math. "Christmas is only thirteen days away."

"In that case you are officially Santa Claus until December the twenty-fifth," said Angie, "and that means I need you in the sleigh in ten minutes, and doing toy deliveries tonight. Your reindeer leaves at six."

Nick turned to Forster, who wasn't even trying to hide his amusement. "You're enjoying this, aren't you?"

"Yes, I am."

"Oh, by the way," said Angie, "that's what I came to talk to you about, Walt. I was able to get an extra truck tonight. You'll be doing a Santa run as well."

Forster stopped laughing. "But I've never been a Santa before. There's got to be someone else who can do it."

It was Nick's turn to laugh.

# CHAPTER TWENTY-FOUR

*Jingle Bells*
*December 13*

The gift giving never stopped. All day people came by with presents. Everyone wanted to help; everyone wanted to know if Laura had been found. There were so many people arriving with gifts that signs pointing out directions to the "Friends of Laura Drop-Off" had to be put up. By mid-afternoon toys began to spill out of the enclosure, and maintenance was called in to expand the storage area.

One suited businessman dropped off a present, and then asked if he could get a receipt for a tax deduction.

Angie said, "We don't have receipts, but we do have this!" And then she handed him a candy cane. He went off sucking the candy cane and looking as if he had been given something better than a receipt.

The media caught wind of the story within the story; their coverage seemed to feed the frenzy that much more. Nick was sorry that Charlotte wasn't among the reporters working, but assumed she was busy looking for Laura.

Many of those bringing gifts also visited with Santa, and Nick was kept busy posing for pictures. Everyone was in good humor, and that made the day pass quickly. There was even a little time for joke telling. As one boy with a winning smile left Nick's lap, he said, "I know why you have three gardens, Santa."

Nick bit at his joke. "Why do I have three gardens?"

"So you can hoe, hoe, hoe."

Nick ho-ho-hoed. The boy's joke reminded Nick of a long ago garden he had planted. It had to have been at least twenty years ago—the planting bug had bit him hard, and he had pored over seed and nursery catalogs. His vegetable garden ambitions were equal parts fantasy and remembrance, spurred on by childhood memories of a lush garden bed his mother had worked every summer.

Nick hadn't just thrown seeds in the ground. He had carefully cleared the earth of weeds, and then he had double dug the trenches and added compost. Every day Nick spent time in that garden, humming as he worked (he had heard you were supposed to talk to your plants, but he couldn't bring himself to do that, so he hummed instead). Nick's garden thrived and grew to bounteous proportions. The tomatoes were plump and red, the cucumbers thick and green, the peppers so big they looked like watermelons, the eggplants pendulous and glowing, the squash irrepressible, and the strawberries fat and luscious. He'd ended up giving away so much produce the other cops started calling him "Nick the Green" instead of "Nick the Greek."

That was the only time in Nick's life he went all out in his gardening. In the years since he had never grown anything more than a few tomato plants, and since moving into the apartment he hadn't even grown houseplants.

Laura's gift pile, he thought, was like his garden. It just kept growing, with seen and unseen forces sprouting hope and life. But Nick knew it was too early to be admiring the harvest. There was still a lot of work to be done.

When Angie finally pulled out the "Santa Is Feeding His Reindeer" sign, Nick heaved a sigh of relief, but she barely gave him time to stretch. Once they were out of the public's eye she suddenly became a truck dispatcher. Clipboard in hand, Angie organized the toy deliveries. Nick barely had time to down a glass of ice tea and eat a burger before being told to hit the road.

"Ready to roll?" she asked. "Your truck is loaded."

"Ten-four," Nick said with a twang. "And where might I find my *rig*?"

"Your driver's waiting for you in the back loading zone. You'll be driving in Vixen tonight."

———— ✳ ————

Four trucks with toys were being sent out that night, and Nick had to walk by Dasher, Dancer, and Prancer before getting to Vixen. The names were spelled out in colored masking tape affixed to the sides of the U-Haul trucks. For once, Vixen was going to be the first reindeer out.

As promised, Nick's driver was waiting for him. The tinted glass obscured his view of the trucker, preventing Nick from seeing much more than a Padres cap. He opened the passenger door, took a big step up, and then almost fell over when the trucker said hello.

He recovered quickly, and tried to mask his surprise. "Got your Teamster's card?"

His attempt at nonchalance didn't fool Charlotte. "Don't need one to fly a reindeer."

She passed him a clipboard that had a map and a list of their stops. "You navigate."

"Can't we do it like Peter Pan? Look at the stars, and take the 'second to the right, and then straight on till morning.'"

"I'm afraid Santa's flight plan is a little more specific than Peter's."

Nick held the clipboard up and looked to see where they were going. There were two stops, a youth center and a church. Nick had patrolled those areas off and on for years. They were poor neighborhoods, the kind where the police made a lot more visits than Santa. Their last stop would be at a Resource Center in Claremont, a mostly middle-class area, but he knew there were always more invisible needy than anyone ever suspected.

Charlotte started up the truck, looked out her side mirror, and then swung it onto the road.

"So," Nick asked, "are you on assignment?"

Charlotte shook her head. "I'm a volunteer like everyone else."

"Does this rig have an air conditioner?" he asked, fanning himself with his beard.

"You've got to be kidding. I was thinking about turning on the heater."

Nick opened his window, and made a contented sound as the breeze rolled over him. He heard some clinking and tinkling, and asked, "What's that sound?"

"Jingle bells," said Charlotte. "Someone got the idea of hanging bells on the bumpers of all the trucks."

Even over the sounds of traffic the bells could be heard. Nick found them lulling. The two of them might not be sitting in a one-horse open sleigh, but their surroundings still felt cozy to him.

"Bells sound nice around Christmas, but not so good the rest of the year. I once had this neighbor who had wind chimes up everywhere. They drove me crazy, especially when I'd work graveyard shift and try to sleep during the day."

"Give me chimes over birds any day. My neighbor has three macaws. Whenever I go out to get a little sun it sounds like I'm in the heart of the jungle."

Nick shifted around in his seat and tried to get comfortable. He wished he wasn't in uniform, but Santa Claus was part of the gift delivery. Though he didn't want to admit it, he was also stiff from his run-in with the three toughs.

Charlotte noticed his discomfort. With one hand, she rummaged around in her purse, and then extended her right hand his way. "Here. There's some water in the cup container. After last night it looks like you could use some pain relief."

"Who told you?"

"Angie did. Since you don't have a cell phone or an answering machine, I count on her to keep me up to date on your activities."

"Consider the source," said Nick.

He took the pill from her hand, and wondered if she felt the same electric charge he did from the contact of their flesh. Nick hid what he was feeling by looking at the pill.

"Take it, tough guy," she said, "and consider yourself lucky. I don't think it was very smart to set yourself up as a victim without any backup."

"You're probably right."

"If that's the case, why are you looking so self-satisfied?"

Nick lifted his arm to swallow the pill, winced, and lost his smug look. Charlotte nodded as if to say, "I told you so."

"I imagine you had a busy enough day without agreeing to be my chauffeur," Nick said.

"It was a madhouse." But the admission came with a smile. "The story's taken on a life of its own."

"I know. I did about half a dozen radio and TV interviews today."

"You'll probably do even more tomorrow," said Charlotte. "Our spot is going national."

"You mean like network news?"

"That's exactly what I mean."

"Congratulations," he said, but his grimace said something else. "What's the problem?"

"The more media attention," Nick said, "the more reporters, and you know how I feel about them."

"All of them?" she asked. Her Padres cap was tilted so he couldn't read her expression.

Nick acted as if her question needed thought, and after going through some exaggerated facial musing finally said, "There might be one exception."

"Anyone I know?"

"Could be."

It had been a long time since Nick had flirted for real. He needed to remember the dance, two steps forward, and then one back. For too long he had just done the backward steps.

"I've got the same problem with cops you have with reporters," Charlotte said. "They make me feel uneasy."

"Why is that?"

"It probably stems from too many traffic tickets when I was younger. That's why I'm uncomfortable around them."

"All cops?" Nick asked.

"Every one," she said.

The silence filled the air for several seconds, and Nick was beginning to think Charlotte wasn't kidding when she added, "But I do like men in uniform, particularly a Santa Claus uniform."

"Is that so?"

"It is."

Nick felt pressure in his upper chest. He wanted to dare the moment, to take another step forward, but wasn't sure how. Then he noticed Charlotte's right hand was on the seat instead of the wheel. Nick reached over and put his hand on top of hers. She turned her hand over and their fingers intertwined. As if to announce the moment, the bells suddenly rang out in loud chorus.

# CHAPTER TWENTY-FIVE

*God Rest Ye Merry Gentlemen*
*December 14*

The Christmas countdown had brought out the Saturday crowds at the mall, and with it more and more Laura presents. It seemed as many people were arriving with packages as were leaving with them. Judging by how many presents were being dropped off at the North Pole corral, the Laura story was on the mind of many San Diegans.

For whatever reason, though, not as many people were visiting Santa's sleigh, and that left Nick and the elves with too much leisure time. In an attempt to keep occupied, they started playing a version of *What's My Line?*, guessing the occupations of people walking by. As the day wore on they grew more and more silly, and now the object of the game was as much to make everyone else laugh as to guess a vocation.

They picked their latest target, a man with slicked back hair, gold chains, and leather pants.

"Undertaker," said Nick. At first he had refused to join in the guessing, but now he was doing more than his share of participating. All the laughter had proved too infectious to resist.

"Used car salesman," said Angie.

"No," said Darcy, "a telemarketer."

There didn't seem to be any agreement, so their eyes shifted to another target.

"President of the Junior League," Darcy said, pointing out a well-dressed woman who was walking along with a very straight back and her nose lifted high.

"Interior designer for custom properties," said Nick.

"Wrong," said Angie. "She writes an etiquette column."

Darcy nodded. "It's called, 'No, Thank You.'"

Everyone started laughing. Their laughter abruptly stopped when six men approached their sleigh. No one had to guess what these men did for a living. For once, Danny Brown was leading the blocking for his offensive line. The men behind him were huge, all of them well over three hundred pounds. They looked mean and intimidating.

They were here to see Santa Claus.

"Hello, Santa."

"Hello, Danny," said Nick.

"Brought you a game ball," the quarterback said, and handed Nick the ball.

Nick looked at it, and then at the quarterback, not quite knowing what to say. "Thank you," he said. "I feel honored. I also feel like I don't deserve this."

"Savannah made sure I brought it to you," Danny said. "I think she was looking at it as insurance. My baby was thinking if you get the ball, then she'll get all the presents she wants and then some."

"Smart girl," said Nick.

"You can tell who calls the signals at our house."

A crowd had gathered to gawk at the huge men. Danny leaned close to Nick and spoke so only he could hear: "Hey, the guys kept saying that you came through for us last week, and since tonight's my night for treating my line to a steak dinner—my way of keeping on their good side—darned if these boys didn't decide that maybe we should come and see you before we go eat."

Nick wasn't sure if he liked the idea of being a good luck

charm. What would happen when the luck ran out? Getting on the bad side of men who weigh half a ton isn't the wisest thing to do. Individually, these behemoths would have drawn stares. As a group, they were now bringing mall traffic to a standstill.

"We're not expecting you to guarantee a win or anything," said Danny, "but we figured that coming and seeing you couldn't hurt, especially with Denver in town."

Nick knew that many athletes were superstitious. Some made a point of going through the same ritual before every game. The Sea Lions, he thought, must have decided that he was their rabbit's foot.

"Well," said Nick, "it *is* my job to ask what people want for Christmas."

The quarterback took that as a signal. He looked back to his henchmen, but they were avoiding eye contact. "Well," said Danny, "go on you guys."

The huge men showed a sudden bashful interest in their shoes.

Danny said, "Don't tell me I have to hold your hands like I did with my little girl?"

Still, nobody moved.

Danny shook his head. "What's Denver going to think when they hear you guys were too scared to see Santa?"

The quarterback's taunt worked. One man, the biggest of them all, broke from the group and walked toward the sleigh. He had a shaved head, a black goatee, and a gold earring. He looked like a four-hundred-pound pirate. For someone so huge, the man moved very gracefully. He bypassed the stairs, lifting one of his huge legs, and then the other, up and over the edge of the sleigh. Everything in the sleigh was vibrating, including Nick.

"Wait a second!" shouted Nick.

The big man paused. Nick stood up, and then motioned for the man to sit. "If you don't mind, I'll sit on you."

The man glowered at Nick for a moment, but then nodded and

took a seat. The sleigh shook so much Nick had to hold on to keep his balance. The gathering crowd laughed and cheered as Santa took a seat in the man's lap. In most pictures Nick knew he looked huge next to the children. This was a role reversal for him. The lineman dwarfed him, making him feel like a child himself. Despite that, Nick had the adult questions to ask.

"What's your name, young man?"

"Tank Mobley," he said. The athlete's voice was so deep it sounded like a growl.

"Tank's your nickname, isn't it?"

Nick thought the man nodded his head, but it was hard to determine where Tank's head stopped and his neck began. He didn't offer his real name, and Nick didn't ask.

"So what would you like for Christmas, Tank?"

"I want to beat Denver tomorrow."

This time Nick wasn't about to guarantee a victory. Tank and his teammates might not take kindly to a broken promise. "Well, Santa will have to see what he can do about that."

Darcy approached the giant with not a little trepidation. "Do you want your picture taken with Santa, Mr. Tank?"

From the cavern of his huge chest came the answer: "Yeah."

Darcy set up the shot, telling Tank to look at the camera. He stared as if he was sizing up the lens to eat it.

"Beat Denver," Nick said.

Tank's expression changed. A huge smile came over his face, and Darcy clicked the picture.

As other players followed Tank's example, an impromptu spirit rally broke out. Angie fished pom-poms out of her Christmas bag, and started shaking them.

Nick didn't have time to be surprised. He was too busy hearing the same Christmas request of every lineman—a victory over Denver. More and more spectators gathered to watch the players visiting with Santa. The onlookers crowded the floor and hung over the railings, and Angie began leading them in cheers. Cell phone cameras were clicking away, and flashes were going off.

At the crowd's urging, the Sea Lions and Nick posed for a group picture, and the flashes erupted. The visit to Santa put big smiles on the faces of all the football players. Everyone was laughing, even Tank Mobley.

Angie made sure the spectators had as good a time as the players. Shaking her pom-poms, she yelled, "People in the front, let me hear you grunt; people in the middle, shake it just a little; people in the back, show us where you're at."

There was grunting, shaking, cheering, and clapping. At some point Forster had arrived and now he sidled up to Nick and the two of them watched the Elf move back and forth. Forster said, "I'll bet that makes you want to dance, Nico."

"Not even a little."

As Darcy lined up one last picture of Santa and the players, Nick faced the team and said, "After you guys win tomorrow, it's Santa that needs a little favor."

Danny Brown spoke for them: "What can we do for you?"

Nick pointed over to the toy enclosure. "We got a toy drive going on for kids who really need a Santa Claus in their lives, and every night we're sending out trucks filled with toys and a Santa. I'm hoping one night next week all of you will volunteer for Santa duty and help deliver toys."

Tank didn't even need to consult with his teammates. "Bring us an early Christmas present tomorrow, Santa, and we'll do your deliveries *every night* next week."

---

Game ball in hand, Nick visited the hospital. Raymond was still in the ICU, but Easy had arranged it so that Nick could deliver his present. She had warned Nick that the boy was sedated, and that in all likelihood wouldn't be able to respond to him, but she had also said that Raymond's condition had improved.

As Nick entered the Pediatric Intensive Care Unit, all he could think about was how much he wanted to get out of there before his heart broke in the midst of so many critically ill children. There were enough monitoring devices inside to make it resemble the Pentagon War Room. As soon as he stepped through the curtained area to see Raymond, Nick felt claustrophobic. It was like being inside a shroud, and what he saw intensified that feeling. The emaciated child on the bed wasn't Raymond. He couldn't be. There was a resemblance to be sure, but this boy was a pale imitation of Raymond. Machines moved this boy's lungs. Equipment pushed and sucked.

The boy showed no signs of consciousness, except that every so often parts of him twitched. There were little jerks of his arms, legs, and eyes. The movements kept startling Nick. He looked at the boy, not quite knowing what to do. Finally he placed the football under Raymond's inert arm.

"It's a game ball, Raymond, signed by Danny Brown himself."

Raymond didn't respond to his words.

"When you wake up," Nick said, "I got all sorts of stories to tell you. We had these huge football players that came to the mall. That crazy Elf I told you about was doing all these funny cheers. And you can't believe how many people have left presents for that girl who wrote me the letter."

The boy's eyes didn't open, and Nick's voice trailed off.

"Yeah, lots of stories to tell you," Nick whispered.

He rocked on one foot, and then another. Nick wondered if Raymond was able to hear him, or whether he was just talking to himself.

"Next time I hope you're awake, kid," Nick said. "We can toss the football around, and drive the nurses crazy."

Nick lightly patted the football cradled in the boy's arm, and then he touched Raymond's cheek. "Whenever you decide to go long," Nick whispered, "I'll be there to toss the ball your way."

—————※—————

All Nick wanted to do was go home and sit in his easy chair, but he had the commitment of toy deliveries.

He walked into the locker room and saw Angie's three Santa recruits already getting dressed. Without even thinking about it, Nick quickly put on his costume. By now it was second nature to him. He looked over and saw that two of the men were applying makeup, heavily rouging their cheeks and nose. They looked more like clowns than Santa.

"I'd reconsider that makeup," he said. "If you leave it on, it's going to get on your beard and wig, and stand out like Rudolph's nose."

It was a small room, and everyone heard. The locker room grew quiet. The men stared at Nick expectantly, and he wondered when he had become the voice of experience on being a Santa Claus.

The third man stepped forward, pointed to his white facial hair, and said, "I'm having trouble with my mustache drooping. How'd you get yours to stay up?"

"White bobby pins," Nick said. "You do 'em from behind so they don't show. I've got some extras if you want them."

Another man held up an unruly white beard. The fibers were going every which way. "Any way to tame this beast?"

"There are a couple of ways to smooth out your beards and wigs," he said.

Nick took off his cap, and ran his hand along the fur. "I usually run the back of my cap down along my beard like this. Short of a cold iron, nothing seems to work better.

"Now, did any of you bring water bottles? Because you're going to need water tonight, trust me. And sodas won't do. They'll stain your beard and make it sticky. And I'd suggest that before you put on your pants you take a long restroom break. You're going to find that it's not easy getting in and out of your costume . . ."

# CHAPTER TWENTY-SIX

*I Saw Three Ships*
*December 15*

The phone rang just as Nick was about to leave for the mall. When he picked up, Charlotte didn't even wait for him to finish saying "hello." She shouted, "I think I found her!"

Nick held the phone away from his ear and she asked, "Nick? Are you there?"

"I am," he said, "but I might have broken an eardrum."

"I'm sorry," Charlotte said. "It's just that . . ."

"I know," he said. "That's great news."

"I'm meeting with the girl this afternoon at two, and I'm hoping you can come with me."

"I wish I could," Nick said, "but I'm working at the mall until five. Santa Bret is doing a matinee."

Charlotte's voice announced her disappointment. "I can try and reschedule," she said.

"No need," said Nick. "I'll be there in spirit."

"I've signed up to be your driver tonight," Charlotte said. "If things go right, how about we celebrate with champagne?"

"I don't think I've ever heard a better plan," said Nick.

The North Pole was busy all morning and through lunch, but

then foot traffic noticeably lessened. The frantic driving force of Christmas-is-ten-days-away seemed to be on afternoon break.

"Where is everybody?" Angie asked.

"It's almost game time," said Nick.

It was the Sea Lions', final home game of the season. If the oddsmakers were right, midnight would soon be chiming on their Cinderella season.

Nick felt a twinge of guilt for thinking like that, as if he had betrayed them. He was now emotionally involved with the team. They had come to him, or at least to St. Nick, and had asked for his blessing. It was ridiculous, of course, but that hadn't stopped him from participating in the charade.

Not that the players really believed in St. Nick, but the ritual had worked for their quarterback, so they were willing to give it a try. It was a show of unity, a way of keeping the faith—and their playoff hopes—alive. It had been too many years since the Sea Lions had made the playoffs, a drought felt even in laid-back San Diego.

"If the Sea Lions win," he told Angie, "there's something you should know."

"What?"

"We're going to need a tailor to custom make some Santa suits. Some really, really big Santa suits."

———❋———

Late in the fourth quarter a gloomy Nick said, "I guess you don't have to worry about finding that tailor."

Nick and the elves were listening to the game on a radio they had borrowed from an electronics store. Denver was up by fifteen points, and threatening to score another touchdown.

"Why do you say that?" asked Angie.

"Are you listening to the same game I am?"

"You know what they say," said Angie. "It's not over until the fat man dances."

"You mean it's not over until the fat lady sings."

Angie shrugged and smiled. "Whatever," she said. "Do you want me to bring out my pom-poms and cheer?"

Nick shook his head.

The radio announcer, Tom Hammell, was an unabashed homer who'd had little to cheer about. Now it sounded as if he was covering a funeral. "Denver on a first and goal from the Sea Lions five," he said. "Nader on the handoff goes straight ahead. He's to the four, the three. He's stopped. FUMBLE! FUMBLE! The Sea Lions have the ball! They still have a pulse!"

To dream the impossible dream, Nick thought.

The clock kept ticking while the Sea Lions eked out two first downs, every one of their yards hard gained. There was no hope. Still, Nick hoped.

"Denver is showing blitz," said Hammell. "Brown backpedals, he's being rushed, he throws. Lincoln's got it at midfield! He's at the forty, the thirty, the twenty, the ten! TOUCHDOWN!"

From around the mall pockets of screams erupted. Not everyone had turned off the game yet.

"The Sea Lions are going to have to go for a two-point conversion," Hammell said.

And they would need *another* touchdown after that to keep their playoff hopes alive, Nick thought. That took their odds from the improbable to the next to impossible.

"Sea Lions looking to narrow Denver's nine-point lead," said Hammell. "Denver twenty-one, the Sea Lions twelve. Three minutes and thirty-four seconds remaining in the game. Brown finishes conferring on the sidelines. Seventy thousand fans are on their feet!

Brown's coming back to the huddle with the play. Listen to the crowd! They're lining up for the snap. Danny's backpedaling. He's looking right. He's moving out of the pocket. Great protection, but no one's open! Brown's running the ball. He's trying to turn the corner! Blockers ahead of him! To the four, the two, he's airborne. He's IN!"

Nick tried to restrain his excitement, unlike those around him. He didn't want children to wonder why Santa was screaming at a radio. The North Pole was now crowded with listeners; no one was there to see Santa.

The mood of the crowd quickly changed when Denver received the ball and broke off a long run. The groans turned to cheers when the play was called back on a penalty. The Sea Lions defense held and Denver was forced to punt with less than two minutes on the clock.

"It's a high punt that's drifting back," said Hammell's voice over the radio. "Horn's not signaling for a fair catch. He's got it at the fifteen, the twenty. He breaks a tackle. He's at the thirty, and brought down at the thirty-three.

"The Sea Lions are sixty-seven yards away from pay dirt, and they have ninety-two seconds to push it in. Brown brings the team up to the line."

Nick couldn't stand it. He had to take a walk. He was half a dozen steps away from the sleigh when he heard the groans of disappointment. The sounds weren't totally despairing, though. A half minute later he heard the same sad, but not quite devastated, wails. Probably another incomplete pass, he thought.

He wished Danny Brown hadn't asked him for a victory the week before; it was even worse that Brown and his teammates had come back hoping for seconds. And Raymond should never have asked him for snow. And Laura shouldn't have written a letter to Santa. Anyone old enough to write should have known that Santa

Claus didn't exist. Everyone had their hand out for a miracle. Didn't they know miracles were in short supply?

Glad shouts interrupted Nick's thoughts. They weren't the ecstatic kind of screams that accompanied a touchdown, but they were at least first-down material.

Nick waited for more auditory clues. Nothing. Commercial break, he supposed. He started pacing, and thinking, again. He didn't dare to believe. Bah, humbug came much easier to him. It was ridiculous for people to expect miracles out of the holidays. The wonder of the season, Nick thought, was that people sometimes remembered to show care and concern beyond their own selves. And that was that. To expect anything more out of the holidays was foolish, not to mention the perfect way of setting yourself up for a fall.

People started calling out again. Something was happening in the game. Loud cheers turned into disappointed moans. It had to be a dropped pass, or a penalty must have brought the play back.

Nick decided it was easier listening to a game than interpreting it through others. As he walked toward the radio a wild celebration broke out. Everyone began shouting the same word: TOUCHDOWN!

Santa Claus jumped in the air, but he was by no means alone. For half a minute the North Pole was bedlam, even if the celebration was premature. The drama still wasn't concluded. The Sea Lions were still a point down.

Ted Hammell said, "Danny Brown is conferring on the sideline with head coach Ed Farley. Will the Sea Lions kick for one and take their chances in overtime, or will they throw the dice and go for the two-point conversion?"

"They'll kick, of course," said Nick. "They have to play the percentages."

"Sometimes life isn't about playing the percentages," said Angie. "They'll go for two."

"Angie," said Nick, "you might know the elf business but you don't know football."

Hammell shouted, "It looks like they're going for two! No kicker is coming out on the field. Brown brings everyone into the huddle!"

"It's just a ploy," said Nick. "They're trying to get Denver to jump offside."

Instead of answering, Angie just gave him her Mona Lisa smile.

Nick said, "Can I bite someone else's nails? I'm afraid I don't have any left to chew."

There was some nervous laughter that was quickly hushed. Everyone stared at the radio, concentrating on it as if they could control the words being reported to them.

"Two yards separate the Sea Lions and their playoff hopes," said the announcer. "Danny Brown brings his team up to the line of scrimmage. Johnson is in the backfield. The two tight ends are in close, the two receivers out wide.

"Brown gets the snap. He's in the pocket. Heavy rush coming. Pump fake, the throw—deflected!"

Pent-up breath was expelled. Tortured hands fell limp. There was a momentary radio silence that seemed to last forever as announcer and fans took in the trajectory of the deflected ball.

"It's caught at the four! Yes! Yes! Yes! Yes!"

Hammell screamed over the noise of the crowd. "On a broken play the Sea Lions come away with two points! Danny Brown's pass, meant for Matthews on a slant pattern, was deflected by Toby Cornell into the hands of big number ninety-two, Sherman *Tank* Mobley. And Tank was not to be denied. Three Broncos tried to stop his charge, but the Sherman Tank bulled through to the end zone. Oh my, the Tank just delivered a wonderful early Christmas present to all of San Diego! The Sea Lions wish you a Merry Christmas! Final score: Sea Lions twenty-two, Denver twenty-one!"

Angie caught Nick's eye and winked. "I'll have the tailor working on those uniforms first thing in the morning."

So many toys had continued to come in that Angie arranged for a fifth truck to go out that night. When Nick heard the name assigned to that fifth truck, he claimed it for his own. He and Charlotte would be going out on Cupid.

Charlotte was waiting for him inside the truck. When Nick opened the door she gave him a smile, but he could tell she was masking her true feelings.

"We'll ice up that champagne for another night," he said.

"I was so sure," she said. "Pride goeth before a fall, I guess."

"Don't beat yourself up."

"The girl had the right name," said Charlotte. "She lives nearby, enjoys the same favorite books, and only has a mother. Last year the mother was hospitalized, and the family was in financial straits. The teacher even told me what a good writer she is."

"I can see why you thought you found her," said Nick.

Charlotte nodded. It looked to Nick as if she didn't trust her own voice.

"Hey," Nick said, "You got to believe. After the Sea Lions win today I think I now believe in Santa Claus."

Charlotte said, "You know what Angie calls someone who doesn't believe in Santa Claus?"

"I give up," said Nick.

"A rebel without a Claus," said Charlotte.

Nick groaned and shook his head. "You have got to stop hanging around with Angie."

"If it weren't for Angie, I wouldn't know where you were half the time. And speaking of improving our lines of communication, I got something for you: Merry Christmas."

Charlotte handed him a wrapped present.

"You shouldn't have," said Nick.

"Don't get excited," she said. "It's what you call a practical present."

Nick shook the package, puzzling over what it could be. "It's not a tie," he finally said.

"That's the best guess you can come up with?"

Nick shook the package again. "Clock radio?"

"Not even warm."

"I don't know. A toaster?"

"I thought you were supposed to be a detective."

Nick shook the package a little more, and then shrugged.

"Go ahead then," she said. "Open it up."

As he started pulling off the wrapping Charlotte said, "These gifts are probably more for me than you. I mean they're not exactly exciting."

"Gifts?" he asked, "As in more than one?"

"They're sort of the same general theme."

Nick finished with the wrapping. In one hand was an answering machine, and in the other was a cell phone. "I'm overwhelmed," he said.

"Now you have no more excuses not to take my calls."

He leaned over and squeezed her shoulder. "Thanks for waking Rip Van Winkle up. Thanks for everything."

Their first stop was at a church in San Diego where they were greeted as conquering heroes. Nick and Charlotte joined hands with the elders while the pastor offered up a prayer of Thanksgiving. Half the gifts were quickly unloaded, and a chorus of blessings was called out to them as they were leaving.

As Cupid took to the road again Charlotte said, "It almost feels as if we *are* flying."

Around them, though, were neighborhoods where the gravity pulled hard on the human spirit. Even flying reindeer couldn't escape the tug. Nick reached over and locked Charlotte's door, and then his. He explained his actions by saying, "I've been a cop a lot longer than I've been Santa Claus."

Charlotte turned onto Imperial Avenue. Nick continued in his cop mode, his head moving from side to side. The view on both sides of the road was bleak, the rare beacon in the darkness usually turning out to be a well-lit liquor store. And yet every so often they came upon a string of Christmas lights. Hope's candle still flickered.

Nick continued to be vigilant. The change of uniform hadn't changed what he was. When they finished with their last delivery, Nick directed Charlotte on a roundabout route that took them over to Mission Bay. Out in the water they saw a flotilla of blinking lights. All the boats sailing the waters were dressed in Christmas colors.

"I thought the Parade of Lights was last weekend," Charlotte said.

"It was," said Nick, "but most of the sailors like to keep the lights on all during the holiday season."

He motioned to her to pull off the freeway so they could get closer to the ships. They found an overlook near the water and parked. Ship after ship passed; sailors had decked out their ships in traditional and not-so-traditional holiday displays. Many of the captains were sailing around the Bay wearing aloha shirts and Santa caps. There was a range of ships, from million-dollar yachts to floating bathtubs, with the only thing in common their Christmas lights.

Some of the boats were even wired for sound. Nick and Charlotte watched as a yacht passed by, and they heard the familiar lyrics of "I Saw Mommy Kissing Santa Claus."

Nick wondered if he should push the moment, but he was so out of practice in the romance game that he felt like a beginner again. He had thought Charlotte was way out of his league, and was sure she couldn't be interested in a beaten-down old cop. Nick was only four years older than she was, but Charlotte was what Nick's friends would have called "classy." She knew how to look, and act, and dress. Nick felt deficient on all those fronts. But somehow they still clicked.

He cleared his throat. "You know," he said, "I had to pull some strings to get this particular reindeer tonight."

"Did you?" asked Charlotte.

"I even added an accessory."

"And what might that be?"

"It's hanging overhead between us."

Charlotte looked up and spotted the mistletoe. Nick wasn't breathing. In his heart he knew this was the moment of truth. She could pretend the mistletoe was a joke and laugh, or she could offer him her lips. His whole world seemed to be holding in the balance; it was all there, Christmas past, Christmas present, and Christmas future.

And then Charlotte was leaning toward him. Her eyes were closed, but her lips were open. Nick met her halfway and they kissed.

# CHAPTER TWENTY-SEVEN

*We Wish You a Merry Christmas*
*December 16*

When Nick awakened in the morning something felt different. At first he didn't know what it was, but then it came to him: he was actually looking forward to the day. It had been a long time since he'd awakened feeling like that. It was almost like he had rid himself of weights pulling him down. Some purpose—and hope—had returned to his life.

Charlotte had something to do with his new outlook. She was planning to bring takeout over for dinner, which prompted Nick to start in on some overdue cleaning of his apartment. He opened windows that had been closed too long, and tried to make the living room look presentable. There wasn't time enough for a deep cleaning, but he could at least tidy things.

Nick looked for the right spot for his answering machine gift, and decided on the end table in the living room. He thought about what message he should leave, and on his first try said, "This is Nick, leave a message."

When he played it back, Nick didn't like what he heard. He sounded too abrupt, so he attempted a more casual tone.

"Hi, you've reached Nick's machine," he said, "please leave a message."

He played back the recording and again wasn't happy. People didn't need to be told they were talking to a machine. He needed to think of something that didn't sound so stupid. Maybe he could do something funny. Nick considered a few lines, and then came up with the idea of doing a riff on giving a suspect his Miranda rights. Aloud he said, "This is Nick, you have the right to remain silent, but I'd prefer it if you left a message."

Too cute, Nick decided. It would probably be better just to identify his telephone number, and ask for a message to be left at the beep. But did his new machine even beep? He was trying to investigate the beep when the phone rang. Nick was glad for the reprieve.

He heard a by-now familiar voice identify herself, and Nick held his breath for a moment, but he needn't have worried. Easy was calling with good news.

"I wouldn't be calling so early," she said, "except a friend of yours insisted that I ring you up. He wanted you to know he was out of intensive care."

"You tell that friend," said Nick, "that I'm coming to visit him tonight."

"I'll do that," said Easy.

Nick placed the phone down on its cradle and faced his answering machine with a smile he couldn't contain. He didn't need to think about a message anymore; it had arrived with the phone call. He pressed a button and spoke into the microphone: "This is Nick. Ho, ho, ho, Merry Christmas! Leave a message at the jingle!"

————⁂————

The team meeting was held in the overcrowded locker room. The room was big enough for about a dozen normal-sized people to dress, but it was in no way big enough to handle eight football players in their new uniforms.

The cramped quarters had been reason enough to keep media waiting outside. Nick was glad of that. The morning newspaper had picked up on the Laura story, and printed her letter to Santa on the front page of its local section. As if that wasn't enough of a spotlight, a radio station had also taken up residence at the mall and was broadcasting from Santa's Workshop for the entire week. They were touting their shows as the "Seven Days of Christmas," and were using promotions to bring in more toys. All of the added publicity had made for a busy day, and now the evening's spectacle had brought out all the local media.

The participating football players were being called the Santa Diego Sea Lions, and everyone in town seemed to be getting on the bandwagon—or the sleigh. Danny Brown and his offensive line were making good on their promise, and would be delivering toys all week. Nick was doing his best to transform the players into Santa Clauses. Like a general inspecting his troops, Nick navigated through the crowded locker room going from player to player to make sure each looked the part.

As big as his Santa suit was, Tank Mobley could barely squeeze into it. He was one Santa who didn't need padding. Nick paused to touch up the man's eyebrows with some of the white stick, and noticed that Tank was nervously wringing his hands. They hadn't been able to find white gloves big enough for Tank's hands, but Angie had altered some white stretch hosiery so that he could have gloves.

"How do I look?" asked Tank.

The big man's nervousness surprised Nick, but then he remembered his own fright the first day he'd put on the suit.

"You look great," said Nick.

He looked around the locker room, and saw that Tank wasn't the only one experiencing stage fright. Nick had the feeling that the players were approaching their Santa stints as if they were preparing for a big game. If that was the case, Nick knew they needed a coach to guide them. He stood up on one of the benches so that all the players could see him.

"You all look great," said Nick.

His announcement resulted in clapping and nodding.

"I expect that some of you are a little nervous right now," said Nick. "That's understandable. It's not every day you step into the shoes of a legend. But you'll all do fine if you just remember that Santa Claus is about caring. It doesn't matter if you forget your workshop is in the North Pole, or you blank on the names of your reindeer. The only thing you have to remember is to care about that child you're talking to."

There was more clapping and shouting. Over their encouragement, Nick shouted, "Tonight you are not the San Diego Sea Lions! You are the Santa Diego Sea Lions! Now go out there and win!"

The huge Santa Clauses stormed out of the locker room, and ran to their waiting reindeer trucks.

Nick opened the door to the dark hospital room. There was enough light coming from the window that he could make out the head turning toward him. Raymond was awake.

"Hey," Nick said.

"Hey."

The football had traveled with Raymond. It was on his bed, right next to him. Nick walked over and touched the ball, patting it like he would a loved one. For Nick, it was easier to show affection to an object.

Raymond said, "You left me the football, didn't you?"

Nick nodded. "There you were, wide open, so I tossed it to you. You ran it in for a touchdown."

Raymond smiled.

"You look like a future prospect to me. I've been telling the Sea Lions they should add you to their roster."

The two favorite words of all skeptical children are: "Yeah, right." Raymond said them.

"I've got something to prove it."

Nick pulled a jersey from a sack, and began to unfold it. The process was akin to unfolding a bedspread. The jersey was huge, tentlike. Raymond's mouth dropped when he saw it spread to its full expanse.

"Wow."

"Number ninety-two," said Nick. "Tank Mobley's number. I told him I was visiting a sick friend tonight and he wanted you to have this. Tank is the biggest man I've ever seen. Thing is, he looks even bigger in his Santa suit than he does in a football uniform."

"Santa suit?" said Raymond. "What's he doing in a Santa suit?"

"He's helping out with a toy drive to bring presents to children who might not otherwise get them."

"Like that girl who wrote you the letter?"

"Like Laura and others like her."

"Have you found her?"

"Not yet. We're still looking, though."

Nick placed the jersey in the boy's hands. "Take a close look," he said. "See all the signatures? He got his teammates to sign it for you."

"Can I wear it?" asked Raymond.

Nick looked skeptical. "Wear this? You might as well wear a bedspread."

"I like big shirts," said Raymond.

"This isn't a big shirt. This is a circus big top."

"Come on, Nick."

Nick knew when he was beaten. "I'll go check with Easy," he said.

Easy moved the IV stand to the side and helped Raymond put on the jersey. "You sure you want this shirt?" she said. "I think it would look great on me."

"It's Tank Mobley's jersey," said Raymond. "Nick says he's the biggest man he's ever seen."

The shirt went over the boy's shoulders, and it looked as if he were wearing a tent. The jersey swam on Raymond, hanging below his feet. He looked like a beaming blue and gold ornament. The boy turned to the adults to gauge their reactions.

With a catch in his voice Nick said, "Perfect fit."

Neither Nick nor Easy knew whether to laugh or cry, so they both coughed and looked away from one another.

When Nick got into his car and saw the time, he pushed hard on the accelerator. He hadn't forgotten about Charlotte coming over, at least not exactly. He had been preoccupied, though, with the Sea Lions and Raymond, and somehow time had gotten away from him.

He was almost an hour late by the time he reached his apartment. He anxiously scanned the courtyard in front of his complex, but didn't see Charlotte waiting at the gate. His stomach muscles tightened involuntarily. Her car wasn't in visitor parking either. She had left. Nick didn't blame her. He doubted whether he would have stayed around waiting in vain for an hour.

It was a dark December night. Nick didn't like the winter months because it was always dark too early. By five o'clock it seemed like midnight. It was almost eight o'clock now. Maybe he could still make this up to Charlotte. He would find a way for her to accept his apology, and then take her out to a fancy restaurant.

As he approached his doorstep a shadow moved and Nick instinctively raised his fists in a defensive posture.

"I come in peace." Charlotte stood up and stretched. "I wondered when you were going to show up."

Nick realized his fists were still raised. He dropped them. "I am so sorry I am late."

Charlotte smiled. "I probably shouldn't admit this, but that's what I was going to say to you. In fact I did say it to you, or at least to your message machine. I just got here ten minutes ago, but I called your cell a few times to tell you I was running late."

Nick offered up a second apology as he unlocked the front door. "I'm afraid I left the phone in the charger. It's going to take me a few days before I get used to carrying it."

As he opened the door, he remembered yet something else to apologize about. "I didn't have as much time to clean this morning as I would have liked."

Nick turned on the hallway light. "I probably shouldn't admit this, but when my ex and I split five years ago I moved in here thinking it was temporary, and I furnished the whole place with garage-sale decor. I always figured one day I would go hunting for a place where I really wanted to live, but that never happened."

Charlotte stepped inside and Nick went around turning on other lights. Each new, shining bulb spotlighted how barren his apartment was. There were no pictures, or photos, or memorabilia. Those were all in boxes in the guest room.

This isn't me, Nick wanted to say, but he wasn't sure if it was or not. At least the place was relatively clean.

Charlotte followed Nick into the kitchen. His microwave was an old boxy model that didn't have a working turntable. Charlotte tried to figure out how to work it, but then stepped back and motioned for Nick's help.

She handed Nick the take-out food, and he put it in and started up the microwave. It sounded like a badly tuned radio station. The load on the electrical system was in no way reassuring. Overhead, the kitchen lights dimmed.

"Dinner dress is usually optional lead lining," Nick said.

"In my apartment a modern microwave is a necessity. I'm afraid that's how I cook most of my meals."

"That sounds like gourmet eating to me," said Nick.

Charlotte pulled out a bagged salad. "You do have a large bowl, don't you?"

"I've got something close."

Nick opened a cabinet, and pulled out the bowl.

"What about plates, forks, napkins?"

"Now you're really getting demanding."

Charlotte glanced over to the kitchen table to see if it needed to be cleared. Nick noticed the way her expression froze, and he saw what she was staring at. Somehow he had overlooked the gun during the morning cleanup. It had become too much of an everyday fixture, he supposed.

He went over and picked it up, and then stood there awkwardly. What do you do with a gun in your hand?

"There's been a prowler around here."

Even to Nick, his explanation sounded lame. Normal people don't keep loaded guns next to their sugar. Nick didn't look at Charlotte. He didn't want her to have to pretend that she didn't understand what the gun was doing there.

"Let me get rid of this," he said. "It doesn't go with dinner. It's more of a brunch kind of gun."

She offered a little mercy laugh, more than he deserved, and Nick put the gun away in the living room closet.

"I got the gun decoration idea out of *Better Homes and Gardens*," Nick said. "Spice up your table for the holidays, you know."

Instead of playing along with him, Charlotte said, "I must have missed that issue."

Nick decided on honesty over bad humor. "After the shooting, I was in a bad place, sort of stuck in the woods."

"Are you out of the woods yet?"

"You haven't heard of Lewis and Clark and Pappas?"

She smiled, but waited for an answer. Nick leaned one way, and then the other, uncomfortable with the subject. "Yeah, I'm out of the woods," he said, not hiding his eyes, not hiding anything, from her. "The gun's put away for good."

"I'm glad," said Charlotte.

Her words warmed him. They exchanged silly smiles, and then his old microwave gave an alarm-clock clang.

"It's playing our song," said Nick.

# CHAPTER TWENTY-EIGHT

*We Three Kings*
*December 18*

The National Weather Service had predicted another Santa Ana condition would be descending upon Southern California, and they were right.

The timing of the heat wave wasn't good for Nick. The Santa Ana arrived on the same day the Plaza Center's air-conditioning broke down. By one o'clock, it was eighty-five degrees outside, while inside the mall it was even hotter, or at least it seemed that way to Nick. Most shoppers were dressed for the heat and not deterred by the mechanical failure, but Nick in his arctic garb was suffering. Liquids didn't seem to help; the more he drank, the more he perspired, and there was no relief on the immediate horizon. Engineering said they were waiting for a part to get the air-conditioning running, but they had been saying that for hours.

Angie tried to beat the heat for Nick as best she could. She had found a fan in her Christmas bag, and was waving it his way.

"Thanks," Nick said, "but no more. I'm beginning to feel like Cleopatra arriving on her barge."

"I have something else for you then," said Angie.

She returned to her bag, and after rummaging through it came up with a seashell. "Hold it up to your ear," she told Nick.

Nick didn't ask Angie what she was doing carrying around a seashell, but instead took the shell and did as she said. The sounds of the ocean came to him, and he smiled.

"Do you have another shell?" asked Darcy.

Amazingly, Angie did, and for a time Darcy and Nick tuned into the ocean until even that became more of a tease than a relief.

"It's the ear version of a mirage," said Nick, putting aside the seashell. "I can't take any more of an imaginary oasis."

"Then we'll have to do something about that," said Angie.

She tore out a piece of drawing paper, and wrote a note in calligraphy that said Santa and company wouldn't return until the late afternoon. Charlotte appeared just as Angie finished taping the note to the "Santa Is Feeding His Reindeer" sign.

"Break time?" asked Charlotte.

"No," said Angie, "it's recess time, and you're invited. We'll take my car."

"Should I change?" Nick asked.

Angie was already walking away. Without turning back, she shook her head.

"Where are we going?" asked Charlotte.

"Beats me," said Nick.

The two of them followed after Angie and Darcy. Nick waved to people as he walked. Several people said, "Hot enough for you, Santa?"

Nick offered some "ho ho's," but his attention was on Charlotte. "So what do I owe to having the pleasure of your company?"

"Do I need a reason to visit Santa Claus?"

"I should have known it was *him* you were coming to see," said Nick, faking umbrage.

Angie turned back, noticed their smiles and yelled, "Quit dawdling, you two."

The four of them walked out to the parking lot and followed Angie to her car. Nick looked at the MINI Cooper and shook his head. "All four of us can't fit in this candy cane," he said.

"It's bigger than it looks," said Angie.

"It would have to be," said Nick.

"If you want to beat the heat, get in."

"You haven't told us where we're going."

"That's right."

They drove west on Interstate 8. Nick's head was out the window, and doglike he was taking in the breeze. The wind pushed at his white beard and he didn't even worry about the tangles. Other drivers kept honking, and giving him the thumbs-up. They approved of seeing Santa Claus chilling on the road.

The interstate ended in Ocean Beach. Angie drove along residential streets until she found an empty space on Newport Avenue just steps away from the sand.

"What are we doing here?" asked Nick.

"Surf's up," said Angie.

"I don't surf," Nick said.

"Take a dip in the ocean then."

"I didn't bring a suit."

Angie looked at Charlotte and Darcy. "It looks like he's wearing a suit to me."

The women nodded.

"Fine," said Nick.

He stepped out of the car and started walking on the sand toward the water. His black boots crunched along the shoreline. His conspicuous figure drew the attention of sunbathers and surfers, and cheers followed him toward the water. Behind him he could hear the elves and Charlotte laughing. If he'd had any doubts about what he might do, they vanished. Without any hesitation Nick continued his walk into the water, and didn't stop until the water was up to his ribs. The water soaked through his layers of clothing and padding, and Nick heaved a sigh of relief. He fell back into the ocean and floated around like a red whale.

Darcy, Angie, and Charlotte were standing just beyond the surf line. The three women were laughing so hard they could barely stand.

"Shall we?" asked Angie, extending a hand to both women.

The three women joined hands and ran into the surf.

———— ❈ ————

Nick had picked the short straw. Any hopes that someone else might be working disappeared when he saw who was waiting behind the counter. The man's eyes widened when he recognized Nick.

Trying his best to be deferential and polite, Nick said, "I'd like one-hour service, please."

Nick did his best to ignore the giggles coming from just outside the dry cleaners. The three women were dressed in work pants and work shirts. They were now calling each other Luis, Hector, and Mack, the names on the shirts.

Still attempting decorum, Nick put the plastic bags on the counters. The Asian man peeked into one bag, and then the next. Seeing the sodden contents made the man frown that much more, and of course, that made the women lose it.

Nick was biting his lip to keep from laughing. "One hour?" he asked again.

The shopkeeper slapped a laundry slip down on the counter. "Fill out," he commanded.

Nick did as asked, and then slunk out of the cleaners. Naturally, the air-conditioning in the mall was now working. In fact the temperature at the mall seemed downright brisk, but that might have been because of their trip to the beach.

"Come along, Luis, Hector, and Mack," he said to the waiting women. "It's time we all changed."

"It's a good thing I keep a spare outfit in my car," said Charlotte. "I can just see trying to do the news wearing this."

As if to comment, Charlotte's cell phone began ringing. "I jinxed myself," she said. "Never talk about work when you're playing hooky."

She looked at the display and said, "I better take this call."

The three of them gave Charlotte some space to take her call, but Nick couldn't help overhearing some of her conversation as they walked. It sounded as if she was carefully answering the questions, and would have preferred saying nothing at all. Nick heard her reference "Santa" several times; it didn't sound promising.

The call ended just as Angie and Darcy went off to go change into their elf outfits. "I think we had better sit," said Charlotte.

"That bad?" asked Nick.

"That was Geoff Stadler of the *Union-Tribune*," Charlotte said. "The supposed purpose of his call was to get an update on the search for Laura, but during our talk he started asking questions about Plaza Center's Santa Claus. He tried to disguise his inquiries, but it became clear to me that he knows who you are."

"So the cop's out of the bag?"

"I'm sorry."

Nick shook his head. "It's not your fault. With all the media attention, I'm surprised no one picked up on my identity until now. Even though SDPD didn't advertise it, I've been dreading that someone would realize I was the one who took down our bad guys."

"I guess it was to be expected, but I was hoping we'd both luck out. I'm going to have to get back to the station and confess to my boss that you are not only the Plaza Center Santa, but also the cop involved in the Chrissie Taylor shooting."

"How much trouble are you going to be in?"

"He's not going to be happy, but I'm going to explain that in return for my silence you agreed to help me on the Laura story. That story is big enough to give me some leverage."

What she'd be telling her boss was true, even if it wasn't the whole truth. The day before, Nick and Charlotte had spent several hours together tracking down leads. Of course they had also spent several hours together not tracking down leads.

Charlotte was in trouble because of him. "You don't need to confess," he said. "Why don't you go to your boss and say you just figured out who I am. I'll even let you interview me about the shooting."

She smiled, and reached a hand out to his cheek. "Thanks, but no thanks. Do you think I'd want to admit that you pulled the wool over my eyes?"

"Beard," said Nick.

"Besides, now that we have a personal relationship it wouldn't be ethical for me to interview you."

Relieved, Nick said, "I guess not."

"But when the reporter contacts you," said Charlotte, "and I'm sure it will be today, I think you should agree to do an interview with him."

"Why would I want to do that?"

"Because it's time the public heard what really happened that night. Your silence hasn't helped you, Nick. It's time people learned you were a hero that night, not some cowboy spraying lead. Geoffrey's a good reporter. He'll corroborate that you weren't drinking, or gambling to excess. You can tell him how Chrissie Taylor's condition demanded immediate attention, and necessitated your leaving the crime scene."

The warmth Nick felt wasn't from the hot day, or his stifling Santa suit. It was from having someone else care about him.

"I'll think about it," he said.

She heard something in his answer that made her smile, and that made him smile.

# CHAPTER TWENTY-NINE

*O Little Town of Bethlehem*
*December 20*

Nick arrived later at the hospital than expected. Charlotte had been right. The reporter had turned up at the mall, and rather than put him off, Nick had talked to him after his Santa shift. Reliving the shooting hadn't been easy. The reporter had done his job, asking Nick specifics and forcing him to remember all that had happened. Nick took a deep breath and let a shudder pass. At least Chrissie was better now. The reporter had seen her earlier in the day and said she was on the road to recovery.

Maybe I'm even better now, thought Nick.

Charlotte had been right to encourage him to talk. He had bottled up so much inside that finally speaking out felt cathartic.

Nick quietly pushed open the door, not wanting to disturb Raymond if he was asleep. He needn't have worried. The boy's eyes were immediately on him. Raymond was still wearing Tank Mobley's shirt. Nick wondered if he had ever taken it off.

"Don't you ever sleep?" Nick asked.

"I don't want to sleep."

Nick took a seat in the chair next to the bed and reached for the Advent calendar on the nightstand. Only four doors now remained unopened. What had seemed so many was now so few. Nick could hardly believe Christmas was almost upon them.

"Whoa, what's this," said Nick. "You ate my piece of chocolate today?"

Raymond didn't pick up on his teasing tone. "I gave it to my dad," the boy said, "before he left for his flight."

"I was just kidding, kiddo. I'm glad you gave it to him."

"He and my whole family are flying in on Christmas day."

"Are they coming by reindeer or by airplane?"

Raymond smiled at Nick's lame joke. "Let's open number twenty-one," the boy said. "You can have that piece of chocolate."

*Number twenty-one.* Not *the twenty-first.* Young children had their own way of expressing numbers.

"Nope," Nick said. "It's not going to be midnight for a few hours, so you'll have to wait until then. Or better yet, why don't you get some sleep now and save it for the morning."

"I'm not sleepy."

Maybe Raymond was afraid to go to sleep, Nick thought.

"Will you take me out in the wheelchair?" the boy asked.

"It's too late," said Nick.

"I'm not sleepy," Raymond said again.

That's what Nick's kids had always said to him, even when their eyes were all but closed. But Raymond really did look awake.

"I'll go check with Easy," Nick said.

————— ✳ —————

Hands on hips, Easy looked down at Raymond with her sternest face. "What's this I hear about your wanting to go out on some crazy late night ride?"

Raymond wasn't buying her act. "Just for a little while."

The nurse shook her head and said, "I don't know."

Nick and the boy knew it was an act. She had already set up the wheelchair with blankets and a pillow, and now she was lifting Raymond into it.

"You better stay covered up," she said.

"I will," said Raymond.

Easy gave Nick a tough look. "And you, sir, better watch your driving."

"Yes, ma'am," said Nick.

"I expect you both to be back within fifteen minutes."

They nodded, all of them putting on an act for each other.

As soon as he was out of Easy's sight, Raymond shed most of the blankets.

"What are you doing?" Nick asked.

"I'm hot."

Maybe he was. Or maybe the boy was showing off his jersey.

"Can't you go any faster?" Raymond asked.

Wheelchair in front of him, Nick started trotting down the hall. Raymond began to laugh, a sound Nick had never thought he would hear out of the boy. He started to run all the harder, making him laugh even louder.

At the end of the hallway Nick slowed down, though over Raymond's protestations. Their touring became more sedate. The hospital was quiet, but now and again Nick and Raymond encountered staff and patients. Everyone offered them a smile.

They had no route, walking the floors and stepping in and out of elevators on a seemingly haphazard basis. They stopped at odd spots, observing flower displays, and paintings, and busts of people unknown to them.

More by accident than design, Nick chauffeured Raymond to the Maternity ward. Not since his own children were born had Nick been in Maternity. There was a nurse on duty who allowed them entry, and Nick and Raymond just stood there for minutes looking into the enclosed area. They stared at the tiny babies in incubators, laughing at their expressions and movements. For the most part their eyes were closed, but now and again one would blink suspiciously at the strange new world around them. Man and boy were entranced by the display of life.

Nick finally wheeled Raymond away. There were more sights to be seen. To Nick, it almost felt as if they were sleepwalking together, or experiencing the same dream state. They took some time to appreciate the large noble fir in the lobby. Hanging from its thick branches were clusters of silver bells, and when a delivery door was opened the silver bells played for them.

*Every time a bell rings an angel gets his wings,* Nick thought. He liked to think he was a confirmed cynic, but every year he still ended up watching *It's A Wonderful Life.*

When Raymond's head started dropping, Nick steered his charge back to the Pediatric Oncology ward. They made a final stop in the waiting area to watch the trains going round and round. Santa was still conducting the train, and all the cars were filled with toys.

As a boy not much older than Raymond, Nick and his friends used to go to the train tracks and lay down pennies. And now and again, Nick had reached deep into his pocket and pulled out a nickel. The trains flattened pennies, but not nickels. The nickels usually got picked up by the wheels, and rode the rails. It was Nick's youthful offering, his young way of traveling out into the world. He wished he could put down a nickel on the track for Raymond.

The boy was asleep now, taken into his dreams by the trains. Nick was reminded of Roger Miller's Christmas song "Old Toy Trains," but Easy appeared while he was still trying to remember the words.

"I'll take him from here," she whispered.

Number ninety-two was wheeled away. Nick wished he could get the standing ovation he deserved.

# CHAPTER THIRTY

*I Heard the Bells on Christmas Day*
*December 21*

It had been twelve days since Nick's last visit to the library, but he'd called Dawn Lambert several times in the interim. As promised, Dawn had sent out copies of Laura's letter to all the libraries in the area, and had asked the other librarians to be on the lookout for potential matches. She also included copies of Nick's contact information in case anyone knew anything about Laura.

Dawn had told Nick that she was working on another plan to find Laura, but had been tight-lipped about the particulars. The day before, though, she had invited him to visit the library for what she termed "the unveiling."

Nick arrived before the library officially opened, and Dawn unlocked the doors to let him in. She led him over to a covered easel in the central lobby. Apparently she was going to keep her plan under wraps until the last possible moment. It was clear the librarian enjoyed challenges, and, in this case, the accompanying intrigue that went along with it.

"As you might imagine, I read Laura's note a number of times," Dawn said, "and I ended up devising a strategy based on her favorite reading. Because she specifically identified the Magic Trunk Tales and the Four Seasons Quartet as treasured reads, I decided to take all those books out of circulation. As it turns out, there are eight different Magic Trunk Tales, and four books in the Four Seasons fantasies."

Nick did the math. "So you took twelve books out of circulation," he said.

Dawn shook her head. "I actually took every book in the City and County of San Diego out of circulation, which is well over two hundred books. For the last ten days no one has been able to check out any of those books, and anyone wanting a copy could only get one by putting their name on the waiting list. I had hoped that would bring Laura or her mother face to face with a librarian, and allow a better opportunity for your note to be passed on."

"Good thinking," said Nick.

"I thought so too," said Dawn with a smile, "but then after a few days I began to doubt my strategy. If Laura is as good of a reader as I suspect, and if she likes these books as much as she says, then it's likely she's read them all several times."

Nick chewed on his lip and nodded. Yet another good idea had been shot down.

"But," added Dawn, "as it turns out, we might be lucky after all. There is a new book in the Magic Trunk series that's due out next month."

Dawn reached over and ran her hand along the white cloth covering the easel. "I am hoping that this is the cheese that will bring in our elusive mouse."

She pulled off the covering, and Nick found himself looking at a display that featured the front cover of a book titled *Stowaway Bag*.

"Beginning today," Dawn said, "these posters will be on display in every library within a twelve-mile radius."

Nick read the block writing beneath the blown-up poster: "Reserve Your Copy Today!"

"Let me guess," Nick said, "in order to reserve this book you'll have to put your name on a waiting list."

Dawn smiled and nodded. "And whoever signs up will get a copy of the note Laura left Santa, as well as your personal information."

Nick was nodding happily. "I think you should have been a cop instead of a librarian."

"Oh, I don't know about that," Dawn said, "but I must admit that playing detective has given me quite a thrill. I think one of the great pleasures in life is curling up to a good mystery."

"Especially one with a happy ending," said Nick.

# CHAPTER THIRTY-ONE

*The Mistletoe Bough*
*December 22*

Nick had promised to spend the afternoon with Raymond watching the football game. The boy was suddenly a huge Sea Lions fan. He arrived at the hospital just before kickoff.

"You should have seen it, Nick," said Raymond. "They just did a story on the Santa Diego Sea Lions on television, and they showed you on TV promising Danny Brown a victory."

"I'm glad I missed that," said Nick.

"And then they showed the Sea Lions helping out with the toy drive and everything."

For the previous four nights Nick had been relieved of toy run duty by the Santa Diego Sea Lions. Involving the football players had kept the toy drive in the news, and had kept the presents coming. There had been such an outpouring of presents that Nick was scheduled to continue deliveries through Christmas Eve.

"That's why I have to leave right after the game," said Nick. "With the Sea Lions out of town someone's got to deliver those presents."

"The Oakland fans are dressed up like goblins and worse," said Raymond, "but we don't have to worry: the Sea Lions are going to win."

"The Sea Lions PR department actually called me up and wanted to fly me to Oakland to see the game," said Nick. "They wanted me to stand on the sidelines in my Santa suit rooting for the Sea Lions."

"Why didn't you go?"

"I told them I was going to be watching the game with my buddy."

The answer pleased Raymond. "The Sea Lions are going to the Super Bowl."

"I hope you're right."

"If they offer you a ticket to the Super Bowl," said a very serious Raymond, "you should take it."

"All right," laughed Nick. "I will."

The camera swept the stands. Most of the Oakland faithful were dressed in black and silver, but the camera focused on a small island of red and white. Around two hundred and fifty Sea Lions fans had traveled north; all were wearing Santa caps.

The announcer said, "The Sea Lions believe in Santa Claus, but Oakland says all they're going to get is coal in their stockings."

Raymond touched his jersey. "Tank Mobley is going to flatten them," he said with absolute confidence.

Nick opened the truck's door.

His driver was already at the wheel. Nick flashed Charlotte a smile. "Sorry I'm late," he said. "Raymond insisted I give him a piggyback ride around the hospital after the Sea Lions won. I think he wanted to show off his Tank Mobley jersey."

"I just got here myself," said Charlotte.

She returned his smile, but it looked forced. "Is something wrong?" he asked.

"I'm just a little disappointed," she said. "I'm beginning to think Laura is more quicksilver than little girl. Just when I think I have a grip on her, she slips through my fingers."

"What happened?"

Charlotte shook her head. "It's not worth talking about," she said. "Just another lead that didn't pan out."

"You're not the only one. I thought my hotel idea would lead us to her when I heard about a housekeeper with a daughter named Laura, but it was just another mirage."

"We're out of clues and time."

"The libraries were closed today," said Nick, "but maybe Laura will see one of those displays tomorrow, or the day after tomorrow."

The day after tomorrow was Christmas Eve. The hourglass was beginning to empty.

"Are the libraries open on Christmas Eve?"

Nick nodded. "They just close a little early."

"So we're waiting for a call from a librarian, or from Laura."

"It's either that or we stake out some libraries and ask every little girl who walks inside if her name is Laura."

"I'm almost at the point where that sounds reasonable. I hate to say it, but I've pretty much exhausted my leads."

"If we don't find her by Christmas, we'll just have to continue our search after December twenty-fifth."

"That's right."

Neither was very good with a concession speech. Nick figured reporters were obsessive like cops. To break a story or a case, you had to dig for answers. There had been times when it felt like he'd dug all the way to China, but it still wasn't enough. That was the way it seemed with Laura.

Nick opened his window and looked up. Blinking stars filled the sky. He exhaled, and it was cold enough that he could see the trail of his breath. Santa Ana conditions often brought on hot days and cool nights.

"See a star signaling the way to Laura?" asked Charlotte.

"If I see one, you'll be the first to know."

He looked up to the skies again. No Star of Bethlehem, he thought. Maybe Laura didn't exist. Maybe God didn't exist. Nick exhaled, and his steamy breath momentarily obscured the stars.

"Raymond's always looking out the window," Nick said. "Even during the game today I caught him looking out. I don't know what he's looking for, but I hope he finds it."

Nick closed his window and turned his gaze to Charlotte. He had thought he was too old, too cynical, too world-weary, too suspicious, and too ingrained in his habits to fall in love, but now it felt like he had been given another chance in life.

"Given up on your stargazing?" asked Charlotte.

"Found something that doesn't make me want to look anywhere else," he said.

# CHAPTER THIRTY-TWO

*O Christmas Tree*
*December 23*

"I'm getting kind of tired of reading about you in the newspaper, and seeing you on the news," said Forster.

"You and me both," said Nick.

"You're becoming a legend."

"You've got me mixed up with the character I play."

"I don't know. If today's newspaper is accurate, maybe you're the new Saint Nick."

"Never believe what you read."

Nick had expected the worst, but was pleasantly surprised by the story that had run in the *U-T*. For once, all the facts were correct. There were interviews with fellow officers and friends, and they told a different story than what had been publicly aired. Nick felt a sense of vindication, whatever the police review board's decision about whether to reinstate him.

"If I hadn't known who that reporter was writing about," said Forster, "I would have sworn that story was on a nice guy who got a raw deal."

"I suppose the article misquoted you," said Nick.

"I'll be demanding a retraction," said Forster.

Forster had been quoted as saying that Nick was both a good cop, and a good human being. And he had told the story of how Nick had saved his life.

"Something you need to know, Walt," Nick said.

"Yeah?"

"You know that story you told about how I saved your life?"

Forster nodded.

Nick managed to say the words without his voice cracking: "Thanks for returning the favor."

Forster nodded, and then turned around and started toward the locker room door. He didn't turn around again, but did pause at the door. With a husky voice he said, "I better not keep you from making some poor kid cry."

Nick approximated a grunt. It was a relief to get back to busting each other's chops.

The newspaper article had played up Nick's changing from a police uniform to a Santa suit. They had even managed to accompany the article with pictures of him in both outfits. Nick didn't like admitting it, but he actually looked better in the Santa suit.

"Time for those crying kids," he whispered.

As he made his way over to Santa's Workshop, Nick noticed a different pace to the mall. Panicked shoppers were scurrying about, and everyone appeared rushed. The reality that there was only one more shopping day until Christmas had struck home. He listened to computers and registers ringing fast and furious. To Nick's ears, they sounded like a crazed version of Handel's *Messiah*.

When Nick sat in his sleigh, he found that even the children were being rushed through their Santa visits. A small boy was brought up to see Nick, his mother pulling him hurriedly along. As she relinquished her hand, and gave up her son to Nick, she recited his history in the rushed tones of a paramedic handing off a critical patient to an emergency room doctor.

"Carl is four years old, Santa. He's been a good boy. We've assured him that you already know what he wants. All we need is a picture with you for his grandmother."

"Hi, Carl," said Nick.

The boy looked very uncertain about getting into Nick's lap. Even before he was settled his mother was saying, "Smile for the camera, Carl. Smile."

Nick tried to ignore the mother. "What do you want for Christmas, Carl?"

Mom interrupted. "We know what he wants. We don't have time . . ."

Angie tried to diplomatically intervene, and began talking with the woman. Nick didn't envy her that job.

"Was there some special toy you wanted?" Nick asked.

"Army men," the boy said.

Carl seemed more relaxed with his mother not yelling, or trying to hurry him along.

"Army men," Nick said. "Was there anything else?"

"Flutterby house."

It took Nick a moment to make sense of what the boy was saying; having heard other children voice similar requests helped him interpret.

"A Butterfly House?"

Carl gave an enthusiastic nod.

The Butterfly House was a nature kit that provided butterfly pupae, and allowed children the opportunity to see the final stage of a butterfly's metamorphosis.

Slightly removed from them, but not far enough away, Nick heard Carl's mother voicing her displeasure. "What are they talking about butterflies for?"

If only, thought Nick, some humans could go through their own metamorphosis.

"You like butterflies?" asked Nick.

The boy nodded. "They're pretty. And they fly."

"Yes, they are pretty. Did you know that before they become butterflies, they're caterpillars?"

The boy looked interested. His mother didn't. "We're late," she said, stepping around Angie. "We don't have time to talk about worms."

Nick tried to ignore her. "You know what Christmas present you could give me, Carl?"

"What?"

"Why don't you give a big smile to that camera right there?"

Nick pointed to the camera, and the boy gave him his Christmas present.

As Carl's mother retrieved him, she said to the boy, "What's this about army men and butterflies? You never said anything about wanting those things."

Nick wondered if that was the case, or if she hadn't taken the time to listen. He signaled to Angie that he needed to make a call and would be back in a minute.

"Laura update?" asked Angie.

Nick nodded. Angie was as invested in his search as he was.

He walked over to the nearest department store and went into the men's changing room. Now that he had a cell phone he didn't need to do his dialing from the back office.

When Dawn Lambert answered the phone Nick said, "At this point, you'd probably rather be hearing from a crank caller."

"I thought I was."

There was something in Dawn's voice that started Nick's adrenaline pumping. He could hear her suppressed excitement.

"There are already a dozen people on the waiting list for *Stowaway Bag*, Nick, but it doesn't look like any of them have any connection to Laura. But a volunteer named Doris helps out in our children's section a few afternoons every week, and she said there's a girl who comes in regularly that likes the same kind of books that Laura does. The girl's very precocious, Doris said, and very shy. She's always brought in by a young woman in her twenties that Doris doesn't think is her mother. According to Doris, the girl never leaves without a pile of books."

Laura's note to Santa had likely been left by a woman that met that description, Nick remembered. His gut told him they were getting close.

"Does the girl check out her own books?" asked Nick.

"No. The woman accompanying her checks them out for her."

"What day do they come in?"

"Doris wasn't sure, but she thinks it's usually on a Thursday. They come in toward closing time. Doris said it looks like the woman comes from work."

Thursday, he thought. This coming Thursday would be the day *after* Christmas. Nick groaned out loud.

"What?" Dawn asked. "I thought you'd be pleased with the news."

"I am. I'm just not pleased with the timing. If this girl is Laura, we won't be able to get her the presents until after Christmas."

"It can't always be a Cinderella story," the librarian said. "Sometimes things happen in their own time."

"You're right," Nick said.

Dawn's was the sensible outlook, but he still wished he'd been a better detective—or a better Santa Claus—and found Laura before Christmas.

No, it wasn't a Cinderella story, he thought. And besides, happily ever after wasn't the modern ending.

Nick went back and took his place in the sleigh. From his perch, his attention fixed on the mall's Christmas tree. Even now, weeks after being cut down, the large tree retained much of its beauty. Of course it was masked with garlands, icicles, and ornaments.

"Penny for your thoughts," said Angie.

Shaking his head, Nick said, "They're not worth a penny. I was just remembering my family's Christmas tree tradition."

"Is this one of those drive-out-to-the-country, drink-mulled-cider, take-a-sleigh-ride, and harvest-a-special-tree-at-a-picturesque-farmhouse kind of story?"

"Hardly," said Nick with a laugh. "It's about the opposite."

"Do tell, then."

Nick looked around, and made sure no young ears were nearby. "I was the youngest of three brothers. The tradition started the year my parents gave my oldest brother Tom some money to go out and get our Christmas tree. Well, Tom spent that money on something other than a tree, so he came up with an alternative plan. He went shopping for the kind of tree that wasn't for sale, and then enlisted my brother Paul and me to help him get it.

"The tree Tom picked out was growing in a nearby park. We dressed up for that first midnight mission in dark clothing like we were some kind of ninjas. While my brother went and chopped down the fir tree, I kept watch. My instructions were to make the sound of a hoot owl if anybody was approaching. It was probably a good thing no one came along. My hoot owl sounded more like the call of a sick cat.

"Tom was smart. By involving me, and swearing me to secrecy, and bribing me with some trinkets, I never told on him. In fact, every year I became more and more involved in the tree rustling. The tradition continued for the next five years. My brothers and I began to think of that Christmas tree money as our annual bonus. Of course, being the youngest, my brothers always treated me like their personal foot soldier. I was thirteen when they decided I was old enough to handle the Christmas tree duty by myself.

"They didn't care that I wasn't old enough to drive, and had no means other than my own hands to transport the tree. They had already taken their cut of the money, which was all that concerned them, and they left the entire operation up to me.

"I made what I thought was a logical choice. Our neighbor's property had a bunch of fir and pine trees, and there was one among them I thought would do nicely in our living room. So on a dark December night I went over and chopped down their tree, and then dragged it over to our house.

"I was sleeping in the next morning when the police came calling. My brothers, as you might expect, instantly disappeared. Faced with the evidence, and I had left a lot including a trail of pine needles from my neighbor's house to our front doorstep, I did a reluctant George Washington and confessed I had chopped down the tree. That was the end of the Pappas brothers' Christmas tree tradition."

"What happened to you?"

"I got a trip to the woodshed and a paddling I'll never forget. I also had to spend my own money to get a replacement tree for the neighbors. And, as might be expected, my mother refused to display the tree I'd chopped down, so my brothers and I had to buy another Christmas tree.

"Maybe one good thing came out of that Christmas, though. The police who came over to our house were decent sorts. In the midst of all my troubles I remember how one of the officers winked at me. No one else saw it. The cop was telling me that as bad as things were, everything would be all right. I think that wink somehow put me on the road to being a cop."

Nick shook his head. "Now, with the way things have turned out, I'm wondering if that cop might have just had something in his eye. Or it's possible I just imagined his wink. That would be real poetic justice, wouldn't it? My calling in life might have been based on one big mistake."

"No mistake," said Angie. "You chose the right job, and you helped a lot of people."

Nick had somehow gone from being a villain to a saint, and didn't feel comfortable being either. They didn't have a chance to continue with their conversation. Darcy was bringing a girl with pigtails, and shoes more ruby red than Dorothy's, up to see him. Nick held out his hands and welcomed her.

"This is Alison, Santa," said Darcy.

Alison was coached along by her mother. She checked with Mom for all her answers, from how old she was, to what she wanted for Christmas. When Nick finished with Alison, he wanted to tell her to go follow the Yellow Brick Road, but instead he directed her to Darcy.

Angie was already waiting with the next lap-sitter. "This is Corinne, Santa."

Nick started when he heard the name, but that was nothing compared to his reaction when he saw his own daughter standing there.

"Hi, Saint Nick," she said, the waver all too apparent in her voice.

Nick hadn't seen his daughter in the better part of a year. He tried to croak, "Merry Christmas," but the words were unintelligible.

"Corinne," he said, and opened his arms.

# CHAPTER THIRTY-THREE

*It Came Upon a Midnight Clear*
*December 24*

Dark storm clouds had hovered over San Diego all day, but the rain hadn't started falling yet. It looked to be only a matter of time, though. It was only five o'clock, but you wouldn't have known it by the darkness. The clouds and the short day had seemed to bring Christmas Eve early.

Forster and Nick were helping with the final loading of the presents into Rudolph. Toy giving had slowed down in the last two days. People were busy just before Christmas, and there had been no more stories about the Santa Diego Sea Lions. Laura and her letter to Santa seemed to be fading from most people's memories. But not his, Nick thought, not his.

"All loaded," yelled Forster. He patted the side of the truck.

The driver waved. Nick and Forster stood together and watched Rudolph drive off into the night.

"The last of ten thousand gifts," said Forster.

"That many?"

"At least that many, according to Angie; imagine, all that giving spurred on by one little letter."

"One special letter," said Nick

"I'm feeling pretty good about this Christmas, Nico. How about you?"

Nick nodded. "I might not have found Laura, but I found my own daughter again."

Corinne's visit was the best Christmas gift he could have asked for. She'd read about her father in the newspaper. They hadn't said much to one another—each was too choked up to say much—but Corinne had invited him over for a family brunch on Christmas Day.

"You better hold her tight and not let go this time."

"You can count on that."

"So, you want to explain all those roses I saw you carrying out to your car . . ."

"One dozen."

"And what about that package from the jewelry store?"

"It's a Christmas present, not an engagement ring."

"That might be true, but that doesn't discount the glow in your eyes. You're talking with your children again, you got a good woman who actually seems fond of you, you've gone from a sinner to a saint in the media, and we just saw Rudolph fly off into the night. It doesn't get much better than that, does it, Nico?"

"What's your point?"

"I'm surprised I even need to tell you. Can't you hear the drum roll? This is the perfect time for your victory dance."

"I don't dance."

"It's Christmas Eve, Nico. Somehow an old grump like you turned into a real Saint Nick and helped to bring thousands of kids Christmas presents. You know you want to dance, so you might as well give it up. You can consider it your Christmas present to me."

"Not this Christmas, not ever."

Forster feigned disappointment. "You know you're just denying yourself."

Nick looked at his watch. "I got to go. You have a Merry Christmas, Walt. Give my best to Maggie."

"She was counting on you coming over for some eggnog."

"I got other plans," Nick said. He experienced a moment of déjà vu, remembering his friend's Thanksgiving invitation. "This time I really do."

The two men shook hands.

———✳———

Like some grand windup toy, Plaza Center was shutting down. Santa's Workshop had closed at two o'clock. It wouldn't do for Santa to be late for the busy night ahead of him.

The smaller stores had closed at five o'clock. Only the department stores were still open, but even they were closing up shop. It was last call for Christmas shopping.

Angie had stayed late, boxing up what she could of Santa's Workshop, and seeing to the last details of the toy drive. She was dropping off a box in the mall's administrative offices when the phone rang. Everyone else had already gone home. It was Christmas Eve, and her family was waiting for her, but Angie still reached for the receiver.

———✳———

*'Twas the night before Christmas.* The rhyme kept going through Nick's head. Even in this cursed hospital, he thought, it was the night before Christmas. Activity looked to be at a bare minimum. Nick figured no one stayed or worked at a hospital on Christmas Eve unless it was absolutely necessary.

When Nick walked into Raymond's room he saw in a glance that he was doing poorly. The boy's eyes were glassy, and he had the kind of pale usually reserved for ghosts. His breathing was labored, each breath sounding as if it was providing a last moment of suspense. His football jersey had apparently been retired for a hospital gown. The jersey was neatly folded on the nightstand, packed up as if he were going on a journey.

"How's it going?" said Nick. He knew it wasn't going well, but he didn't know what else to say. Nick went and took a seat next to Raymond's bed. The boy shifted, causing him to groan, and his sounds of pain made Nick reach out to try and help him, but he realized he could do nothing. For a moment his hand just hovered there, until he dropped it at his side.

"I'm sick of being sick," Raymond said.

Nick wasn't sure if the boy was talking to himself, or confessing something. But Raymond wasn't too sick to notice the bag Nick was holding.

"What did you bring me?" he asked.

"How do you know I brought you anything?"

"Because there's something in the bag."

"It could be my dirty socks."

"You know it's not."

Nick shrugged, as if to indicate it might very well be.

"Is it?" asked Raymond.

"No. But that reminds me. I do need to do a load of laundry."

"What's in the bag?"

"A present."

"For me?"

"Could be."

"Can I open it?"

"You got to wait until tomorrow," Nick said.

"No. Now please."

Nick looked unsure. Raymond offered an echo: "Please."

The box had been gift-wrapped. Nick placed it in Raymond's hands and the boy started pulling at the paper. In his weakened condition, even tape was a formidable foe.

"Sometimes that paper's kind of tricky," Nick said, leaning over to help him.

Together, they stripped off the paper, and then opened up the box. Nick pulled out a plastic canister. Raymond squinted to try and make out what was inside of it.

"What is it?" he asked.

"How about I turn on a light?" asked Nick.

Raymond nodded, and Nick reached over and flicked on an overhead light.

"I know you're not allowed pets here, but Easy said these would be okay. Can you see what's in here?"

The objects were small and dark and thin, not quite an inch long. They were mostly still, and surrounded by silky cocoons. Raymond put his face close to the plastic.

"Are they fuzzy-wuzzies?"

"That's right," said Nick. "Caterpillars. Five of them. They're in what's called their larval stage. Each of these caterpillars is going to grow into a kind of butterfly called a Painted Lady. See, I got you a booklet here that tells you about them. It's got lots of neat pictures and diagrams."

Nick handed Raymond the container, so that he could display the book. "This goes through the whole life cycle of these critters. See, that container's going to be their home for the next couple of weeks. The green stuff on the bottom is the nutrients they eat. In about a week, these caterpillars are going to climb to the top of that canister, attach themselves, and hang there. You got to leave them alone when that happens, 'cuz they have to shed their coats. That's when they'll start getting pretty. It's sort of like that ugly duckling story, you know. They're brown and nondescript now, but when they change into a chrysalis they'll start showing their colors. You see, they got a picture of how they'll look right here."

The boy looked from the small, brown caterpillars to the picture. "They look so different."

"That's only the start. You're going to put the chrysalides—that's what they're called at that stage—into their butterfly house. And in about a week or ten days later they're going to come out as pretty butterflies."

Nick put his finger on a picture of a Painted Lady. The butterfly had vibrant brown, black, and orange markings that looked as if they had been painted on.

"Will I let them go then?"

Nick shook his head. "Not this time of the year. It needs to be a little warmer."

"But how are they going to eat?"

"We're going to make them a nectar drink. Butterflies are kind of like little boys. They like sugar. So what we'll do is mix some sugar and water, and sprinkle them on some flowers, and put those in their house."

Raymond kept watching the caterpillars. "This is really cool."

Nick had been in luck. The mall's nature store had just happened to have some of the caterpillars on display. Normally you had to send away for them, but Nick had been able to talk the manager into selling him the display model.

"Do the butterflies live very long?"

Nick shook his head. "Not very. Two to four weeks."

"Oh."

Nick wondered if that was the kind of question only a very sick kid would ask.

Raymond continued to look at the caterpillars, gently turning the container round and round. The turning gradually slowed and then stopped.

"You want me to take that from you?" Nick asked.

A small nod, even though when Nick reached for it, the boy's fingers seemed reluctant to give up their prize.

"You'll look after them?" asked Raymond.

"We will."

Raymond's eyes closed for a long moment.

"You tired, big guy?" Nick asked.

"Just a little. But don't leave yet. Let's go look at the trains."

"I'll see if that's okay with Easy," Nick said. "If it is, I'll get the wheelchair."

"We don't need the wheelchair. You can carry me if you want. I'm not very heavy. Tonight I feel real light."

It didn't surprise Nick that Easy was working on Christmas Eve. She probably wouldn't have trusted her charges with anyone else.

"We bend rules on Christmas Eve," she said, laughing. "We bend them good."

Easy released Raymond from the tubes and drips that sustained him, and then Nick got his arms under the boy's legs and back and lifted. Raymond was right. He wasn't very heavy, but Nick pretended he was.

"My back," he groaned. "What have you been eating? Lead?"

"Hospital food," said Easy.

Nick carried Raymond out to the sitting room, and set him up in one of the chairs. Together, the two of them watched the trains. There was something lulling about the toy trains. Raymond's eyes kept narrowing, but he never quite let them close all the way. He was fighting off sleep.

His eyes were still on the trains when he asked Nick, "Did you ever talk to Santa Claus?"

Not now, thought Nick, not tonight. "You mean about what you wanted?"

The boy turned his head this time, looked at Nick, and nodded. "The snow."

"No, I didn't. I'm sorry."

"That's all right. I have my snow globe, and my Sea Lions shirt, and the butterflies. Those are the things I really wanted anyway."

Raymond sounded as if he almost believed what he was saying. Nick tried to think of something to say, but he was short the words, and the explanation.

"What colors will my butterflies be?" Raymond asked.

"Orange and brown and black."

"Those are pretty colors."

"Yes." But not Christmas colors, Nick thought.

They continued to watch the trains. There was something therapeutic about them. The pain on Raymond's face appeared to ease, and his breathing didn't sound as labored.

"Did you ever find that girl who wrote you the letter?" Raymond asked.

"We're still looking for her," said Nick.

Sick as he was, Raymond still found the compassion to think about someone else. The kid always amazed him.

"What time is your family flying in tomorrow?" Nick asked.

"Mid-afternoon," said Raymond. He didn't sound too happy with their time schedule.

"Is something wrong?"

"I wish I was home. I wish they were here."

"Your family wishes the same thing."

The little boy in Raymond emerged: "No, they don't."

"Yes, they do," said Nick. "I'm sure sending you here was the toughest decision your family ever had to make, but they did it because they wanted you to get better more than anything in the world."

Raymond didn't answer, but he did appear to be listening.

"I know how hard it's been on you not having your family around all the time," said Nick, "but it hasn't been easy for them either. Your parents have had to juggle work, your brothers and sisters, and your illness. Right now your family is missing you as much as you're missing them. You know that, don't you?"

Raymond shrugged.

"Don't underestimate their love, son. I know I wouldn't want my kids to have the same doubts about me. If they did, I am going to make sure they never do again."

"Maybe you should be spending Christmas with them."

Nick blinked hard a few times, and then bit the inside of his cheek. Raymond was willing to sacrifice his own time with Nick so that he could be with his kids.

"As it so happens," said Nick, "I'm going to be getting together with them for a late morning brunch." His tone changed, and became equal parts indignant and playful. "What? Are you trying to get out of spending Christmas morning with me?"

Raymond shook his head with surprising vigor: "No."

"You better not be."

The two of them sat back in their chairs; both felt a little better for having talked. They took in the sights and sounds of the railroad, and Raymond's eyes grew heavy. Music was being piped into the sitting room, and Nick recognized the tune from "It Came Upon a Midnight Clear." Without thinking about it, he joined in the chorus:

> *"Oh ye beneath life's crushing load,*
> *Whose forms are bending low,*
> *Who toil along the climbing way,*
> *With painful steps and slow;*
> *Look now, for glad and golden hours,*
> *Come swiftly on the wing;*
> *Oh rest beside the weary road,*
> *And hear the angels sing."*

Nick's voice was anything but angelic, but the song's magic worked. Raymond's eyes were closed.

"Nick? There's a—Oh."

Easy stopped talking when she noticed Raymond was asleep. Nick crossed the room to her, moving as quietly as possible.

"You have a telephone call," she whispered.

Nick took the call at the reception desk. He kept his back to Raymond, and tried to keep his voice low, but was hard-pressed to restrain his excitement.

"I'm sorry," Nick said into the phone, "I forgot my cell phone again." A moment later, he added, "That's great, but I'm afraid I can't get away right now."

Whispering draws the attention of all children, and Raymond was no exception. "What is it?" he asked.

Nick turned from the phone. "It's nothing."

"Tell me," said Raymond.

"We already got our evening planned."

Sick as he was, the boy's eyes never left Nick's. They demanded an explanation, and Nick capitulated. "There might be a new lead on Laura," he said, trying to downplay his words.

"I'm ready to sleep anyway, Nick. Go find her."

"Are you sure?"

Raymond nodded. Nick hesitated for moment, taking a long read of the boy before lifting the phone and speaking into it. "I'll be at the mall in half an hour, Angie. Does that work for you?"

He listened to her answer and started nodding. "If we luck out I'll need my Santa suit. Could you? That would be great."

Remembering something, Nick suddenly looked at his watch. "Are any of the stores still open?"

He didn't like Angie's answer. "I was afraid of that. How do you think she'll feel if Santa Claus arrives empty-handed on her doorstep?" He listened while Angie spoke again, and then said, "You're a miracle worker. Okay, I'll see you in half an hour."

He hung up the phone, and turned back to Raymond who was clearly awaiting an explanation.

"I'm not quite ready to believe yet," said Nick, "but it's possible we might have finally tracked down Laura's whereabouts. And Angie—that's the Elf I've told you about—is running over to her house to get some toys for her. I guess Angie must have figured out we'd find Laura sooner or later. Or maybe she just pulled them out of that bag of hers. Did I ever tell you about that bag? It's got everything in it but the kitchen sink."

Nick shook his head. "And here I thought this would be a Christmas Eve where the two of us just played a few leisurely games of checkers. We'll do that tomorrow morning, though, okay?"

Raymond nodded. Nick rubbed the boy's hair before scooping him up. Once again he was struck by how light Raymond was. It was like holding air.

As they walked down the hallway all was quiet. It was like that poem, Nick thought. Not a creature was stirring. When Nick eased Raymond into his bed, the boy asked to see his butterfly house. He peered closely at the caterpillars.

"When will they get their wings?" he asked.

"About three weeks."

"I liked your singing," Raymond said.

"You're the first person who ever has. What'd you do, fake me out? I thought you were asleep."

"I sort of was, and sort of wasn't."

The boy's words were weak. His breathing sounded labored. Nick didn't like what he was seeing and hearing.

"You know, buddy," said Nick, "maybe a doctor should come and take a look at you."

Raymond shook his head. "No doctor. He'll want to move me to the ICU, and I don't want to be moved, not on Christmas Eve. The view's not as good from there."

Nick hesitated.

"Just wait until tomorrow," Raymond said. "I'll be okay, you'll see. You don't have to worry. And I promise I won't go anywhere without saying good-bye to you first."

*Go anywhere.* Raymond was too young to be using euphemisms. He was too young to die. But he had lived longer than anyone had thought possible.

Nick let himself be convinced. He let out some pent up air. "Okay. I'm going to find Easy and tell her to tuck you in. But remember your promise to me. I'll be here first thing in the morning."

The boy nodded, and Nick turned off the light. But he didn't move to leave, not yet. Raymond was looking out his window.

"You need to sleep," Nick said.

"I will."

"If you don't, I might sing again."

Raymond smiled, and Nick was encouraged to whisper, "Peace on the earth, goodwill to men, from heaven's all-gracious King. The world in solemn stillness lay, to hear the angels sing."

Either Raymond was a good actor, or the words lulled him to sleep. The boy's head was on his pillow, and his eyes were closed.

Nick tiptoed out of the room.

# CHAPTER THIRTY-FOUR

## O Holy Night

Nick spotted a lone figure huddling outside the Plaza Center. Angie had draped the Santa suit around her like a stole, but she was still shivering. Gaily wrapped presents sat on the sidewalk all around her.

Angie's MINI Cooper was the only car Nick saw in the mall's parking lots. He had never seen the place so still, and the quiet was disconcerting. It was just a little past nine, but the place looked like a ghost town.

Nick pulled up to the curb, and got out of his car. "Sorry if I kept you waiting."

Her elf suit wasn't much protection from the cold. Angie's face was red, and she was shivering. "I d-didn't expect it to be this c-cold," she admitted.

Angie undraped the Santa outfit and handed it to Nick. "I keep trying to retire this suit," he said, "but it has a habit of following me."

"Maybe you should take that as an omen."

"Maybe I should just bury the thing."

He hung up the suit in his car, and then began helping Angie stow away the presents. "You still haven't told me how you managed to get all these gifts."

"No, I haven't," she said.

"And they're even wrapped," said Nick. Suddenly suspicious, he stopped loading the gifts. "These aren't Noël's presents are they?"

"No," said Angie. She took a breath and then said, "They're her sister's. I'll have to put new labels on them for Laura."

For the first time Nick noticed the name on the tags. One label said: "To Penny, the best little girl in the world." Another said: "To our Pretty Penny."

The bumper sticker on her car that read "My Other Child is an Angel" suddenly made sense to him. Nick stood immobile, not sure what to do or say.

"It's time these presents found another home," said Angie. "My friends put them away in boxes in a closet. I knew where they were, of course, but I never really looked at them. A few times I made vows that I would give them away, but I never could bring myself to do it."

"You don't have to . . ."

"I want to. I had planned to give the gifts to the toy drive. I really had. But I never got around to it, or at least that's what I told myself. Now I'm glad I waited."

"I can take care of the tags," Nick said. "You shouldn't be spending your Christmas Eve like this."

"There are worse ways to spend Christmas Eve." Angie spoke with the conviction of someone who knows only too well. "The accident happened five years ago on Christmas Eve. Penny was driving with a friend and her mother. It was one of those fluke, awful things."

Angie shook her head and sighed. As if touching a memory, she reached out and put her hand on one of Penny's presents. The gift-wrapping didn't show how long the package had been waiting to be opened. Now that Nick looked closely he could see the tape was slightly yellow and brittle, but that was the only giveaway to the passage of time.

"I went overboard that year," Angie said. "I should say *we* went overboard. Jack was just as bad as I was."

"Do you want to keep some of the gifts . . . ?"

"No. I feel so happy about where they're going. It all feels so right."

Angie smiled at a happy intersection of past and present. "I would guess that Laura is now about a year older than Penny was, but I think there are plenty of presents here that she'll enjoy."

Nick nodded. His Adam's apple felt about as big as a watermelon, and his throat was so tight he could barely swallow.

"Let's get in the car," said Angie. "I'm freezing."

Nick didn't trust himself to answer. He sat behind the wheel and turned up the heat. Angie leaned forward and gratefully rubbed her hands. The roads were quiet. Most people were at home hunkered down in front of their Christmas trees.

He didn't know what to say to Angie. Should he be offering sympathy? Was it appropriate to ask questions? Remaining silent seemed the easiest, if not best, solution. Still, he wondered how Angie had managed to embrace the holidays again after such a tragedy.

Angie must have guessed Nick's dilemma. "When Penny was taken from me," she said, "it felt as if my heart had been yanked out of my chest. For two years the pain overwhelmed me. Christmas brought on the kind of despair you can't imagine. And then I heard this prayer of Mother Teresa's: *God break my heart so completely that the whole world falls in.* Those words resonated with me. My heart was broken, yes, but not completely; I was left with pointed shards, and those shards pierced me so that every day I bled anew. I needed to have my heart completely broken, so that's what I prayed for. And my prayers were answered, and the whole world fell in."

"That's a lot of company," said Nick.

And she answered: "The heart was made to accommodate a lot of company."

They drove in silence for a minute before Nick said, "After giving so much you shouldn't be giving up your Christmas Eve. I'm sure your husband and Noël want you home tonight."

Angie smiled. "They know Santa and his elves have to work late tonight of all nights."

———※———

As Nick and Angie walked toward his apartment she explained the chronology of the eleventh-hour events. "Heidi called Dawn," said Angie, "who tried calling you, and when she couldn't reach you, called the mall."

Nick tried to make sense of her explanation. "Who's Heidi?" he asked.

"She was the librarian on duty today. At just before two o'clock, a young woman and a girl came into the library. Because it was Christmas Eve, the library was closing early and most of the staff was already gone. Anyway, this girl noticed that poster you told me about, and she went to tell the young woman who had brought her in that she wanted to reserve a copy of the book. With everything closing down it was chaotic, so at first Heidi didn't ask any questions. She just took down the woman's name for the waiting list, but then she remembered to hand out your information sheet, and that's when she learned that the girl with the woman was named Laura, and that this woman was not her mother but a neighbor. Heidi tried to get her to call you from the library, but the woman said she was in too much of a rush. The woman did promise to call you at your home number later tonight, though."

"Promises to keep," whispered Nick.

"Heidi tried calling you, but didn't have any luck. Then she called Dawn Lambert to tell her what had occurred, but she had to leave a message because Dawn was out Christmas shopping. When Dawn finally got the message she tried calling you, and after she didn't reach you she called the mall and got me."

Nick put his key in the lock. "I guess this is what they call the moment of truth," he said.

———————✴———————

His new message machine was blinking. Pen and pad in hand, Nick hovered over it. The display said there were four messages. Nick reached for the "Play" button. His finger was shaking. It could probably do a drum solo by itself. He pushed the button.

The first beep sounded.

"Mr. Pappas? This is Heidi Boehm at the library. I know you've been dealing with Dawn Lambert, but all the staff here has been on Laura watch. The library's just closed, so I'm afraid you can't call me back, but I wanted you to know that a girl just came in who might be the one you're looking for. I talked with the woman who brought her in, but I can't give you her name, what with confidentiality laws and everything. However, I did give out that information with your name and telephone number. She was late for a family dinner, but she did promise to call you tonight. I hope she does. Well, good luck and good-bye."

Beep two.

"Nick? Are you there? This is Dawn Lambert. Heidi said she already called and left a message. I tried your cell but couldn't get you. Maybe I can still get you at work, though. Anyway, call me and tell me how this all turns out, would you?"

Beep three.

"Nick, this is Charlotte." Her voice was high-pitched and breathless. "I just got off the phone with Angie. I'm at home, but I'm also carrying my cell. Call me when you get home. I don't think I have to tell you that I'm ready to meet you at a moment's notice."

Angie and Nick stared at the machine, awaiting that last message. Beep four.

"Nick, this is Gerry Finnegan."

Finnegan was a rarity, someone who had been on the force longer than Nick, even though Finnegan was now one of the downtown suits. "I thought you'd like to hear some good news before the holidays," he said. "The official report won't get released until next week, but the Department's decided to lift your suspension and put you back on active duty. Merry Christmas, Nick."

Nick felt numb. He had never really thought he would be reinstated. He was going to be a cop again. But it still wasn't the call he really wanted.

Angie said, "That's wonderful news, Nick."

Nick nodded. "Tonight, though, I wanted to be Santa more than I wanted to be a cop."

He walked to the kitchen. "Can I get you anything to eat or drink?" His words were overloud, as if by volume he could fill the void of not getting that call.

"Nothing, thanks."

Nick wasn't hungry or thirsty either, but he poured himself a glass of water just to have something to do.

He dreaded having to call Charlotte, but it was something better done sooner than later. As he reached for the phone, it started to ring. Nick pulled back as if he had been stung. With suddenly shaking hands, he grabbed the receiver.

# CHAPTER THIRTY-FIVE

*Joy to the World*

Nick hurriedly finished putting on his Santa suit. He took a look in the mirror. His eyebrows were dark and he didn't have any of the white color stick to lighten them. He'd have to be an imperfect Santa, but then he always had been.

Angie was his navigator. When he got to the car she had already mapped out their route. Santa Claus had one more delivery for the night.

"Will Laura be expecting us?" asked Angie.

Nick shook his head. "Sofia never called Laura's mother. We're a surprise."

"Sofia's the neighbor who took Laura to the library?"

Nick nodded. "She lives in the same apartment complex. Sofia told me that Laura's a latchkey kid. She said Laura's mother works and goes to school, so Sofia helps with some of the driving."

"I guess the mother was too busy to follow the news and hear about the Laura story," said Charlotte.

"I guess so," said Nick. "Sofia also mentioned that Laura's going to a new school. She is a good girl, Sofia says, but shy. Because of that, Sofia says she hasn't really made any friends."

"She's made thousands of friends," said Angie, "but just doesn't know it yet."

"Amen," said Nick.

"At the next street," said Angie, "make a right."

"Are we there yet?" asked Nick. He asked it with the same impatience of a child on a road trip.

Nick steered one-handed, first his right, then his left. He kept cupping his free hand, and blowing into it. Angie was also rubbing her hands. Their nervousness, and the cold, combined to make them shiver.

"Feels like the North Pole," said Nick.

Angie didn't answer. She was intently checking out the street numbers. "It should be the next block."

They had come so far to get here, Nick thought. But he still didn't feel ready. "What am I going to say?"

"You'll know what to say."

"That's what you told me the first time I went out as Santa Claus."

"And I was right."

Angie pointed. "It's on your left side just up here."

Nick looked in his rearview mirror. No one was on the road. He could make a U-turn. As he turned the car around, Nick started laughing.

"What?"

"My reflection," he said. "I was looking in the mirror and it struck me that here we are on Christmas Eve, and you're dressed up as an elf, and I'm dressed up as Santa Claus, and we're delivering toys to this special little girl, and my heart's beating hard, and I'm so excited, and I know this sounds stupid, but I really feel like *the* Santa Claus."

"You are *the* real Santa Claus. I wouldn't have given up Penny's gifts to anyone else."

———————✸———————

Charlotte was waiting for them at the curb. Not all of the gifts would fit in Nick's Santa bag, so Charlotte and Angie filled their arms with the presents.

"The three Magi bearing gifts!" said Angie.

The apartment complex was worn, but not dilapidated. They walked through an exterior security door that probably hadn't worked in years and went in search of Apartment 125. There was just enough lighting to make out the numbers. At Apartment 125 there were no exterior lights on, nor was there a welcome mat, a Christmas wreath, or any holiday ornaments.

Nick knocked on the door. The sound carried. It was a little after ten, but it seemed much later. The night sky had gotten even darker, the storm clouds blotting out the stars. Angie and Charlotte were both shivering.

Nick knocked again.

He heard some movements from inside, and then a woman's suspicious voice: "Who's there?"

"Santa Claus," said Nick.

Laura's mother had likely not had an easy life. It would be no wonder if she had little enough belief in the goodness of mankind, let alone any belief in Santa Claus.

"Go away or I'll call the cops."

I am a cop, Nick almost said, but at that moment he wasn't. He was something much more.

"Go ahead and call the police," said Nick. "I'll still be here, and I'll still be Santa Claus."

"I'm not kidding. I'm calling the cops."

"And I'm not kidding either. I'm holding a bag full of gifts."

"Who are you?"

"I told you, I'm Santa Claus."

The answer wasn't mumbled. It was announced loudly, and proudly. It was unequivocal. It left no room for disbelief. No door could stay closed to that proclamation.

"Santa Claus?" This time a girl spoke, and Nick knew that voice though he had never heard it before, knew it with an absolute certainty.

"I'm here, Laura."

# CHAPTER THIRTY-SIX

*The Hallelujah Chorus*
*December 25*

It was just past midnight when Nick arrived home. Christmas, he realized, Christmas.

At Laura's apartment he had felt like one of those movie heroes of old who arrive on the scene in the nick of time, and then at the end they ride off into the sunset, or in this case, into the night.

She had loved Penny's presents, but Nick told her he hadn't forgotten about the other gifts she had asked for in her Christmas letter. He said that his sleigh had been just a little too full to bring them on this visit, but that she'd get everything in the next few days.

Nick sat down in his easy chair. He took off his cap and beard, but was too tired to take off the rest of his Santa suit. Besides, it was such a cold night all the padding felt good.

In another minute Nick would get up. His chair sure did feel comfortable, though. It had been such a long day, such a long season. But Laura's smile had made it all worthwhile; the day, the past month, everything. She had danced around the room, danced for joy. And Nick had laughed the kind of great belly laughs that Santa is known for. There had been no need for him to act out his mirth. The laughter had just come flowing out of him.

And while she had danced, Laura kept saying, "I knew you'd come, I knew you'd come, I knew you'd come."

Angie and Charlotte had talked to Laura's mom, who told them she'd been downplaying the holidays, preparing Laura for a lean Christmas. Seeing her daughter so happy had made her cry for joy.

Nick found himself nodding off. He knew he should get up and go to bed. Whenever he fell asleep in his easy chair his back always paid an awful toll the next day, but the chair felt so comfortable . . .

---

Nick awoke with a start. The first thing he noticed was that he hadn't closed the curtains. He looked at the clock. It was a little before seven. It was light outside, brighter than it should have been for a December morning. At that hour it still should have been dark, but there was a brightness reflecting from outside.

Nick tried to focus. What he was seeing looked like a fuzzy TV picture. He squinted a little, not believing what he saw.

It was snowing.

No. Nick knew that was impossible. It didn't snow in San Diego. He'd lived in Southern California for more than thirty years, and had never seen more than a few flakes fall. What he was seeing now was real snow. The sky was filled with flakes.

Nick got out of his chair, and his back didn't seem to be too much the worse for having spent the night there. He walked to his window and looked out to the courtyard. The snow blanketed the area, giving it a charm and grace never seen before. There was maybe an inch of snow on the ground, and Nick thought he had never seen anything quite so beautiful.

He opened the door, stepped outside, and cupped his hands to catch the snowflakes. They didn't even feel cold.

Nick felt something rather than saw it. He looked up, sensing something, but it wasn't there. Nick swiveled his head around. Not there, either. The area was deserted. But that didn't explain the voice calling to him.

Raymond's voice.

The boy was in the courtyard, just a few steps away from him. Nick didn't understand how he had gotten there.

"I've come to say good-bye," he said.

Raymond looked different. He wasn't sick, and pale, and bony. This boy was strong, the Raymond that should have been. There was a glow to him, and a smile the likes of which Nick had never seen.

"What do you mean?" asked Nick.

"I told you I wouldn't leave without saying good-bye. But it's time now."

"I don't understand."

"You will. Thank you for the snow."

"I had nothing to do with it."

"Oh yes you did."

"That was artificial snow. This is real, isn't it?"

Smiling, the boy nodded. "It sure is. Good-bye, Nick."

Raymond started walking toward a sleigh, a sleigh that hadn't been there moments before, but then neither had Raymond.

"I'm dreaming," said Nick.

It was Santa's sleigh, complete with reindeer. And sitting in front was an all too familiar character. Santa Claus waved at him. Dream or not, Nick didn't want to be rude. He waved back.

Santa offered Raymond a hand up, but the boy didn't need one. With a single bound, he jumped inside the sleigh. He was the healthiest of little boys. Nick noticed he was wearing his Sea Lions jersey. Raymond didn't fill it out—his change hadn't been that miraculous—but somehow it fit him better.

Raymond turned his head to Nick, and smiled. There was so much joy and peace radiating from his smile that Nick wished he was wearing sunglasses, not only because they would have shielded him from the glare of the smile, but they would have hidden his tears as well.

"Good-bye, Nick. Good-bye!"

The sleigh lifted. Santa and Raymond never stopped waving until the sleigh disappeared high into the sky.

With a start, Nick's head came up.

He was in his easy chair.

It was only a dream.

His cheeks were wet. He'd been crying in his sleep over some wishful dream. Nick took a deep breath. Everything had seemed so real. If only it were. He turned his head and looked out the window. The curtains were open, just as they had been in his dream. That, at least, was real. And there was something else.

Outside it was snowing.

This time Nick slapped himself. He wanted to make sure he wasn't having a dream within a dream. His smarting face told him he wasn't. What he was seeing was no dream. He rubbed his eyes, but the mirage didn't disappear.

It really was snowing.

Nick got out of his chair. This time his back hurt. He walked to his front door and threw it open. The courtyard was as beautiful as he remembered it. In fact, it was just as he had dreamed, with the exception of Raymond and the sleigh.

Without closing the door behind him, Nick ran back inside. Seeing was believing. With one eye he kept looking at the snow, and with the other, he dialed the hospital. He was connected with the Pediatric Oncology ward, and Easy came on the line.

"Easy, this is Nick Pappas. It's snowing! I mean you probably know it's snowing, but I don't know whether Raymond knows. He's got to see it!"

Easy's voice didn't sound right. "He saw it, Nick. He was the first to see it. He called for me, and together we watched the snow falling, and then he said I needed to wake up everyone else so that they could see. And so I went and did that—"

"Tell him I'm coming down now. Tell him I'm going to make him a snowman. I'll even bring a snowball up to him, and let him drop it on my head. I'm going—"

"He's gone, Nick."

His "oh" was part sigh, part acknowledgment, part moan.

"I only left him for a minute, but while I was telling the other children about the snow he must have decided it was time to go."

Nick had known it, of course, but hadn't wanted to believe it. Raymond had come to him and said good-bye. Nick had heard of the dead making a last call upon the living, of people getting a final message from the departed, but he had always assumed those stories were just a lot of wishful thinking. Now he knew differently. Raymond hadn't left without saying his good-bye.

It had been more than a dream, much more.

"I came in just as he was leaving. He went out so gently, Nick. There was a smile on his face, and he looked so at peace, so harmonious. It almost looked like he was floating."

"He was, Easy, he was."

Nick hung up the phone. He wasn't sure what he felt. Everything was all jumbled inside. He wanted to laugh and cry all at once.

It was still snowing. Nick walked out to the courtyard, and let the flakes fall down on him. He reached up and caught one, and then another, and then another.

He moved his hands and feet, and kept snatching the snowflakes out of the air. His body spoke for him, telling of his joy, and pain. Nick was laughing and crying at the same time, and all the while he kept reaching up faster and faster, and higher and higher.

And then Nick realized he wasn't reaching for snowflakes so much as he was dancing, but he didn't stop. He just kept on dancing.

# ABOUT THE AUTHOR

Stathis Orphanos 2012

Alan Russell is the bestselling author of ten novels, including *Burning Man*, *Shame*, *Multiple Wounds*, *The Hotel Detective*, and *Political Suicide*. His books have been nominated for most of the major awards in crime fiction, and he has won a Lefty award for best comedic mystery, a *USA Today* Critics' Choice Award, two San Diego Book Awards for best mystery novel, and the Odin Award for Lifetime Achievement from the San Diego Writers/Editors Guild. He lives with his wife and children in Encinitas, California.

This book was originally released in Episodes as a Kindle Serial. Kindle Serials launched in 2012 as a new way to experience serialized books. Kindle Serials allow readers to enjoy the story as the author creates it, purchasing once and receiving all existing Episodes immediately, followed by future Episodes as they are published. To find out more about Kindle Serials and to see the current selection of Serials titles, visit www.amazon.com/kindleserials.